LAURA BARBER

Just Between Friends

First published by Independently published 2021

Copyright © 2021 by Laura Barber

All rights reserved. No part of this publication may be reproduced, stored or transmitted in any form or by any means, electronic, mechanical, photocopying, recording, scanning, or otherwise without written permission from the publisher. It is illegal to copy this book, post it to a website, or distribute it by any other means without permission.

This novel is entirely a work of fiction. The names, characters and incidents portrayed in it are the work of the author's imagination. Any resemblance to actual persons, living or dead, events or localities is entirely coincidental.

Laura Barber asserts the moral right to be identified as the author of this work.

First edition

For anyone still looking for closure.

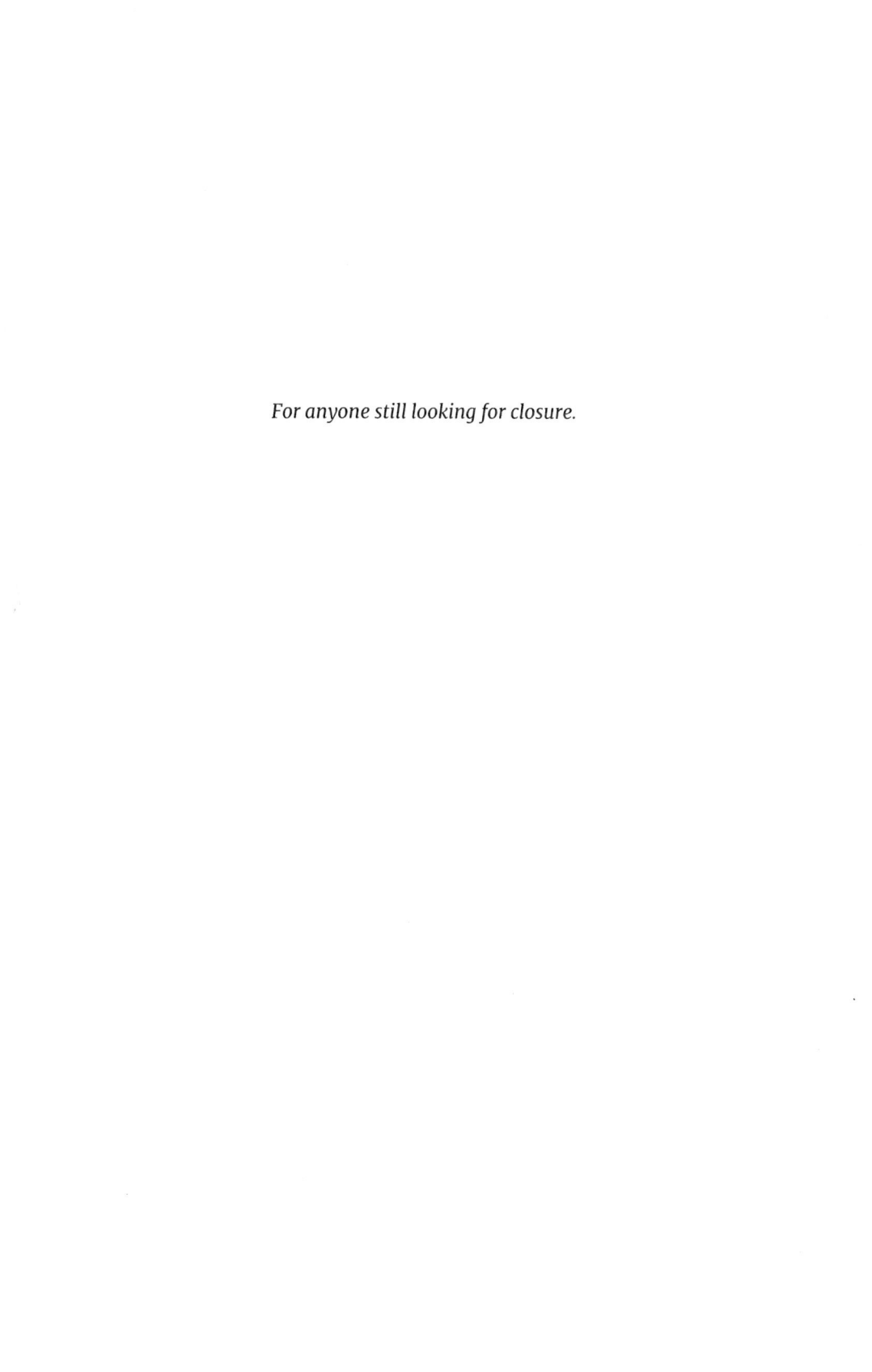

Part One

"Your whole life is ahead of you, don't you ever forget that." —
Jackie Collins

Chapter 1

Walking through the revolving doors, Ivy pulled her boarding pass out of her travel wallet with her teeth whilst dragging her mum's scuffed, blue suitcase behind her. She looked up to see the airport wasn't particularly busy and was relieved since she hadn't grown out of the occasional nightmare where she was trapped in the departure lounge.

They wouldn't be back for five weeks, so Ivy had booked some hold luggage as well as the carry-on duffle bag she hooked onto the handle of her case. Sam, of course, only had a backpack slung over his shoulder which Ivy could only assume contained a phone charger, condoms and three t-shirts. He leaned against the metal frame that demonstrated how big your hand luggage should be. With his eyes closed, he waited for her to drop her suitcase at the desk.

He wasn't superhuman after all, Ivy thought, looking to her best friend. Sam was one of those friends who you wanted to hate because everything came easy to him, including not having hangovers despite the copious amounts of alcohol he drank, but you couldn't hate him if you knew him. Mainly because he had a self-destructive streak that usually undid all of his good luck, but also because he was so aloof and untouched by anything you just forgot to keep hating him. She, on the other hand, had woken with a splitting hangover this morning that was just beginning to die down.

They had left the bar together at around 3 a.m., not among the last out, but they weren't far off. Neither of them were ready to call it a night yet so the pair kept walking until they reached a large green that was popular with homeless people and weed smokers, which Ivy found ironic as it backed onto the city's council building. Ivy sat on the grass while Sam went over to a twenty-four hour Tesco to buy them some drinks. Her head was spinning but she still felt in control of herself.

She lifted the case on the conveyor belt and felt an ache as the weight of the case strained against her hand. Greenish bruises were setting in around her knuckles and more pieces of her night started surfacing in her memory.

She had been sitting on the green, waiting for Sam to return with their beers when she heard voices to her right and looked up to see a man holding a girl against a wall across from where she sat. At first, she had dismissed it as some drunk couple, but something about the girl's voice sounded panicked and Ivy was pretty sure she could hear her crying. This guy wasn't her boyfriend. He was forcing himself on her. Before she could register she was doing it, her feet were pounding on the wet concrete floor in time with her hammering heart.

He had his back to her, so relying on her instincts, she grabbed his shoulder intending to throw him around, but he barely moved. Thinking quickly, she wrapped her hand around his neck and managed to push him against the wall and punched him square in the face as he turned.

She hadn't ever really hit anyone before, except her sister when they were younger, but not like this. It was surprising how much it hurt to be the one who threw the punch, but the light buzz of the alcohol was still there so she knew it was going to hurt more later and she wasn't wrong.

"You'll get no sympathy from me," Sam said, "three points for feminism remember?" He tugged at her sleeve, pulling her towards security. She scrunched her nose up and remembered their conversation.

"I mean fair shout for doing that, but what the fuck?"

"What?" she asked innocently.

"You shouldn't have gone storming into a situation like that without thinking."

"I was thinking," she said, pouting for emphasis. "Man bad. Girl sad. Me help." she said and looked up at Sam in a forgive me sort of way. Which of course he would. "Plus, I did it all in high heels," she said, clicking her heels together and smiling. "Three points for feminism."

She winced a little at her drunken boasting but fell into step behind him. She was glad it was Sam she was out with last night, not her older sister Agatha who would have thrown a fit if she had seen the bruises on her hand today.

CHAPTER 1

Luckily she seemed to have already left for work before Ivy had woken up.

They tagged onto the end of the queue for security and Ivy pulled her travel wallet out of her pocket in anticipation. She wore flip flops and no jewellery to make sure the painful process of security was less so. She only needed to add her hoodie, wallet and phone to the tray, dumping her duffle directly onto the belt behind it. Sam added his wallet and phone to her tray, plus the contents of his pockets which included lighters, keys and some loose coins.

Ivy walked through without a problem but heard Sam set the machine off behind her. He took his shoes off and put them into a new tray and was waved over to an x-ray machine.

"You can't wait here, Miss. You'll have to go on through." Ivy acknowledged the direction with a curt nod and picked up Sam's things as well as her own and walked through to the duty-free. She browsed the sunglasses section and tried a few pairs on while she waited, still thinking about last night.

It wasn't very like her to go all superhero like that, but the liquid courage and the thought of escaping life for a while loosened her usual caution. After so many years, perhaps Sam's reckless behaviour was rubbing off on her, but that might not be such a bad thing. This trip had been his idea after all *just you, me, sun and fun,* he had said.

"I like the red ones best," Sam said, coming up behind her. She turned on the spot and handed him his wallet, phone and keys in a pile into his hands. He stuffed them back into his pocket.

"I believe I also had some change."

"Finder's fee," she replied absently as she put the sunglasses back. "Besides, it was about 80p," she said, zoning back in and looking at his face properly for the first time since they left her house this afternoon. He wouldn't be out of place in an early eighties punk band all he needed was a smear of eyeliner and studs on his jacket. That was part of his appeal, one part wild, one part apathy with just a smidge of charm and after almost ten years of friendship, Ivy was grateful to be immune. "Come on, let's check when they're gonna announce our gate," she said.

The screen in front of them showed THAILAND DELAYED in capital yellow letters.

"Well, that's a good start," Ivy said, sucking in her cheeks and biting down on them in annoyance.

"More time to drink" Sam replied, patting Ivy on the shoulder with a quick drumroll.

"Airports are expensive though." Ivy whinged, pulling a face at Sam.

"Just go find somewhere to sit," Sam said. So, she did.

There were no free seats in the area they were in, but she didn't want to leave that section in case Sam couldn't find her. She sat on the floor near a plug socket so she could keep her phone charged up. Who knew how long they would be delayed?

She decided to facetime her sister. The cheaper, Tuesday flight meant travelling during normal people's office hours, so she hadn't said goodbye to her. It was past 5 p.m. so she should be home from work by now. One thing Ivy was glad to get away from was work. She didn't think she had the stomach for temp work anymore – at least not in administration. *Should probably look for a better job when I get back. If I decide to come back that is.* She had dropped out of uni in her second year. Unlike Agatha, who excelled at her studies, Ivy had little motivation to do well and had been temping over the summer to try and figure out what she wanted to do with her life. She still didn't know what that was, but when Sam suggested they go to Thailand for a month she thought maybe she could at least go enjoy herself to break up the monotony. Just as Ivy was about to hang up, Agatha answered.

"Hey!"

The picture came in of Agatha lying on her front in bed typing on her laptop. The phone was propped up against something to the side and Agatha wasn't looking at the screen.

"What's up? You're bored of Thailand already?" Her sister said jokingly, but Ivy could tell she was distracted. By what she didn't know.

"We haven't got there yet. Our flight's delayed, but even if it was on time, we're about thirteen hours away from being there." Ivy replied.

"Sounds great," Agatha replied, still not looking at the screen.

"What, the delayed part or the thirteen-hour plane journey?" Ivy replied confused. She usually felt so in sync with her sister.

CHAPTER 1

"Oh, you're delayed? That sucks. What are you going to do?" Agatha asked.

"Drink," Sam said, sitting down next to her and handing her a pint of lager.

Sam had requested extended leave from the mechanics he worked for, so he would have a job to come back to when he got home. He had always been good with cars and fixing things in general, so the mechanics suited him for now. How long that would last, she didn't know. Knowing how flaky Sam could be, he would probably be off to the next thing that took his fancy soon enough.

They tapped their plastic glasses together saying an exaggerated cheers for the camera, which Ivy screenshotted to add to her Instagram story later.

"How was work?" Ivy asked Agatha.

"Work like." She replied. They never really spoke in full sentences because they didn't need to, but this was clipped even for them. "I'm gonna go. Not all of us are on holiday. Some of us have real-life things to do," Agatha said smiling.

Ivy smiled back. "Yeah sure. I'll see you in a few weeks."

"Be safe," Agatha said, then hung up.

Ivy continued to stare at her screen for a few beats before lowering her arm and putting it in her lap. "Weird," Ivy said more to herself than Sam. Sam just shrugged at her.

"She's fine, she's probably just jealous she can't come with us," he said and gulped down most of his pint in one go.

Ivy nodded but she wasn't so sure about that. Agatha was, as her mum called her, a ball of light. She was always wondering how you are and what was going on with you and remembered even the most trivial of details. She actually thought her dismissive behaviour might have something to do with what she had said when she had last seen her. Agatha had commented on how she had been staying out a lot recently with Sam and now she was going to be on the other side of the world for five weeks so she wondered whether her sister might feel a bit abandoned.

"She will probably write some angsty poetry about it and be over it tomorrow. Besides, she's too nice to hold a grudge," he said, bumping her shoulder.

She smiled at him. *He's right. She will be there when I get back so I just need to spend some more quality-sister-time with her then.* A few texts and calls from

Thailand probably wouldn't go amiss either.

Ivy carried on sipping at her beer. Rearranging her things, so Sam's backpack was between her and the wall, she put her travel pillow around her neck, leant back and started reading on her phone. Sam spent his time wandering back and forth to the Irish themed airport pub for the next hour. He finally settled next to her for a moment around an hour later and plugged his earphones into his phone and started scrolling. Ivy swivelled herself and put her head in his lap, partly for comfort but mainly to stop him from getting up again. All his toing and froing was getting on her nerves. He always had to be doing something, rarely content to just sit with himself. They stayed like that until their flight was eventually called, two hours after it was originally supposed to depart.

Ivy tried to sleep on the plane, wedging herself and her travel pillow into the window. She dozed on and off but didn't really sleep. Mostly due to Sam's incessant ringing of the steward bell to order gin and tonics. After a few hours, she gave up and ordered herself two vodka cokes on the steward's next visit. Sam looked at her with a raised brow.

"What? I need to catch up, don't I?" she said, swallowing most of the first one in one gulp.

They passed the time mostly in silence playing thumb wars with each other. Ivy couldn't remember where they picked up this little pastime, but they always did it when they were bored. They didn't take notice of who won, just enjoyed passing the time like they were still kids. When they got bored with playing, they watched videos on Sam's phone, until they landed another nine hours later.

* * *

Everything seemed much louder in Koh Samui. The sounds of the streets contrasted so aggressively to the almost silence of the plane. With car horns blaring, motorcycles rumbling, people talking and street vendors shouting, it all felt like an assault on Sam's ears. Its strong humidity, burning flames and smell of spices was all that distinguished it from being a regular busy town

CHAPTER 1

back home, like London. It also felt brighter, which was odd considering it was eleven at night, the streets were lit up with multicoloured fairy lights and fluorescent fly zappers.

They got a taxi to their hotel, which was in Chaweng, just off the local strip full of bars, clubs and even a few restaurants. The room was bare, except for a small table and chairs near the bathroom, the bed and two bedside tables. There was also a silver box TV in the corner that didn't seem to work, but that didn't matter. They had hardly come to Thailand to watch TV. No artwork adorned the yellowing white walls but it still managed to look dated. They both dumped their bags on the double bed in the centre of the room.

"Isn't there supposed to be two beds?" she asked. He pulled out some deodorant and used it before chucking it to Ivy. She caught it with both hands. "Is that your way of telling me I smell like B.O.?" she asked but rubbed it on without waiting for the answer and threw it back on top of his bag.

He bent down and lifted the layers of bed sheets at the bottom of the bed. "It's two singles, they've just pushed them together."

"We can pull them apart later — I'm starving," she replied as she changed into a pair of wedges that laced up her ankles and a small, cotton playsuit while he changed his t-shirt but kept his jeans on.

They wandered down the street from the hotel and stopped at a side street that was full of market stalls, the fronts covered in food. The smell of fried meat and noodles made his stomach rumble. And they took turns choosing something from each stall to try and everything was delicious. Sam bit into a giant prawn which tasted like it had been caught that evening and the saltiness made his mouth water. He spotted Ivy coming back from the next cart with what looked like fried meatballs on sticks.

"So, this is *yai* and I think *gai* means *chicken*," she said, handing a stick to him. Chicken or not, it was good, he thought. Going back for seconds while small, scruffy dogs ran around their ankles, begging for scraps.

When they couldn't eat anymore Sam guided them into a bar. He ordered them both a cocktail while Ivy found them a small table outside. Balancing two extravagant red drinks, topped with pineapple, cherries, an umbrella and curled straws, he sat down opposite her and handed a drink over. Ivy took it from him and began slurping at the drink.

"Woah, woah hang on drunky," Sam said, holding out his glass.

Ivy mirrored his behaviour and said, their usual mantra: "Friends and lovers" to which Sam replied, "Fuck the others." and they clinked their glasses together.

He felt especially bloated from inhaling so much food before their drinks. Ivy drank her fruity drink slowly, then told him she wanted to explore the area a little more. They made their way down to the beach at the end of the strip. The bars on either side of them were bustling but the beach was quiet. Ivy looked out as if she could already hear the call of the sea despite the fact it was drowned out by the sound of the conflicting music around them. He watched as she stood on the edge of the concrete path and took her wedges off, hooking her fingers through the backs.

"Let's swim." She said before running towards the water, clutching her heels to her chest as she did. He saw her reach the water, and stop to wait for him to come panting behind her.

"That's a real work out that, running in sand." he puffed but she ignored him and dropped her shoes in front of her. She took off her playsuit and tucked it into one of her wedges. Then hooked her fingers on her underwear, pulled them up over her hips and walked into the water.

He was quick to follow and was already pulling his t-shirt over his head. His trousers around his ankles. The water was surprisingly warm, and it felt like silk draping his legs in contrast to the balmy heat that was still in the air. They carried on walking until he could only just touch the seafloor with the tips of his toes.

By the time the water was up to his neck, Ivy was floating next to him. He watched her dunk her head back into the water, bringing her legs up so she was starfished on top of the water and copied her pose, bobbing next to her, bringing his face close to hers.

They lay there still for a moment, the only noise: the tide coming in and out and the distant thud of the nightlife not too far away.

"Something's going to bite me in a minute," Sam said, breaking the silence.

"Like a shark?" Ivy asked.

CHAPTER 1

He rolled his eyes. "No not like a shark, V, but doesn't it freak you out a bit not being able to see what's in here with us?" He turned his head to look at her.

"We're in the sea, there's a lot in here with us," she replied, lifting an eyebrow. She was being purposely obtuse he knew. "I'm not scared of what is in the water."

He heard the water ripple and felt her pinch a small bit of skin on his arm.

"Ha-ha, very funny." He said looking round in her direction.

"I don't know what you're talking about." He could hear her smiling sweetly even though he couldn't see her. "In a strange way I feel safer than I ever have, there's no one here to disappoint,"

Sam cleared his throat forcefully, to indicate himself and lighten the mood slightly.

"You have to admit. No weekend to drag ourselves towards, no expectations, just freedom. This place is paradise."

"We've only just got here," Sam replied. "Tell me that after three weeks. I bet you'll be bored."

"No, I mean, we're so far away from everything we've known. It's nice" she said quietly.

Sam turned to look at her. He didn't respond, but he was glad. He knew how lost she had felt lately since dropping out of her business degree so he was glad he could spend five weeks partying in Thailand and give her a break from reality. Two birds, one stone thrown six thousand miles away. His eyes adjusting to the dark meant he could just about make out her profile. The light of the moon hit the edges of her nose and lips, her eyes fluttered slowly as she blinked, water droplets hanging on her lashes. He turned his head back to look at the night sky.

They floated there for a while, just looking at the stars until their skin was pruney and wrinkled.

"Come on, we should get out," Sam said. "It's shark season." He smirked. Knowing Ivy she probably rolled her eyes, but she followed him out of the water. He looked around and realised they were still alone but only a few feet from civilization.

He pulled his jeans on smacking the sand from them as he did. He could see out the corner of his eye, she had turned her back to him and had unhooked her bra to wring it out. As he pushed his head through the neck of his t-shirt he saw her crouching low to the sand using one hand to hold her boobs and her free hand to search for her playsuit.

Sam watched her search for a second, before walking over to where she had left her clothes, which were only just out of her reach and threw them at her.

"Thanks." She said, straightening and wriggling into the outfit. He caught a glimpse of her one and only tattoo as she did. It was a simple line drawing of a crown, the size of the tip of his thumb on her left bum cheek. If you weren't looking closely, you could mistake it for a mole or a birthmark.

He remembered going with her to get it. She wouldn't tell him what she was getting or where, but she was excited. He looked down at the snake tattoo that wrapped around his hand that he got that same day. She had come over to him beaming while the tattooist was still working on the outline of his snake and pulled down half of her shorts to show him this tiny tattoo, in a place that no one would see, that she was very proud of. He smiled at the memory.

That very much summed them both up: Ivy was endearing and quietly rebellious whereas Sam was eager to show his disobedience as plainly as his hands with no forethought to how it would serve him later down the line. Ivy would have considered that small crown for years and kept it to herself until she was ready to commit but every one of Sam's tattoos were on a whim. Each time he added to his collection it was a permanent reminder that no matter how many times he marked his body, his parents would never notice or care. His smile faded. *That got dark real fast. I must be sobering up.*

He looked up and saw that a group of people were heading towards them now.

"We should head off." He gestured to the group walking towards them with his head. Ivy looked up and nodded. She picked up her shoes and tucked her bra into the back of his jeans, which quickly began soaking through his pocket, weighing it down. They walked up the sand to where the path met the beach and he watched as she thought about putting her shoes back on. Anticipating her dilemma, he bent in front of her and said, "jump on."

CHAPTER 1

So, she did, and he carried her like that, up the strip, all the way to their hotel, with her heels knocking against his shoulder with every step.

Chapter 2

Ivy walked into the dark room, lit carefully with sparkling blue lamps. She had heard some other tourists talking about it as she was buying her ticket. The exhibit was called *Raining* and the room was filled with strings of white porcelain hearts reflected in the mirrored walls. All other visitors had left, making her the only person left in the room now, and she smiled at the solitude. Spinning in the centre of the room quickly, turning and turning trying to take it all in at once until she felt dizzy. *Agatha would love this*.

"This exhibit is on loan from Bangkok. It was created during the mourning period after the passing of King Rama IX." She heard the voice approaching the room and looked up to see a tour guide leading a couple into the room.

"The artist wanted to convey what the Thai farmers felt when His Majesty's initiative to develop natural water systems in rural areas led to rain. They called it *The Royal Rain*," she continued.

"It's beautiful," one of the tour takers replied.

Ivy smiled as she passed them and left the room before moving into a new wing of the museum, brightly lit and filled with paintings adorned with gold, baroque frames.

They had spent their first week sightseeing. Ivy wanted to make sure she didn't waste this trip on just partying and drinking so she allowed some time to visit temples and old cities. By the end of the week, she was practically dragging Sam to try and get some culture. But he was usually very hungover so when he did agree to come, he made sure to carry a hip flask of some local whisky around with him. When Ivy teased him, he would just say it was hair of the dog to ease his banging head, but Ivy could feel the judging stares of others whenever he pulled the flask out.

By the final day of her sightseeing itinerary, Sam had had enough and went back to the hotel for a mid-afternoon nap and left Ivy to get on with it. She took a taxi to a local art museum and spent the afternoon with herself, appreciating the air conditioning. The local taxis were yellow on top and red on the bottom like a Little Tykes car. They looked like they had been in an accident and they had to make do with whatever parts they could get hold of.

She almost couldn't remember a time when he didn't drink and sometimes she wondered whether for Sam life would be worth living if he wasn't self-medicating in some way. He once told her he had too many thoughts for one brain, his head was full of noise that he needed to quieten before he could find a coherent strand to follow. She wasn't sure how true that was. Having been in his home, even the walls there screamed of the silence. His mum, Vicky, avoided him, like just his being in the same room burned her and Ivy thought that it was more likely the silence he wanted to dampen. In the same way, she knew they spent more time at her house than his because her house was always full of familial sounds.

Turning her attention to the next painting, she studied the brushstrokes that created two skeletons in a romantic embrace between the trees of a dead forest. It was a shame that Sam was missing out, but she was glad he wasn't here. She appreciated having the time to herself, silencing her own noise as such. Looking at the paintings she wanted to look at and not feeling rushed by Sam's presence. They hadn't spent much time alone since arriving in Thailand, and it thrilled her being somewhere new, exploring and finding her way, relying only on herself.

She treated herself to a cocktail after the museum and only began to meander back when the sky was painted a vivid orange and she felt the day slipping through her fingers. Her mind turned to her sister and she wondered what Agatha was up to at this moment. This was Ivy's first holiday without her. She checked the time on her phone and counted back the hours. It would be 11 a.m. so too early to catch her on her lunch break, she made a mental note to video call her on the weekend.

When she arrived back at the room, Sam was up and showered. He was walking around with just a towel on and his wet hair was dripping onto his shoulders and down his back.

He turned to look at her while rubbing the hand towel into his hair, ruffling the small springy curls he had on one side of his head. The other half of his head was normally shaved fairly short, but he seemed to be growing it out for the moment.

"How was the 'art'?" he asked as if art was a made-up concept.

"Great. I feel *supes* cultured right now," she replied sarcastically. "Where are we going tonight?" she asked.

"Let's grab something quick from downstairs food-wise, and just bar hop down the strip. If we hit it at the right time, there's those two for one offers they do," he said rather bored like.

Ivy nodded her agreement and went to the bathroom to get ready. She spent minimal time getting ready for the night. She let her hair air dry, got changed and put a small dab of aloe vera on her face to cool her. Avoiding the mirror on the way to the door, just in case she looked a mess and it slowed their escape from the room.

Perfectly uniform bushes skirted the edge of the hotel. She hadn't noticed the gardeners cutting them once during their stay but they look just as they had when they arrived. They ordered some chips from the hotel bar and ate them with cocktails. There wasn't any ketchup, so Sam was pouting. When they'd finished eating, they charged the bill to their room and strolled down towards the strip of bars and clubs where they had spent most of their evenings. As with every night so far, the place was full of tourists taking advantage of the cheap thrills of Thailand.

Ivy could barely hear Sam over the blurring noise of multiple different songs and the chatter of the crowds. But they were content to talk and laugh into each other's ears and they shared a few fishbowls in the first two or three bars. They were sitting outside at their fifth bar and by this point, it was finally dark, but the heat was still in the air. There was a large group of what Ivy thought were probably gap year students. Their strong American and Australian accents rose across the air and their frequent laughter drew Ivy and Sam to keep looking over at them, like the two kids that weren't invited to the party.

"Why don't you join us?" A voice said with a long drawl. Ivy and Sam both looked at each other wondering who they were talking to. "Hey, you two. Lovebirds." Ivy and Sam looked up to this almost too quickly. Ivy opened her mouth to object, but she was relieved when she was cut off by the American girl calling to them again "I said why don't you join us?"

The girl was beautiful, Ivy thought. One of those girls who was probably awkward in school but signed a modelling contract the moment she left. Her lips and eyebrows were so prominent as if whoever painted her had exaggerated them. She was angular and had long half-closed eyes that looked almost dreamlike with the huge fluttery lashes that framed them. Long blonde hair was scooped over one shoulder and Ivy spotted a ring through her bottom lip which she spun with her tongue.

"We were beginning to think you wouldn't say anything so I thought I should be the one to welcome you to our little group," she said as if performing for the table. "I'm Alice," she said proudly, locking eyes with both of them individually before moving on. "This is Chad, Paul, Dom, Gemma and Alex," she said reeling through the names.

"Ivy," Ivy said, trying to match her confidence. It wasn't unusual for her to feel intimidated by someone else, but Alice's whole demeanour made her nervous. She was so forward and seemed to hold the attention of everyone around her. Ivy couldn't help but feel like she wanted to impress her even though only a few words had passed between them.

"And this is Sam. Who is not my boyfriend by the way," she added, annoyed with herself because she couldn't help adding this end bit, she knew it didn't matter what others thought, but she hated being labelled as one of Sam's throwaway girls.

"Oh, good for us then I guess," Alice said more to her companions than to Ivy and Sam. "Anyway sit, sit. Tell us all about yourselves."

Sam sat down before Alice finished her sentence, in the gap between Alice and Gemma so Ivy, feeling a little more confident, strode around the table to the only other space, opposite Alice.

Dom drum rolled the table loudly next to her and sprang up. "What are we all drinking? Fish Bowls?"

"Sure. We were drinking the red one. Dunno about you guys." Sam replied.

"Five red ones, please!" Gemma said, louder than was probably necessary. She laughed and Ivy realised she must not get drunk that often. Her thin, monolid eyes were almost completely closed from drinking. The rest of the group seemed pretty sober by comparison.

"I'll come with you," Ivy said, getting up and walking to the bar with Dom. He seemed nice, very attractive, with dark skin, a tight afro and deep dimples in his cheeks. He was fresh out of uni or 'college' as he put it and was living it up here before he went back to work at some law firm his dad owned.

She was surprised to hear that Dom didn't know any of the others before he got to the bar. They all seemed so close-knit when they joined the table, but she felt more at ease knowing they weren't some clique of forever friends experimenting on her but just trying to find similar people to have fun with. Sam wouldn't be concerned with why they were hanging out with them, especially as both Alice and Gemma were attractive and had probably caught his attention.

She carried two of the fishbowls to the table, sloshing some of the sticky liquid onto her chest as she walked. She leant over the table and put the bowls down in the middle of it. Gemma seeing her glistening chest shouted "Oooh. Spillage is lickage." and laughed.

Ivy turned her body to Chad who was closest to her and held her hands up in mock surrender. He was a little older than the others with dark hair and eyes that stood out against his paler skin.

"Be my guest." She said. Chad leant forward and licked the cocktail from her cleavage to which the group whooped and clapped, bringing a blush to Ivy's cheeks she hoped no one could see. Although Ivy was letting loose a little, she was still self-conscious being the centre of attention.

They spent the next few hours drinking and talking as if they were old friends, to the point where Ivy forgot they had only met that evening. Alice leant over the table to whisper in Alex' ear before interrupting the conversation of the group.

"We're going back to the hostel for a party," Alice said and they all exchanged knowing glances.

"We like parties," Sam said, speaking for both of them.

He slammed his plastic cup down on the table, the mouthful of liquid left sloshed up the side. Ivy gave him a sideways squint to show her distaste, but she wasn't sure if she was annoyed that Sam spoke for her or whether it was because he knew what her answer was before she did. This was usually the point in the night where Ivy would dip out and Sam would take over but she felt bolder in Thailand like she could do things she normally couldn't. *Why not?* she thought.

Alice stood, leaned her body over the table towards Ivy and brushed her lips lightly against hers before looking her in the eye and kissing her deeply.

Ivy was surprised but returned the kiss eagerly. She devoted herself completely to the kiss. *Girls' lips were always so soft.* But she remembered where she was the moment she heard the rest of the group whooping around them and broke the kiss coming back to reality.

When she opened her eyes, Alice was smiling sexily at her.

"Wanna come to our party?" She asked, speaking loud enough for the whole table to hear but quiet enough Ivy felt like they were having a private conversation.

"OK," Ivy said.

Sam downed his drink and stood "Come on then. Let's go."

The group stood up from the table almost at once and began walking down the side of the curb towards the five or six mopeds they had hired. Ivy jumped on the back of Alice's bike, grabbing her around the waist and wishing for a helmet. She looked over to Sam who was jumping on the back of Chad's bike, hooking his fingers around the edge of the seat behind him.

"Let's take the long way round," Gemma shouted from the back of one of the other mopeds.

They rode through the city together. The red and white striped curb flickering as they rode by. Alice and Chad raced each other down the streets so the lights all blurred into one either side of them. Electrical cables threaded between the balconies of the buildings overlooking the roads, creating a canopy of wires that weaved their way back to the masts.

Ivy loved it. She felt so free. She wondered if Sam did too. She looked over to try to steal a glance at him, but he must have felt it because his eyes locked on hers.

Her mind pulled back to a moment when she and Agatha were younger. Their mum had sent them away from the table at a restaurant, when, growing bored of waiting for their meals, they began playing with the salt on the table. They were swinging themselves around a bannister to the staircase that led to the toilets when they spotted a young couple at a table that caught their attention enough to make a game of spying on them. They were playing with each other, which was something Ivy didn't know adults did. Making faces at each other, then hiding behind their menus and laughing, each one trying to top the last face made. Their hands remained entwined the entire time. Agatha pulled on her dress and pointed to her parents who were arguing. Agatha had said years later that she thought their parents only ever seemed to argue about them and Ivy wondered if that was why her dad left them. She remembered looking back at the couple and thinking: this is what love should be, love should be easy. Looking back at her parents she didn't think it was ever easy for them. Reflecting on it now, she wondered if maybe love was supposed to remain young, not stand the test of time.

Her reverie was interrupted by a bump in the road which pushed her up closer to Alice, she could smell coconut in her hair. Looking across at Sam again, he crossed his eyes and puffed out his cheeks at her as if he were aware of her thoughts. He turned back to talk into Chad's ear. *Maybe Sam had the right idea: live fast, have fun and deal with the consequences after.*

This is how Ivy ended up having an orgy in a hostel. She knew she had come to Thailand to 'find herself' but she didn't think she would fall into the cliché of sexual exploration that was group sex, at least, not so quickly. An innocent touch here, a small kiss there and suddenly she was on the bed with Alice holding her close and flicking her tongue over hers.

Alice undressed her with ease and stroked the back of her neck, behind her knees, the inside of her elbows and the tops of her fingers; wherever Ivy felt most sensitive. She was surprised at how well Alice seemed to know her body, she knew exactly where to push for her body to respond better than Ivy did herself.

Others around them were in the same throws, including Sam who Ivy could see rolling around with Gemma who was also kissing Chad. The room was electric with sparks of lust, a sea of mouths open, tentative and slow, fast and hard, testing and teasing and finding a willing counterpart.

Alice kissed down Ivy's body while Dom leaned over and started biting on Ivy's nipple. Ivy opened her legs and wrapped them around Alice's head, and stiffened, before relaxing to bask in the warmth of Alice's mouth. She felt so good her brain was starting to fog and she was almost lost to the feeling.

Alice took Dom's hand and placed it between her own legs. The breath caught in Alice's throat as he began to move inside her and this turned Ivy on more than she realised it would. She was close. She arched her back and fluttered her eyes open enough to see Sam driving into Gemma, he was kissing her when Ivy felt his eyes on her.

Ivy came, suddenly and powerfully, frowning slightly as she did without taking her eyes off of him which forced his own orgasm. Her body was flooded with waves of heat and her eyes closed, almost sleepily, for a second and the spell between her and Sam was broken.

At some point, they all stopped, temporarily satiated and lying with each other in a pile sprawled between the bunks and the floor.

***

Alice and Dom dropped them off at their hotel around 5 a.m. The bar was closed but Sam went to the room to grab some Singha beers they had stashed in there and re-joined Ivy downstairs. He found her sat on the edge of the pool with her legs hanging into the water. Sam rolled his shorts up and sat next to her. He opened one of the beers on the edge of the pool and handed it to her before opening one for himself. They sat there quietly for a while.

Sam thought Ivy would feel weird about what they had done, but she hadn't said anything and although she had been fairly quiet since they left their new friends' hostel, he was pretty certain that was due to tiredness more than anything.

He wasn't sure how he felt about it. He had no problem with being naked in front of Ivy or the fact they had just had sex in front of each other. However, the moment they locked eyes with each other, that did unnerve him. Mainly because even though they hadn't touched each other at any point and even though they were both having sex with someone else, at that moment, it felt like they were just with each other.

His ego told him that when Ivy had orgasmed, it was because of him or at least, it was for him. More than that he realised that he wanted that to be true for more than just his ego. He closed his eyes for a second and remembered opening them, mid-kiss to see Ivy flushed and beautiful with Alice between her thighs, her eyes locked onto his. His mind was completely focussed on Ivy while his body acted and responded to Gemma beneath him.

"What would your mum think if she saw us now?" Ivy asked, interrupting his thoughts. "Do you think she would be surprised?"

"I think I would be surprised if my mum was surprised, you know? I don't think she even notices me anymore, let alone has feelings that hinge on my life choices," he replied.

"She notices you. She cares, Sam. She is just a bit scared of you. Scared of how much of her is in you."

A memory flashed in his brain. *"I don't know where you came from Sam, but you're not mine."* he pushed it out. "You think?"

Ivy nodded.

"I don't think we could be more different. My dad on the other hand...to be honest, I'm terrified I will turn into him one day."

"What do you mean?" she said.

"You know, meek and soulless with no mind of my own." Ivy wasn't the only friend to meet his parents, but she knew them more in the way he did than anyone else.

"Why do you think that?" she asked. Although Sam thought she was asking out of kindness.

"Come on, you've seen him. He barely opens his mouth unless it's to say "What does your mother think?" he said, deepening his voice to impersonate his father.

"He just wants an easy life is all. Be grateful he's even around. At least he didn't check out like mine did."

"Maybe not physically, but mentally he has," Sam answered.

Sam lit a crumpled up joint he found in his pocket. He inhaled and held his breath as long as he could bear it, until he felt a pulsing in his ears, and exhaled harshly before passing it to Ivy.

They passed it back and forward in silence like that for a while.

"What do you remember about your Dad, V?" Sam asked.

"The smell of his hair gel and the scratch of his stubble on my cheek. It didn't matter if he had just shaved, his face was always rough against mine. His beat-up brown dress shoes he wore to work. Just Dad stuff… I always wonder why he left us when he did,"

"Because he sucked at being a dad," Sam answered.

"Or I sucked at being a daughter," she replied.

"Don't say stupid shit you don't believe," he said quickly.

"He left because he got himself into trouble and he couldn't stick it out," Sam offered.

"I knew he got himself into trouble, even then, but I still feel like he would have stuck around if we were worth sticking around for. If I was worth sticking around for."

"You deserve a better Dad than either of us have," Sam responded. He paused. "You know, I'm not great at this stuff, Ivy, but you are worth sticking around for,"

"You're right," she said looking at him. "You aren't great at this stuff." She smiled but he felt her pull away from him a little.

They lapsed back into silence for a few minutes. "Let's stay here," Ivy said, breaking the quiet. Before Sam could respond she continued. "You can sell stuff on the beach like boogie boards and snorkels and I could waitress during the day."

"I could bartend. I think I would be an excellent bartender. Plus, I could always hook you up with free drinks" Sam replied.

"Very good point," Ivy said, uncurling one finger from her beer bottle and pointing at him. She took another swig of her beer. A bird called in short sharp rings.

"Let's throw the passports away now, shall we?" Sam said, knowing he would if she asked him to. He was never really sure why he couldn't be this person all the time, but it all seemed to melt away with the daylight. The vulnerability was replaced with bravado and he went back to not caring about anything again. That was why he liked Ivy, she let him have his moments of being himself and didn't hold it against him when he wasn't. Mostly, she was the family that wouldn't ignore him like the family he grew up with. To her, he wasn't worthless.

"Maybe in the morning," Ivy said quietly smiling.

"It is morning," Sam said, looking at the sun rising above the trees in front of them.

Ivy followed his gaze. "Come on, let's get a few hours' sleep before we go out again."

Chapter 3

As they walked up the beach, Ivy focussed on the sound of the waves pushing their way onto the sand and pulling themselves back again. She had forgotten her sunglasses today, so she kept her eyes on the sand that stretched in front of them. The beach was bordered with brown, faux wooden sun loungers draped with brightly coloured towels and passed out tourists who slept last night's fishbowls off in the sun. A Thai seller pushed a clothes rail, the wheels digging into the soft sand. It was covered with a large shawl that was lifted to showcase the collection of Hawaiian shirts and t-shirts underneath.

Sam looked over to the bar on the edge of the beach like his mouth was suddenly dry. "Drink?" He asked.

"Um...yeah. A beer?" Ivy replied, but Sam had already started jogging over to the bar. Ivy shielded her eyes with her hand to watch him leave and as she did, noticed several other heads turn to do the same. One thing she could say about Sam is he was nice to look at, so she could see why he got so much attention, and for someone so slim, he did have a peach of a bum.

Ivy turned back to face the sea, crossed one ankle over the other and sat down in one swift movement, dropping her small bag to the side and kicking her sandals off. She closed her eyes and listened to the tide, blocking out the noise of the few, other beachgoers around her. She thought back to last night and how glad she was to be on this trip. Last night was definitely...an experience. Even in her head, she struggled to not feel weird about it, physically, she felt great and wasn't that one of the reasons she agreed to take this trip? To do things she normally wouldn't, to try new things, to tick things off her list.

But she knew the part she felt weird about was how she felt about Sam. She wasn't sure where it had come from, but she had wanted him last night and she wondered if he had felt the same. The feel of the sun on her cheeks and chest mingled with the flush she was feeling from reflecting on her evening.

Sam interrupted her thoughts by pressing a cold bottle to the back of her neck. Opening her eyes she took the bottle from him, noticing he had a bottle of white wine for himself. Ivy had the impression he had also had a shot or two whilst ordering. His drinking seemed to be increasing these last few months, and the heat and atmosphere of Thailand seemed to be increasing it further still, but she wasn't going to nag. She wasn't his keeper or his mother, which was ironic because she doubted Vicky would have anything to say on the matter anyway. Besides, she'd tried to broach the subject with him before whenever she thought he was partying a little too hard and he would just brush it off, in his usual Sam way.

"So I got chatting to some guy up there, his name was Hai. - Do you think when his friends see him they say, Hi Hai? - Anyway, I've rented a beach hut from him, for the night. Cost me three quid, gotta love Thailand." He swigged the wine directly from the bottle.

"Well how very generous of you. Where is this quaint, little abode?" Ivy asked in a mock posh accent. Sam took another swig from his bottle of wine and half pointed with the hand holding the bottle to her right. Ivy squinted against the sun so she could just make out some wooden bungalows poking out between the trees that enclosed the far side of the beach. Ivy nodded her head in approval and took a sip of her beer before pulling her phone out of her bag and began looking through her emails for the details of the booze cruise they had booked for tomorrow.

"The boat leaves at twelve tomorrow, but they are picking us up at the hotel for eleven," Ivy said.

"That's fine," Sam replied. Although Ivy knew she would have to be the one to turf him out of bed and organise them to make sure they didn't miss the transfer.

They spent the entire day lounging on the beach. Sam had found her a book left at the bar on one of his many trips back and forth, so Ivy alternated between reading and swimming all afternoon. Neither of them had remembered to bring a towel so they both just lay on the sand until they dried. Ivy shook her hair and watched the sand sprinkle out and inwardly rolled her eyes at the thought of washing it. Sam led asleep with an almost empty wine bottle in his hand. Tracing the shape of his arms with her gaze, her eyes stopped at each individual tattoo that laced them. She had gone with him for the first few, but in the space of a year, he seemed to have added a new one every week. It struck her odd that someone who presented himself to the world as a creature so averse to commitment and permanence could wear it on his skin so openly.

"Are you hungry, V?"

Her eyes snapped to his face at the question unsure whether she had woken him or he had been awake the entire time. "Sure," she replied.

Sam pulled some keys out of the pocket of his shorts and handed them to her. "Number four. I'll come and find you," he said getting up and dusting his front off. Ivy pulled a few notes out of her purse and handed them over. Sam pocketed them and strolled off.

Ivy wasn't sure how Sam felt about last night. It felt like he was in that moment with her, but he wasn't betraying his thoughts about it today. If anything, he was acting a little less interested in her than usual. If that was a thing. Not quite distant but decidedly platonic and a little closed off, so maybe that was his answer: nothing had changed for him.

Brushing it off, she picked up her bag and hooked it over her neck, picked up her sandals back to back so the sand stayed on the soles as much as possible and wandered towards the huts.

He had picked a good one, if he had picked it, that is. There was a hammock outside on the porch area, strung between two trees that bent over the side and roof of the structure. The hut next door had a swing instead, probably because it only had one tree accompanying it, but it didn't look like anyone was staying in it. She opened the door and dropped her bag and shoes on the floor and turned around so she could appreciate the view from the doorway.

A terracotta tiled path led around the back of the hut. She followed the path, on the balls of her feet because of the heat radiating from the tiles and found a small shower. It was a welcome sight and although only partially enclosed by a reed fence, Ivy stripped down, turned the old-fashioned tap and jumped in. The water was cold but refreshing in the humidity.

Ivy cast her gaze over the divider that only came to shoulder height and watched three figures paddleboarding on the horizon and idly wondered if maybe one of them was her dad. Something she had done since he had left them, was to imagine seeing him again, randomly bumping into him in his new life. She was curious how long he had to be gone for her to stop doing so. *Because fifteen years wasn't long enough.*

Her hair was plastered against her neck and face, but it felt less wiry and her skin felt better so she turned the water off. She realised she didn't have a towel to use so she stood there dripping for a moment before changing back into her shorts and bikini top. She could have done with a change of clothes for this evening, but it was a bit late now.

Once dressed she stuffed her bikini bottoms into her back pocket and walked back, dripping, to the front of the hut, scraping her hair back as she went. The tiles weren't as hot on her feet now and the sun was beginning to set. She sat down on the front step, bringing her knees up and hugging her shins to her. Leaning her head on her arms while she watched the sun go down. She started wondering about Sam; where he was and whether he would be coming back soon, but her thoughts quickly morphed into his face when he was coming in front of her last night and it immediately made her wet.

The beach was darker than before, taking on a purplish hue, but it was still more than light enough to see tourists walking along the beach, so she went inside and leant against the door. She unbuttoned her shorts and slid her hand down the front of them.

She replayed the memory of last night in the movie that was her mind, but the frame kept getting stuck on Sam. The way his lips parted slightly and his eyelids grew heavy. The one bead of sweat dripped slowly down his right shoulder onto his thigh as he thrust against Gemma. Her shorts were wet and warm, and she extended her fingers inside her lips and imagined Sam inside her instead. She came quickly, the blood pulsing in her ears and a wave of pleasure washing down her body to the tips of her toes, making her buckle slightly.

That was the first time she had thought about Sam while touching herself before. She knew she could choose either to obsess over the fact that she'd orgasmed thinking of him or put him out of her mind, so she decided on the latter — she had done enough obsessing about Sam for today. *Whatever gets you there.*

Sam returned a few hours later with some skewered meats wrapped in foil, some cardboard pots of Pad Thai, which was quickly becoming Ivy's favourite dish, and a carrier bag of what she correctly presumed was alcohol.

She was lying in the hammock outside reading Papillon, the book Sam had given her earlier that day when he dropped the armful of food onto her lap.

"You've been gone a while. I'm surprised it's not cold." Ivy raised an eyebrow at him before folding the corner of the page she was on and putting the book and food to the side of her. She spent a few awkward minutes shuffling herself up so she could sit cross-legged and eat the food. She was starving now.

"The real mission was the gin," he replied with his mouth full and noodles sticking out of the sides.

"I could have done without if it meant the food was quicker." She said hostilely. She opened the kebabs and smelled the fresh scent of ginger and the tartness of lime. She took a bite. It was chicken. Or it could have been pork. She'd noticed the locals love their *moo ping*. Long, wooden skewers threaded with pineapple, tomatoes and thick cuts of pork. She half expected Sam to come back with a scorpion or something equally unusual, so she was grateful it was food that she was used to. When she finished the kebab, she wrapped the stick in the foil and went to eat the noodles.

"Fork?" she asked.

"You'll have to wait, I'm using it," Sam responded between small hiccoughs.

"Why would you only get one fork? Give it here, you can eat with your hands." Ivy said, holding her hand out for the fork.

"So, could you," Sam said, dangling a noodle in her face with his fingers. Ivy smirked and he handed her the fork.

It was getting dark quickly and there was a nice breeze coming through the trees that broke the humidity slightly. Once they had finished eating, she gathered up her rubbish and swung herself out of the hammock, bending down to pick up Sam's rubbish that lay on the sand. She put it all into the bin inside the door and wiped her hands in her shorts.

"What now?" she asked with her arms folded. Sam responded by holding the bottle of gin up in the air. Ivy turned her nose up. "I am not drinking that straight," she said.

"There's some coke in the bag," Sam said, unscrewing the cap and sniffing the liquid inside.

"Gin. And coke?" She said critically.

"I told you, it was a mission. That's all they had."

She pulled two cans of coke out, opening one and turned around to Sam, who was no longer behind her. He had found his way onto the neighbours' swing so she hoped she had been right earlier in thinking no one was staying there. She walked across the sand to where he sat swinging. Taking a long swig on her way over so she could hold the half-empty can out to him to fill. She went to do the same to the other one, but Sam took it out of her hand and dropped it into the sand in front of him. Ivy sat beside him and drank her drink. They talked for a while and played thumb wars until the gin started taking its effect.

It was about 2 a.m. before Sam fell asleep on the swing. Ivy dragged him over to their hut and into the bed and laid down next to him, but she still felt wide awake so went outside and got into the hammock. She tried to read but even though the moon was quite bright, she couldn't quite see the words on the page.

Giving up, she dropped the book on the floor and rocked herself gently in time to the pounding base of distant music she could hear from bars and clubs. Her mind drifted to memories of nights with Agatha. They used to try to sleep in each other's room but would be so loud and giggly their mum or dad would get up and come charging in. The two girls would feign sleep until they heard the door close, but usually, their mum would still be standing there and march one of them out into their own bed. She smiled at the thought and began dreaming of those nights.

She was almost fully asleep when she felt Sam climb into the hammock with her, tucking her feet into his underarm and cradling them while putting his own against her shoulder.

Chapter 4

Ivy told him she woke with the sun. His arm itched with mosquito bites and his neck ached from sleeping awkwardly in the hammock he didn't remember climbing into. He got up and went to the toilet with his eyes closed, still adjusting to the day, then followed Ivy out the door. She handed him the key and told him to meet her on the main road. Hai was nowhere to be found so he gave the key to a guy setting up his hut with snorkels and other sea gear for hire. He said he knew the guy who rented the huts and would get the key back to him. Sam thanked him and jogged up to meet Ivy.

They pulled over a tuk-tuk, even though the beach was within walking distance, to make sure they had more time to get ready when they got back to the hotel. They arrived around 9 a.m. and Ivy got straight into the shower. Sam started digging through his bag for some clean swim shorts and realised as he bent down that Ivy hadn't fully closed the door. She was stepping out of the shower and reaching for her towel with water dripping down her treacle-toned skin.

He glimpsed her breasts as she pulled the towel towards her, and a flush of heat travelled up his neck, into his face. He turned his attention back to what he was doing and cleared his throat to compensate for the fact that all moisture had left his mouth. The cliched noise made him immediately panic that he was being obvious. But that annoyed him more, the fact he would panic at all, especially around V. He had seen a lot of boobs before. He had even seen Ivy's before the other night. He convinced himself he was just a pervert who didn't want to be caught, which somehow seemed the lesser of two evils.

They made the transfer on time and it was pretty quiet, considering they were about to go to an all-day party on a boat. Everyone that got on the bus was around their age and most of them were already drinking. If Sam had realised the bus driver wouldn't have a problem with alcohol on board, he would have done the same.

"So what can I expect from this boat trip?" she asked.

"You're the one who booked it," he replied.

"But you chose it."

"Dunno, it seems a bit Club eighteen-thirties but the booze is included and it will be full of other young twenty-somethings, so your normal Thursday really, just on a boat."

They were seated under the roof deck with drinks when the boat pulled away and they were laughing and joking as they always have. They found it easy to make new friends on the boat and even partnered up with two strangers to join in one of the games.

"So, you all have your partners?" the holiday rep said into the microphone which distorted every word he said. He couldn't have been much older than Sam and that surprised him. He wondered if he lived in Thailand full time or whether he was just there for the season. "Everyone give our five couples a loud cheer! Give them some support while we hand out these balloons." Balloons were passed down the chain of participants so each couple ended up with three and thankfully before anyone could ask, the rep explained what to do with them. "So, ladies, put one in your mouth and two between your legs - so they are pointing both ways. Now the aim of the game is to pop the balloons between you. But of course, there is a catch. You can only pop them by showing us your best sex moves. SEXUAL POSITIONS ONLY!" he shouted this last part. The whole boat erupted in laughter, whoops and whistles. Ivy looked to Sam who was smirking, and she rolled her eyes exaggeratedly before smiling back. "The winner is not just the quickest to pop all their balloons but is also the most entertaining," he said leadingly. This caused more whistles and whoops, but he didn't wait for the crowd to die down before saying "Ready? On your marks, get set - go!"

Before he had time to register 'go', Sam picked up his new partner and placed her down on her back and wriggled on top of her. She was laughing as he gyrated cheesily to the beat of the music. The first balloon had already popped on the way down and the second wasn't far behind when he looked up to see Ivy's partner had spun himself all the way around at the crotch, so they were facing opposite directions. *Inventive* he thought.

With the final balloon pinched between her teeth, his partner pushed him off of her and onto his back and feigned giving Sam a blowjob, with the balloon between them. He heard everyone cheering at that and he hoped it was directed at him, not one of the other couples. He played into it by putting his hand on her head as she bobbed and he watched as she tried to sneakily bite the balloon. It popped and everyone clapped while she helped Sam up. The other couples seemed to be finishing at the same time except the couple furthest away from him who still had two balloons left.

"And you're out!" The rep said pointing to them. "I mean not even close." he laughed. The couple left the makeshift stage and everyone lightly clapped. "Now then, those were some sexy moves, weren't they?" the rep asked the crowd who responded in their usual way. "So, who's moves were the best? Cheer for your favourite. Number one?" he held his hand over Sam and his partner's head. Sam got some loud cheers from the crown which he played up to pulling mock strongman poses. He saw Ivy shaking her head out of the corner of his eye but she was laughing. "Number two?" He held a hand over Ivy's head and the response was louder still. "And number three?" The couple next to Ivy's partner got a fairly reserved cheer which made Sam think Ivy was in with a good chance of winning. "How about number four?" The final couple got the loudest cheer of all and Sam felt a bit disappointed but smiled anyway. "Looks like it's a tie." Sam and his partner both raised an eyebrow at each other, but the rep said "couples three and four! You are head-to-head for a tiebreaker. Thanks couples one and two but go sit down!" and they did. Cheers followed them off and Ivy was handed a drink by a girl next to her who winked at her. She held it up to her in quiet thanks.

"We were robbed," Sam said as they sat down. They still had a pretty good view of the game, but neither were particularly interested anymore.

"I mean, it's obviously fixed. I should have stayed on," Ivy said before taking a sip of her drink.

CHAPTER 4

"I think you're confused. Our cheers were much louder than yours. Why did you get a drink? I want a drink." He got up and left before Ivy could respond. As he returned he saw everyone's attention on the game and could hear groans and laughter. "What did I miss?" he said, sliding back into the seat opposite Ivy.

"I think we should count ourselves lucky we didn't win - look what those last balloons were filled with." Ivy pointed as a girl ran past them with what looked like shaving cream all down her front.

Sam watched her go by and looked back at Ivy "Friends and lovers—" he said.

"Fuck the others." She replied clinking glasses.

They had lunch on board the boat and there was a delicious spread of barbeque food. Ivy was practically drooling. She filled a plate for herself and began ramming food into her mouth like she hadn't eaten in weeks before he had even sat down beside her.

"You have some in your eyebrow," Sam said with his mouth full of a burger.

"I'm saving it for later," she replied after swallowing but when he looked back at her it was gone, she must have waited for him to look away before brushing it from her face. He'd never seen her self-conscious around him before.

The boat stopped not long after lunch in a small patch of sea that was surrounded by cliffs. The water shone like aquamarine.

Ivy walked to the front of the boat and went to jump off the side edge but Sam grabbed her wrist as she did.

"Ah ah ah, didn't anybody ever tell you not to go swimming for an hour after eating." He said teasingly, looking at a fake watch. "I'm afraid you will have to join the back of the—"

* * *

Ivy jumped and took Sam with her as she did, cutting him off. It wasn't often she got the upper hand with him so when they sprang up from the water, he was already trying to dunk her back down, but only for a second because he knew she would hate it.

They swam for a few minutes before joining in with a mass game of chicken. Ivy started hooking her left leg over Sam's shoulder.

"Woah Woah Woah — who said you could be on top?"

"Your fat ass," Ivy replied.

"Don't even go there King, we both know who the one with the fat ass is." Ivy pushed on Sam's shoulders to hook her right leg over. "Well I am doing this in protest, I hope you know." He said in mock grumpiness.

"Shut up and get in there jelly-bum," she said, hitting her heels into his chest like a horse.

He waded over to the pack and on the count of three by a distant voice, they all went at each other trying to wrestle each other until one team was left standing.

Ivy was laughing so much she started choking at one point when water splashed into her open mouth. A guy came up and whacked her on the back for a minute until she gave him an embarrassed thumbs up and lifted her back onto Sam's shoulders before immediately wrestling her back into the water.

She came up laughing.

"Showed a sign of weakness there V. My turn to go on top now," Sam said as he sat on top of her shoulders, tucking his feet under her arms. It didn't take long for Sam to be pulled off and they were both pushed into the water.

Ivy opened her eyes under the shimmering blue-green and stayed a while, looking up to the blinding sun. She thought back to when she and Agatha learned to swim on holiday. One of the few memories she had with her dad in them. They had their own pool in a villa. Her dad took it in turns to hold them while they kicked and paddled. "You're a little water baby aren't you Aggy?" she hears her dad whispering in her ear. He never said the same to Ivy though. Agatha always found it easy, she floated on top of the water from day one. Ivy had to fight for breath with every kick. She got it eventually but only on their last day when their holiday was over.

Chapter 5

They spent the next day on the beach. Mainly because it meant that they could sleep in the sun and recover and, from Sam's point of view, they were close to the bars and restaurants. *Hair of the dog that bit your ass* he had said.

Ivy headed to the water, she wanted a swim to cool off and Sam joined her not long after she got waist-deep. They stood there and spoke for a while, bobbing casually as the waves came in. Ivy kept looking over Sam's shoulder as they spoke, her eyes were fixed on the things they had left on the beach. She pictured the things one by one and thought it was only some cash, towels and clothes but she still felt a bit awkward leaving them unattended.

"Most of the cash is in my shorts pocket," Sam said. Ivy turned to look at him, "Just in case," he finished.

It was always surprising how readily Sam could read her mind, even though she was pretty good at reading his too. Not through any sense of the strong bond they had as friends but more out of familiarity. Despite the fact that they were both very different, they were also very much the same like their differences were equally matched and fitted together perfectly. She couldn't have known as a teenager that Sam would fill the space in her that her father had left. Sam pushed her boundaries and she kept him grounded and this worked for them.

Ivy usually knew what Sam was thinking because she was thinking it too, at least until this holiday when she had struggled to follow his train of thought, but if she was honest with herself, she had struggled to follow her own as well of late.

She thought back to their conversation the night before. They were perched on some stools outside a bar called Savana, drinking the sugary cocktails that were becoming their usual, when a group of guys approached her.

"What's your name, beautiful?"

"Is this your boyfriend?"

Ivy looked between the men and Sam and replied, "Yeah, yeah he is," instinctively putting her hand across the table for Sam to take, which he did.

"Fair enough, no harm meant, mate" one said before walking off.

"You're a lucky man, there," another said patting Sam on the back and the group drifted off into the bar.

"Thanks," Ivy said, when the group was out of earshot, bringing her hand back to her drink.

"I'm surprised, you didn't like the blond one with the muscles, he seems your type."

Ivy choked slightly on her drink and cleared her throat.

"No, they were all too obvious for my liking. Like, show handsome. I mean except for the one with the purple shirt on, didn't he look like Sid from Ice Age?"

Sam laughed, "That's exactly what he looked like, poor fella."

Ivy smiled into her drink.

"Why didn't we ever get together, V?" he asked, catching Ivy off guard.

"Don't be stupid,"

"I'm not. I'm being serious. I'm hot, you're hot, it makes sense," he asked smirking.

"Nothing that comes out of your mouth ever makes sense, especially when you're drunk," she laughed trying to brush his comments off.

"Maybe, but you know that I am much more truthful when I am," he retorted.

Ivy looked him in the eye, not sure whether he was being genuine or not. She remembered the first day she met Sam — had she wanted him then?

"We've been friends since we were thirteen. I know you too well to want you," she said smiling.

Sam leant in, so close she could feel the warmth of his skin even though there was still space between them, and she wondered if she had spoken too soon. That wasn't the whole truth though. She knew that a relationship with Sam would be a pretty terrible idea. If it went wrong, which it inevitably would, he would get bored of her, cheat on her maybe and then she would lose him entirely. As friends, no matter how close they were, she could keep him at arm's length and keep herself guarded.

"Your loss," he said, shrugging and laughing. She laughed too, but when he picked up another girl from the bar and they both walked Ivy back to the hotel, leaving her there, she thought about it. The sound of him kissing his new friend prickled her more than it usually would and she wondered if that was because she wanted it to be her he was kissing.

Bringing her thoughts back to the present, Ivy waded over to Sam and cocked her head to one side, one eye squinting against the sun.

"Come on, let's go deeper then," she said and Sam turned to let her jump onto his back. He walked them out to deeper water and when she figured he could no longer touch the seafloor, he loosened his hold on Ivy's legs and let her drift from him and they let the water sway them as they basked in the sun.

She watched Sam idly as he held his nose and dropped down into the water dunking himself entirely before resurfacing. "You thirsty?" he asked.

"Yeah, a bit," she replied.

"I'll go grab us a drink,"

"O.K., I'll be here," she said and twisted in the water to face the sun again. She listened to him move against the water until he was so close to the shore, she couldn't hear him. Turning and watching him walk up to the bar while she paddled lightly in the water. She was looking forward to him returning with a cold drink. The sea felt like a lukewarm bath wrapping around her limbs, only mildly satisfying. She closed her eyes and dunked her head back into the water and swished her hair around so she could feel the saltwater crunch leaving her hair, knowing it would return when it dried. lying back, she floated on top of the water with her eyes closed against the sun and when Sam came back with her drink, stirring the water around her as he approached, she acted as if she had forgotten he was getting them.

"I have snorkels," Sam announced and held her drink up to show them hanging from his left arm. She looked around to see she had drifted back closer to the beach without noticing. She placed her knees onto the seabed and watched the disturbed sand whirl around her thighs as she took her drink from him.

She sipped the cocktail through the straw for an almost aching minute and stared out to the horizon. She felt awkward like she needed to do something, away from Sam for a minute to allow her to untangle her thoughts from him. "I fancy an ice cream," she said and started to wade out of the sea.

"OK, cool. There's a place up the road—" He started.

"It's fine you stay here, with our stuff. I'm a big girl." Ivy said over her shoulder.

* * *

Sam knew better than to argue with her, but he had obviously done something to piss her off. Usually, she was quite upfront with him, she was never afraid to voice her opinion whether it was something Sam would like or not, but she had seemed more closed off to him these last few days.

He watched her walk purposefully out of the water thinking she was about as gentle as a thunderstorm and looked down at the snorkels on his arm. He had only got them for her. The water was crystal clear anyway, so they weren't needed. He wasn't sure why he cared, but he did. *That's a lie. You know why you care.* Maybe what happened at the hostel had freaked her out after all. He felt like there had always been a wall of glass between them and inside that moment, that wall had cracked. It would only take a gentle touch for it all to come crashing down and Sam didn't think he would be the one to do it. He was afraid of where the pieces would land.

* * *

She was annoyed with herself. Putting her face in her hands, she rubbed her eyes. Why did she make herself so miserable like this, with what-ifs and maybes? Especially when she was in a beautiful country, as far away from home as she had ever been, having an amazing time. Ivy thought that when

CHAPTER 5

she ran away from home her problems would stay there, that the uncertainty and the second-guessing would stay in England, but she should have known, she would always bring herself along to create more.

She had made it to the front of the queue in the ice cream shop while lost in thoughts of Sam and hadn't even thought about what she wanted. Her mouth opened to say vanilla when a voice next to her said: "The salted caramel is the best."

"Salted caramel then please."

It wasn't that she was so easily led but it was easier than making up her mind. She turned to see who spoke and a tall guy with very green eyes stood next to her.

The stranger smiled before turning to the server and said, "make that two please, I'm buying."

"It's fine, I got it," Ivy said. There was no way she was accepting money from a guy she didn't know, she didn't want to owe anyone anything, so she dropped the coins she had onto the counter and left.

He caught up with her a few minutes later. "Have I offended you?" he said, walking backwards so he could face her as she walked back towards the beach.

"Really? Does that work for you?" she asked without stopping, but still with a hint of a smile on her face she couldn't hide.

"Offending women or trying to buy them ice cream?" he asked. *He was definitely a charmer.*

"This whole 'I'm a great guy and oh so charming and cheeky, how could you say no' routine," Ivy said.

"Luke." He said, sticking his hand out in front of him. She couldn't tell if he was being ironic or still playing the part, but she took his hand anyway and let him shake it.

"Ivy." She replied.

"Where are you going Ivy?" he asked and the way he said her name made her cheeks warm. She hoped she wasn't doing anything as fatal as blushing.

"Back to the beach," she said in between licks of her ice cream, feigning nonchalance with a touch of flirting.

"May I walk with you? Or maybe head to the same place at an appropriate distance so that you don't have to go there completely alone, but still maintain a sense of your independence. I feel like that is important to you." he said.

She just laughed. "OK, I can't cope with the try-hard act so if you cut it out you can walk me back." She wasn't sure why she was agreeing to it because even though he was quite attractive, she wasn't really interested. Especially because he came off as if he chatted girls up all the time but was trying to act as if she was the only one in the world, he'd tried these lines on, like she wouldn't see right through them. But she did let him walk her and in fairness, he did drop the act.

They reached the beach and he offered to get her a drink at the bar which she declined and held up her ice cream by way of explanation.

"Meet me tonight then." He said more than asked. "Meet me at Coco's. It's just up there on the main strip — you can't miss it."

"Maybe." She replied and walked back to Sam. She was playing up to him and she knew it. "Hey." She joined him on the towels.

"Where's my ice cream?" he asked her, and she held the cone out to him. There was only a bit left, but he put his hand around hers and bit into both the cone and the ice cream inside.

"He wanted me to meet him tonight," she said. Sam didn't respond. "At some bar called Coco's," she added.

"Are you gonna?" he asked.

"Maybe," she replied, in the same manner as she had replied to Luke.

They did walk past Coco's that night and she saw Luke over Sam's shoulder near the bar on his own, but they didn't stop in Coco's that night, and they both went home together.

Chapter 6

Ivy was dozing but could feel Sam, lying there, still, but awake. His breathing was calm, but he seemed restless. His fingers began to pitter on his chest, almost like a quick tick of a clock he was willing the seconds away. She could have slept but felt uneasy with him awake next to her.

Maybe she should say something, but Sam suddenly sat up, making Ivy jolt a little. He swung his legs around and padded over to the bathroom, closing the door behind him. She rolled to her right and peeled one eye open. The alarm clock glowered at her from his side of the bed in small, red, digital numbers. It was 3:14 a.m. Although the air conditioning worked, the shutters rattled as they rotated and thick strings of dust wavered in the vents. She looked down at her semi bare skin. They had both been sleeping in their underwear, which she normally felt comfortable in, but tonight she felt exposed. *We've been doing this since we were kids so you would expect it to feel natural by now.*

It didn't help that usually, they would just talk to each other about this stuff. Mostly Ivy would talk, and Sam would pretend to only half listen in his 'too cool to care' kind of way, but Ivy knew he did care. At least about her. This thought made her heart flicker in her chest and caught her by surprise because this wasn't new information to her. For some reason, thinking about how Sam felt about her, felt new at that moment. The thought of him caring about her in any way felt good but also anxiety-inducing.

Sam came out of the bathroom, interrupting her thoughts. She cast her eyes over to watch him without moving her head. He was wearing a pair of black boxers that hung low on his sharp hips. He was full of hard edges and corners, she thought. Ivy watched as he put on a black, short-sleeved shirt without doing it up. He let it hang there, exposing his milk-coloured chest and barely-there abs. Stretching up, he curled his back inwards and sighing loudly as he released. Ivy took the time to appreciate the contours of him in the dark. She watched as he slid the balcony door open, grabbed a half-drunk bottle of whisky from the table that sat in the corner of the room, and stepped onto the balcony.

He pulled one of the white, plastic chairs from the table in the corner, to the edge of the balcony, scraping it across the floor as he went, oblivious to the noise he was making. *It's a good job I wasn't sleeping* Ivy thought.

He pushed his head through the centre gap of the small stone pillars that made up the balcony perimeter and stared out for a while, before sitting back and unscrewing the whisky cap and taking four or five gulps like it was water. Ivy was always surprised with how well he could drink, maybe he had no taste buds because Ivy wouldn't even be able to drink a sip without having to wash it down with something else. This was his third or fourth bottle and he was getting a taste for the Thai drink that was served in most bars.

She had a perfect view of him right now from the bed. The low lights of the hotel pool bounced off his still pale skin. *How can he still be so white after almost three weeks abroad?* she thought, furrowing her brows slightly. Without looking, she knew her own skin was a golden brown and would only get darker.

She took the time to drink him in, watching his tiny, tattooed chest rise and fall, and his Adam's apple bob as he drank from the bottle. Lowering her gaze, and tracing the outline of his abs with her mind's eye. Her mouth devoid of moisture, she licked her lips, a somewhat involuntary move that made her feel weird. But her gaze continued down, following his snail trail and to the edge of his boxers.

What was she doing? She was suddenly annoyed with herself. *This was Sam* she told herself. Her best friend and a complete loser most of the time. *This isn't some fairy tale where you find out it was the best friend all along*, she scolded herself.

Sam was selfish, a bit of a drunk and super annoying. *But man, was he hot.* Plus, his 'I'm so cool and uncaring' act did work on her, much to her dismay. He must have felt her eyes on him because he glanced over his shoulder, his eyes catching on hers. Ivy immediately shut her eyes and shifted herself, more from embarrassment from being caught than anything. But it only took a few seconds for her eyes to flicker open again and find Sam was still staring at her intently.

They maintained eye contact like that for a while, seconds that could have been an eternity. She didn't know how she could feel such contrasting emotions, not in the least bit awkward staring into his eyes like that, but crazy scared at the same time about what it meant, if anything.

Sam took a large swig of whisky, never taking his eyes away from hers. He swallowed and stood quietly, before walking softly over to the bed, leaving the bottle on the table next to the balcony doors. Ivy tried to push down the warmth sweeping her chest and cheeks. Sam climbed onto the bed and led beside her. *Weren't we going to separate these beds weeks ago?* His body was facing hers, and still, neither of them said a word, he just stared. Ivy adjusted her face and stared back. His deep, brown eyes seemed to say so much. It was like he was telling her everything in that moment. Or maybe she was imagining it. Maybe he was telling her how tired he was. But she wanted him to be telling her how much he wanted her. If just to feel wanted for a while. She watched his brows turn down at the edges and felt her heart quicken slightly, at the seemingly innocent gesture.

Ivy rolled onto her back as if trying to go back to sleep, leaving her arm to her side, one hand near his face. She felt the warmth of his breath and she exhaled quickly. Trying to breathe and stay calm. She didn't intend to do this. Is this even what she wanted? There was a reason they had been friends for all these years though. He was sometimes kind and always fun. He was fearless too, but she doubted that helped in this instance.

Ivy's thoughts were interrupted when she felt Sam's fingers brush lightly against the back of her hand. Her heart jumped as he began to pull at her fingers, gently threading his through hers.

This was too much. Her mind was racing, filling with more and more thoughts. Thoughts she had no business thinking. She didn't know why but she had to get out, to escape. Not that she was exactly sure what she was escaping from. Grabbing her dress from the floor, Ivy strode out of the room in four steps. She threw the door open, pulling her dress on as she stormed out, not caring if she was flashing other guests as she did and carried on walking with big strides into the balmy, mid-evening air.

Her steps were so purposeful, that it took her a minute to realise what a stupid idea that was. She was walking around a Thai hotel, in only her underwear and as it turned out, Sam's t-shirt which was a bit tight and only just grazed the line of where her bum cheeks met her thighs. She was also barefoot and keyless. Turning a corner she stopped still, leaning against the wall almost as if to hide. She caught her breath quickly and as she did, she realised she needed to go back, but as she turned, Sam was directly behind her. He had followed her out.

"Ivy—" he began, but she was done thinking about it, turning on the spot, she grabbed his face with two hands and pulled him towards her. She kissed him then, hard. No thinking, just feeling, and what she was feeling was overwhelming gratitude for him. Whatever it was buzzing in her brain a moment ago just stopped and it was bliss.

His lips were so soft, and his mouth was so warm and inviting and she resigned herself to the thought that she could live in this kiss forever, even as a memory where for a short while, the only thing they had in common were their two tongues. Sam wrapped his arms around her and pushed her against the wall, grounding her completely to the moment. This was right, he was right, she needed it, she needed the silence he could provide.

Sam kissed the edge of her mouth and trailed hot, whisky kisses down her throat and across her chest that burned her skin at their touch, before returning his mouth to hers. He began running his hand up her throat and pushing into her hair, pulling at the curls at the back of her head a little to make her arch her back, throw her head up and gasp for air just a little. He clearly knew what he was doing, but Ivy batted the thought away because right now he was hers and only hers.

She could feel the power she held over him right now. Like if she said "jump" he would be up on the railings before she could blink. But she also knew not to get too attached to this feeling because of how quickly it would go away and the roles would reverse. In a moment it would be her on her knees saying "I'll jump if you let me." But it felt good, no matter how short-lived, to know that another human being was willing to twist themself in such a way just to please you.

Barely able to breathe, she felt like she needed to consume him, if she could climb into his skin and just live inside him for a while, that would satisfy her. She started pulling at her shirt, or rather his shirt and pushed it over her shoulders. Almost hesitating. If they did this, she was giving in, closing the door on whatever came before, or maybe she had already done that by kissing him. She didn't get to finish the thought though, because the next thing Ivy knew, her feet went out from beneath her. The wall she was leaning on, she was quickly realising, was a door. She was on her back on the same terracotta tiles that ran through the rest of the hotel, clouded by the darkness of the room they had inadvertently entered. Sam landed on top of her in a bit of a heap, winding her slightly with a dull elbow to the stomach.

The pair looked up, almost in unison, to see a confused, tired, Asian man in a robe standing over them. They had found themselves in the doorway of another guest's room who must have heard noises and decided to investigate.

Ivy smiled awkwardly and pushed Sam off of her, scrabbling forward, onto her hands and knees, pulling herself out of the room. Straightening up on the door frame when she reached it. Then, she ran. She laughed as she ran, she couldn't help it, the adrenaline bubbled up in her chest and in her reverie, she didn't feel guilty about leaving Sam behind, especially when she heard his laughter and smack of bare feet behind her. *Of course, that would happen to us*, she thought and a little voice responded *because it was a sign to stop.* She shoved it away and concentrated on finding their room.

Ivy didn't realise quite how far she had wandered off before until she had made it back to the room. She was still sucking big gulps of air, but she had stopped laughing and Sam was close on her tail.

"Open...the door." she panted.

Sam looked at her sheepishly. "Probably should have picked up the key before following you."

Ivy rolled her eyes and they laughed again, but only half-heartedly. *Irresponsible*, Ivy thought hypocritically. That was another thing to add to the Sam

Johnson Cons List. She turned and started walking back down the corridor they had just run up, probably waking every guest in the process and headed for the reception desk.

The woman at reception didn't seem too impressed with their attire. She had a small pinched face and seemed to loom over them from over the counter. Her eyes were heavy with lack of sleep, or age - Ivy wasn't sure which. She also didn't seem impressed with the fact they got locked out of their room in the middle of the night. Ivy mumbled something about how this couldn't have been the first time this had happened. She seemed a bit high and mighty considering the pool was full of skinny dippers the night they arrived. This wasn't five-star family accommodation or anything. But she did eventually phone for a porter to walk them back to their room and open the door for them.

Ivy walked in first and Sam stayed a few steps behind her. Once the door had shut, Ivy turned slowly and looked up at Sam. The electricity around him hadn't exactly melted away, but it had fizzled enough for her to think more clearly now. She wasn't sure what to say, but Sam began to open his mouth to speak and the thought of what he could say scared her enough to blurt something out herself. "I'm going to bed."

"I'll join you," Sam replied, a smile slowly touching his eyes.

"I'm tired, Sam." She looked at him heavily and the smile faded from Sam's eyes.

"OK," Sam said, his eyebrows pushing together and his eyes glassy. He had this way of raising his walls so quickly. Which equally annoyed and pleased Ivy at this moment. It at least meant she didn't have to talk to him about what happened, even if secretly, almost secret from herself, she wanted to.

Ivy turned away and listened to him walk over to the table and pick up the whisky bottle. She couldn't work out how he was feeling but she could feel something radiating off him close enough to anger, to make her want to pull away further.

She climbed under the sheet but didn't take his t-shirt off. Ivy knew he was watching her, and pretended not to notice. She rolled onto her side, so she was facing the door, away from the balcony, and away from Sam. He stepped onto the balcony and sat down, staring out over the hotel pool again.

CHAPTER 6

Ivy felt shitty now, but nothing good would have come of them sleeping together. Even if she was still pulsing with the thought of touching him. Apart from Agatha and her mum, Sam was her only constant and she couldn't risk that. She closed her eyes and willed herself to sleep. Things will hopefully look a bit different in the morning. But instead of sleeping, she spent the next half hour replaying what just happened and imagining what came next, before finally drifting off.

Chapter 7

The sunlight streamed through the balcony glass doors, waking Ivy only once it got close enough to brush her foot with comforting warmth. She opened one eye slowly and, slightly blinded by the bright light that filled the room, she shielded her face before opening the other. She felt groggy and almost physically sick with tiredness this morning. The room was stuffy and stifling.

She clambered up, unravelling herself from the sheets as she went and pushed herself to the balcony, sliding open the doors. Standing there for a moment in the doorway, her hand rested on the handle, while she acclimatised herself to the bright sun and appreciated the breeze gently tickling her skin as it moved her tight curls around her face.

She took a few deep breaths and scanned her eyes across the horizon, appreciating the view of the beach and strip they had visited almost every night so far. Turning from the view, she walked back towards the bed and grabbed her phone charging on the bedside table. 12:34 p.m. Why had she slept so long? She wasn't exactly an early bird and she was used to trying to sleep off a hangover, but they had flown halfway around the world and she wanted to make the most of their time there. Even if Sam's definition of making the most of it meant trying all the local delicacies of Thai drugs, girls or booze.

She looked to the bed at that thought and realised he wasn't there, before casting her eyes over to the bathroom door opposite the bed and seeing it was wide open, and the room empty. She was alone.

Why didn't he wake her? Why go out without her and leave her to sleep the day away? It was then Ivy thought back to last night and took a guess at why

CHAPTER 7

Sam might have left her this morning without a word.

She touched her lips as if the memory of his were imprinted on them. She remembered feeling something when she kissed him last night. He had made everything in her still and she wasn't exactly sure what that meant. After trying to dismiss these thoughts of him without success, she let her mind circle back to his leaving again.

"How childish do you wanna be?" she groaned aloud. *This is how he wanted to behave when nothing had even happened between us?* Although, she was unconvinced by this last thought. It wasn't as if a kiss was nothing to her, but she assumed it was for him, and so her inner ramblings flipped again.

What was I thinking? He is just about passable as a friend right now; I definitely shouldn't be thinking about him as anything more. Even if it's just adding benefits to our current situation.

If Sam wanted to be a dick, I can be too, she thought. She started typing a text to Agatha.

```
Hey, just checking in. I'm having a great time. Haven't really
left the hotel much this week, but I think I'll book a trip to one
of the smaller islands or something tomorrow. Oh, and Sam's a
dick. I may kill him before I get home, but you'll give me an
alibi, right? :)
```

Ivy threw her phone onto the unmade bed and stomped into the bathroom. She tugged Sam's t-shirt from last night over her head and shimmied her underwear down her legs, dropping them on the floor with the tip of her big toe in the bathroom doorway. She reached in to turn the shower controls and let the water run for a minute.

OK, she was being a tad dramatic, she knew. It's not like they haven't separated before and maybe he was trying to be considerate by letting her sleep. *Why am I still doing this to myself?*

She turned to stare at herself in the small mirror above the sink. Waiting for the water to warm, she pulled handfuls of her hair up into a ponytail at the top of her crown and then let it slowly fall around her shoulders again. She pulled at one of the curls at the nape of her neck and watched it spring back, dazed in a daydream, noticing the steam in the air before remembering why she was in here.

Testing the water with her hand, which was just warmer than tepid, she stepped in face first, soaking her hair and with her eyes closed, she tipped her head back and started paying attention to the water running from her hairline down the inside of her nose and catching on the corner of her eyes, so it felt like tears.

She didn't know how much time had passed since she had gotten in the shower or how long he had been there, but the air had shifted in the room. Ivy felt Sam without seeing him. Had she closed the door? If she was mad at him before she wasn't now, she didn't have the energy to be mad at him anymore. She felt him move into the shower and crossing one arm around her, he cupped her left cheek in his hand. She turned her body in his direction but still couldn't bring herself to open her eyes and look at him just yet. He pulled her face around and up to his until she felt his lips brush softly against hers. His chest, millimetres away from hers. She let him kiss her. Although she wasn't entirely sure what she wanted, at this moment, it felt OK to let it happen. Kissing him back she pushed herself forward wrapping her arms around him and running her hands over his shoulders, the t-shirt he was still wearing, folded and wrinkled under her hands. Water dribbled between the edges of their lips and collected in between her cleavage that was pressed against his chest.

He pulled back slightly and when he spoke, she felt his words on her mouth. "Are you sure?"

She responded by kissing him again. Telling herself that all she wanted was one moment with him, just one moment if only to show herself she could. It could live in this bubble of Thailand and nothing would have to change. He was much gentler with her than she thought he would be, but every touch was electric. He pulled his kiss away and lowered himself to his knees, threading his shoulders under her thighs and pushing his mouth into her, so she was balanced on him ready to fall if he let her.

His tongue felt so soft against her and she felt so good she was beginning to pant, the sound of which was drowned out by the water running down her body, even to her own ears. She couldn't help but come wholly which only increased her need for him. Unhooking him from her thighs, she pulled him up by his face and kissed him so hard she wondered if his pale mouth might bruise.

She pulled his hands around her thighs and he braced himself ready to catch her as she jumped, intuitively knowing her intentions. Feeling how hard he was against her stomach made her ache inside.

Sam carried her out of the shower, but she didn't notice they had moved until he dropped her onto the bed and climbed on top of her. She could still hear the shower running which acted as white noise to her brain, which was a small mercy because right now was not a time for thinking.

They kissed each other frantically, their tongues searching and pushing inside each other's mouths, leaving Ivy gasping for air. Her desire taking over, she pulled his wet shirt over his head, struggling against his damp skin. She tried to keep her mouth connected with his skin at all points as if the passion would be broken if she stopped. He threw the top behind her, where it landed with a clap, and his mouth found hers again. She kissed him hard while she pushed her hands down his shorts and eased them off of him, before rolling him onto his back, guiding his body with her hands. Sitting astride him, he sat up, he pressed himself against her and reached to thread his fingers in her wet hair.

She ran her fingers up his arms and shoulders then leveraged herself on him to push herself up and sink back down on him all in one motion and the feeling of him inside her made her gasp in a small way. Sam moaned and the sound vibrated into her lips. She held still there for a half-forgotten second and arched her back before beginning to move back and forth and let him fall into her rhythm.

Chapter 8

Ivy woke to the sound of distant nightlife with a half-smile on her face. Her legs were tangled in Sam's and her head was wedged in the gap between their pillows, close to his neck. She inhaled him deeply and realised he smelled different to her now. Maybe he was letting off some Ivy specific pheromones, but he definitely smelled more...something. But she also wondered, with a slight sadness if he smelled a little less like home than he did before.

The sheet was bunched up at the bottom of the bed and the corner of the mattress sheet was undone, the elasticated edge rolled around her shoulder. She rubbed the inside of her foot up the sheet underneath her and felt the rough texture of sand against her skin. Wondering idly if Sam had been to the beach today or if it was leftover, still there from yesterday.

She unwrapped herself slowly from Sam, careful not to wake him. Rolling onto her back she propped herself up on both of her elbows to assess the damage. Her eyes drifted over her naked body, to the floor where small puddles from their soaking wet feet still glistened. The shower was no longer on, but Ivy didn't remember Sam turning it off. She turned to look at Sam beside her. He had such an innocence about him when he slept as most dangerous boys do.

Looking at him now, she didn't see any of his acting out, his machismo or his self flagellating dependence on self-medicating. She saw the boy ignored by his parents and open only to her. Like that final barrier between them had been broken. She wasn't sure if that would be a good thing.

She got up from the bed, and walked towards the balcony, stretching her

CHAPTER 8

arms above herself and smiling as she did. Ivy noticed some cigarettes hanging out of Sam's pocket so picked one out along with a blue plastic lighter that was missing the protective metal cap. The doors still open from earlier, she walked out onto the balcony to smoke it, without bothering to dress. She felt perfectly at home in her own body most of the time anyway, but right now she radiated an after-sex glow that made her feel infinitely alluring and like it would be a disservice to herself, and others, to cover herself up. It was beginning to get dark by this point anyway.

She put the cigarette to her mouth, thinking back to Sam's lips on her skin, sparked the lighter which produced a huge flame that warmed her face and took a long drag on the cigarette against the flame until it glowed orange. Her body wavered as she felt a head rush before she had taken her second drag and it wasn't the first time today. It had been a few years since she last smoked and longer still since she smoked sober.

She knew she had been kidding herself earlier when she thought she could have Sam just once, but she knew she'd stepped over the line into the darkness of Sam's orbit and now she had a taste for it, the pull was only going to get stronger.

Sounds of Sam beginning to stir behind her caught her attention, but she ignored it and continued to look out over the balcony. Modern, angular villas built into the sides of the hills amongst the fields of palm trees stood out against the low sun. Walking up behind her, he wrapped his arms comfortably around her waist, resting his chin on her shoulder. He had put some boxers on, and Ivy could feel the soft cotton resting against her skin. She held the cigarette over her shoulder, to his mouth and let him take a drag, the smell of smoke, already stale, wrapped around the curls that hung by her ear. He pulled away, still breathing in through his teeth. Lifting his head from her shoulder but keeping the contact by moving his hands to her bare hips.

"We going out?" Sam said, blowing the smoke from his mouth as he spoke.

Ivy's eyes flicked to the glow of the strip of bars in the near distance "Do you want to?" Ivy replied.

"Unless you can give me a reason to stay in?" He questioned and Ivy thought if anyone else had said that she would have found it cheesy as hell, but the way

Sam said it made her toes tingle slightly. Although Ivy couldn't see his face, she could feel his eyes on the back of her neck. He kissed her shoulder.

She took a final drag of the cigarette, which was just filter by now and burned her fingertips as she sucked. She flicked it over the balcony and turned around to face Sam.

When in Thailand. She thought. Took a step towards him and kissed him lightly on the lips. She looked into his eyes, grabbed his hand in hers and took him back to the bed.

* * *

Sam got up and walked to the other side of the room, where his green hoodie was draped over one of the chairs and pulled a little plastic baggie of weed out of the pocket, along with some rizla and tobacco. Where he got it from in a completely foreign country, she didn't know but knew better than to ask if she wanted to skip the big man around town speech, he had probably prepared for her.

He padded back over to the bed and climbed in. He reached across her, his chest softly grazing her nipples, which awakened goosebumps down the sides of her chest. He grabbed *Papillon,* from her bedside table and sat back. He crossed his legs and placed the book in his lap as a makeshift table to roll on.

Ivy couldn't help but zone in on the process of it all, the curling of the paper and the back and forth of his fingers. Especially the way he licked the gummed edge of the rolling paper. It made her think of what they've just done, and she felt a rush of emotions at once. Calm because she felt so at peace with and comfortable with herself and excited at the thought of doing it again but there was a small seed of embarrassment.

Embarrassment at the thought of all those people who said they were never just friends giving her that knowing look, sure, but it was more than that. She was embarrassed for herself. Embarrassed that she fell for Sam's charm, after ten years of seeing how he treated relationships, embarrassed that she had spoiled something so important to her.

Ivy started to feel a cool tingling beneath her skin and she knew the weed was doing its thing. She looked at Sam and began laughing. She couldn't stop herself, she felt it bubbling in her stomach and rising through her throat and the sound was all around her. She knew she was laughing but it sounded so distant, it could have been someone else.

Sam was smiling dopily at her. He had more of a tolerance to weed than she did. *Like he did with everything*, she thought. She had laughed for so long, she was no longer making a sound. Her stomach ached and she fell back on the bed and carried on silently laughing, staring at the off-white peeling ceiling. She wasn't quite sure what she was laughing at, probably the absurdity of the situation, but she thought: no matter what happened next with them, their relationship was forever shaped into something different. What was once a circle, was now a square.

Sam's face appeared above hers and he kissed her, probably just to stop her laughing, but she welcomed it and she started to roll the squareness of their new relationship around her mouth with her tongue. Sam pulled back and asked her, "What?" as if responding to her thoughts, not her words.

"I just...I don't know if I want to be square," Ivy sighed.

* * *

Sam was used to Ivy dropping him into the middle of a train of thought and expecting him to know exactly what she was talking about. She seemed to have most conversations in her head first and only ever came to the conclusions out loud. He wasn't too worried though, because he realised this was a high thought, so the beginning probably wasn't too important.

"What's wrong with square? I quite like squares myself."

"I don't know. They have pointy corners and sharp edges and that seems... suspicious to me."

Sam didn't understand what she meant by this, but he enjoyed watching her try and make sense of this riddle.

"Did you notice on the plane on the way over, that none of the windows had corners?" she took another toke on the joint before continuing. "I mean they weren't window-shaped. They were round." She seemed to consider this for a moment before saying: "Do you know why that is? It's because corners are weak points, so if you're up in the air — she lifted her arm and curled her fingers around before dropping it again — and the pressure gets too much, the windows won't crack."

"What happens if they crack?" Sam asked. He wasn't really sure if they were talking about the aeroplane windows anymore, but she answered anyway.

"Then all the air gets sucked out and we suffocate," Ivy responded in a hurry as if she couldn't breathe again until the words had left her mouth. She turned her head and looked Sam in the eyes and he thought about how beautiful she was.

He finally replied. "Well that's a cheery thought." and they half-heartedly laughed together for a minute before lapsing back into silence. Sam turned himself to rest his head in Ivy's lap. She brushed a stray curl from his face and the intimacy of it made his chest ache. "Corners can be good too, you know. I mean, they are just two straight lines," he drew a corner in the air with the joint above his head, between him and Ivy, "that meet each other and think 'hey this feels pretty good, let's keep doing this'."

"They meet each other and think 'this feels good' yeah, but what about when you shine a light on them huh?"

"What about it?" he asked, handing over the joint.

She took another drag. "Light can't bend around corners. So, there is always gonna be one of those lines in the dark." she had said matter of factly. And as usual, he was taken aback by how quietly clever she was. She clearly paid much more attention than him in school to be discussing the elements of physics while she was high.

"Wow, you are just a bundle of joy tonight, no more weed for you," Sam said, taking the spliff away from Ivy and finishing it in one long drag. He knew exactly what she was saying, but she was wrong. He would never voice it, but he knew she would never be in the dark. What drew him to her, what drew everyone to her, was that she was made of light. He thought back to the silhouette of her naked body sitting on top of him earlier, the sun streaming around her as if it was there just for her. He remembered thinking about whether she wanted him inside her as much as he wanted to be. She always looked so beautiful, but the memory of her eyelids hung heavy on her huge golden eyes and the way she looked at him was almost heartwrenching. He had intentionally slowed her movements, guiding her by her hips, to savour every second, to pray at her altar just a little longer.

The thing with Ivy was, she thought she was this complicated soul, and he knew this was something he perpetuated to not feel so lonely, but she was the most perfect person he knew. Perhaps, perfect wasn't the right word, but she was as close to it as he could see.

"What did you want to do tomorrow?" he asked, changing the subject and pushing his thoughts away.

"I wanna go see the elephants. But not the kind you ride, 'cause they get tortured into letting you sit on them and it's not good for them to have people on their back. I mean, if they were supposed to have people on their backs they would have been born with saddles."

"And maybe big flashing arrows on their heads saying, "human seat here'". Sam replied.

"Exactly," she said, pausing for a second. "Wait. Where was I? Yeah, elephants. I wanna go to an elephant sanctuary where they look after the elephants and bathe them and smooth them and feed them." Ivy said. She stroked the air in front of her to demonstrate.

"Don't they just get tourists in to shovel their shit?" Sam frowned.

"No. But if they did, I think I would shovel their shit. They're just like big dog shits." Ivy said.

"You certainly have a way with words V," Sam grunted. He was feeling tired now. More mentally than physically. Really, all he had done all day was sleep, but he felt worn by what had happened. He had wanted this for so long. It wasn't something he decided but it crept up on him slowly until it just became fact. He had never thought anything would actually happen between them, so he had accepted his role as her best friend. He didn't know what his role was now. But what he did know was, for Ivy, he was part of the periphery; she saw him, but didn't really see him and that truth never really meant anything until right now. "So are you my corner then?"

She shrugged. Maybe together they were square, just like she said, full of breakable corners. He decided then if he could be with her, he might be OK with being in the dark, knowing that if he let her, she could fill his corner with light.

Chapter 9

She left him sleeping in bed with a note on the pillow, scribbled in eyeliner. She woke up starving and was content to get breakfast alone but on her way out the door she stopped herself. Not wanting Sam to think she had ditched him after sleeping with him, she wrote the quick note with the only writing implement she could find. Then kissed his cheek and walked out the door.

It was annoying that she already felt like she had to think about her actions and second guess herself, but she could cope with that for now, because the frustration she was feeling was trumped by the flutter in her stomach that she had every time she thought of Sam's lips on her skin. She stood outside in the open mezzanine hallway. The sun was shining, and she could hear the birds nesting in the huge tree that stood in the middle of the courtyard of the hotel. She walked down the steps and through the bar to the restaurant. She thought it strange that neither of them had eaten there yet, but she reasoned, they were usually out or asleep at mealtimes. She sat down in the almost empty restaurant and pulled a menu out of the holder in the middle of the table. And for a solid three minutes, she devoted her thoughts entirely to the laminated sheet that was curling at the corners, her mind only on breakfast. When the waitress arrived, she ordered the banana pancakes and a glass of orange juice and put the menu back in the holder.

Looking around herself she was surprised to see there were only a handful of other guests there. She wasn't looking at the people, her gaze washed over their faces as it did the pictures on the walls, but Ivy felt all their eyes slide to her one by one. Suddenly feeling like the room was judging her, she straightened herself in her chair and looked at the table, her chest flushed with shame she couldn't place. It was as if they all knew her secret and disapproved.

Ivy tapped the table a few times then pulled her phone out of her front pocket and started typing a message to Agatha. She figured if she wasn't sure whether she could talk to her best friend about this, she could at least talk to her sister. Agatha had known Sam almost as long as she has, and she would get it and hopefully not judge her.

```
So, I did something...
```

Ivy saw that she had read the message almost immediately when the ticks turned green. She saw the three dots come up then disappear. They came up again and then after a few seconds, disappeared again.

Ivy started typing again when she realised the three dots weren't going to come back up.

```
I slept with Sam
Several times actually
And now I think maybe, in the movie of me, it could have been the
best friend all along??
```

She suddenly felt quite vulnerable having typed it out.

```
I don't know, maybe not, but with Sam, it's just easy
```

She could see that Agatha had read the messages or at least still had the screen open on the conversation. Ivy scrolled up slightly and looked at the last message she sent about how she was going to kill Sam and thought about how surreal that last message seemed to her now after what had happened.

Her pancakes and juice were placed in front of her and the waitress disappeared swiftly. So she put her phone on the table and started eating, trying to bat the confusing thoughts of her and Sam out of her head. When she had almost finished eating he strolled through the restaurant and sat down. He took half of the last pancake she had cut in half from her plate and folded it all

CHAPTER 9

into his mouth.

With his mouth still full, he flagged down the waitress and ordered two more plates of banana pancakes and a beer. The waitress told him politely that they didn't serve alcohol in the restaurant, to which he shrugged and ordered an apple juice. When the pancakes arrived, they shared the third plate between them.

"I booked an elephant sanctuary," Sam said between mouthfuls. "Don't worry, it's an ethical one. They're picking us up at eleven."

Ivy looked at the time on her phone. It was already ten, so she had an hour to get ready. "What do we need to bring?" She asked. Sam opened the booking up on his phone and handed it to her while he devoted his attention to the remaining pancakes.

An hour later, they rode in the back of the minibus, to feel like the cool kids. They spoke a little, but not about what they had done the previous afternoon, or the previous evening either. But at some point, one of them had put their hand in the others and they stayed there until the bus had stopped and it was time to get off.

They all stood around the guide in a misshapen semi-circle while he talked about elephant conservation and what they do in a sanctuary. Ivy found she wasn't listening. Her mind kept wandering and she only really tuned in when they began handing out bananas to feed the elephants with. Sam was acting protective over her, and rather than annoy her, she enjoyed the feeling of security and smiled inwardly.

The guide led them over to four beautiful and majestic creatures and they were all introduced to their new friend for the afternoon. Ivy watched as they stroked the guide with their trunks affectionately as she went from elephant to elephant and told the group how to behave with them.

They fed the elephants in pairs and the guide passed between each of the pairings to make sure that everyone including the elephants was at ease. Ivy held her banana up to Jasmine the elephant and laughed when she took the banana from her hand with her trunk and threw it into her mouth, skin and all. Sam had begun peeling his, but she did the same to him too, taking it out of his hand and eating it whole.

Ivy was glad they had come today. She was surprised that Sam had been so thoughtful to book this trip for them on his own. However, she also knew she should try to be rational and not get too invested in one single gesture. At least not until she was sure of what she wanted.

The guide then encouraged them to gently guide the elephants to the nearby river to bathe them. They both helped to bathe Jasmine, splashing the water up onto her skin while she rolled in the muddy water and wiping her with the thin cloth they were given.

They were given large shirts to wear that were bright and boldly patterned and the group sat down to lunch. They mingled with each other speaking a little here and there but they talked between themselves more often than not. When they were getting ready to leave, Ivy took her phone out of her locker and saw that Agatha had finally replied to her. She read the message, but it wasn't the message she was hoping for, even if it was the one she was expecting.

```
Sam? really? I think he's great, I really do, but he isn't exactly
Mr Stable is he? Is it bad to say I want something more for you?
And do you actually have feelings for him? Or is it just because
he's there? Try not to ruin your friendship on a holiday romance.
Be safe and look out for each other. A x
```

Chapter 10

Ivy couldn't be bothered to get ready quickly. Still lying on the bed when Sam walked out the door. Slowly walking towards her open case on the side table, she took out a t-shirt dress that she hadn't worn yet. Pulled it over her head and put her hair into a bun. She was still hung up on Agatha's message. It was the last she had heard from her for over a week now. Ivy hadn't responded mainly because she knew Agatha was probably right — she usually was, but Ivy would never tell her so. She wondered if it was too late to not ruin the friendship. It felt pretty ruined. They had had sex almost every night so far and Ivy had no intention of cutting that off but she no longer knew what was going on in Sam's head and she was starting to miss her best friend.

As lovers, the boundary between what she should do and what Sam wanted to do was becoming blurred and that was never something she had to worry about before. She sniffed some cocaine with him the other night. Not that she hadn't done so before, but not in a foreign country and not in such large amounts. That was never something she would have done if she was thinking clearly, but she did it because he offered it and she no longer knew where to push back.

Opening her phone she reread the message from Agatha. Bit weird for her to add the *A x*, she thought. It wasn't like Ivy didn't know who she was messaging. Agatha was always a bit unsure of Sam, she knew what a mess he could be just as much as Ivy did. She couldn't avoid her sister forever, she was her only close friend now Sam was her...*boyfriend? Sex buddy?* Whatever he was, but she'll deal with what to say to her tomorrow. She put her phone into her bra and looked for some shoes to wear.

She opted for a pair of flat lace-up sandals tonight. Even though she wanted the extra height from heels, she was not prepared to deal with the sore feet later. Catching her reflection, she stopped at the mirror next to the room door and looked at herself. She had a good tan coming on, warming her already dark skin, especially across the bridge of her nose and forehead. A real holiday glow. She tucked a loose strand into her bun and grabbed the key card out of the slot and headed out the door.

It felt a bit weird going out for the night on her own, but she was only a ten-minute walk from the club she told Sam to meet her at. Street vendors roamed the strip offering roses to every passing couple and tourists sat on mopeds, in a domino line, watching the football through the open sides to the sports bars.

She ignored the people shouting at her trying to get her attention, trying to get her in their bar, or restaurant, or bed and walked up to Bamboo and collected her stamp at the doors.

The neon lights and foam machine in the middle of the club took her back to when she was sixteen, pretending to be eighteen with Agatha's passport, she went to her first rave. Sam came with her that night, although he didn't have a fake ID. She couldn't remember why, but that wasn't a problem, he just walked straight in. Agatha had followed her in a few steps behind with her own driving licence.

Her sister was always there, taking her under her wing and showing her the world as she grew up. She never felt scared because Agatha was sensible, she knew what she was doing and seemed to know everything. They danced together all night. Coming out she felt disorientated. It was 7 a.m. the birds were singing, and the sun was up. She remembered feeling like she didn't belong. Like she had intruded on a time of day that was reserved for birds and not people.

She saw Sam at the bar and walked casually up behind him, slotting her arm through the gaps in his, to take the drink he just bought from under his nose. Sam turned to look at her and watched her gulp it down with faux innocence in her eyes. Before wandering over to the dancefloor and beginning to dance. She felt oddly vulnerable in that moment which frustrated her. Aren't *I self-*

CHAPTER 10

sufficient? Why would I need someone else to dance with? She thought. But she was reassured when Sam came over, grabbed her by the waist and started dancing with her. She took another big gulp of the drink and turned around, balancing her arm on Sam's shoulder while she danced against him.

His lips met hers but it felt like it wasn't her lips he was kissing, as if there was a degree of separation between them, though she could feel his hands in her hair, *maybe someone else's hair?* The foam was released into the crowd and she could hear cheers faintly in the distance and taste soap on her tongue. She suddenly felt a bit sick so pulled back from Sam and her eyes rolled to the ceiling. All of the lights were stuttering across her vision. Her mind was buffering like a video. She could see more than one of everything and felt a pounding in her ears, that felt like it was hitting her from both sides. Pushing Sam out of her way, she went straight to the toilets.

There was a queue of four or five women waiting to go, but she pushed past them and hung her head over one of the sinks. She ran the tap and scooped some water to her mouth before remembering she couldn't drink the tap water here and spat it back out.

She ran both hands under the running water and rubbed it into her face. Ivy stared at her reflection. She studied her features as if to check they were all where they should be, and all belonged to her. The pulsing sound in her ears began again and she started to feel something, something good. She was coming up.

"The fucking idiot," she laughed to herself. Sam must have spiked his drink, but right now Ivy didn't care. She stumbled out of the bathroom, with her drugged-up heart focussed on Sam. But her thoughts quickly turned to Agatha's text. *Maybe this was a mistake.* Does she want Sam because he's Sam? Because he wants her? Because they were on holiday and the sun was getting to her? Holiday romances are always super intense. You live in a bubble that quickly pops when you step off the plane on the other end. She wasn't sure if those rules applied here or not, but the biggest question she had was whether she wanted Sam because she actually loved him and had done so all along.

She went over to the bar and asked for three shots. Before she could specify what she wanted, the bartender put three glasses down in front of her and threw some honey-coloured liquid in each and held up three fingers. She gave him a handful of notes that she pulled out from her bra and let him take three hundred baht from them, returning the change.

The first shot burned so she ended up swallowing it in two. She was more prepared for the second one and managed to drink it in one but felt the acid reflux follow its route back up. She tapped someone on the shoulder next to her and handed them the final shot before turning around and headed for the dancefloor. She had made it halfway across the small crowd that was grouped around the foam cannon next to her when she saw Sam. He was dancing with a group of girls and smiling. She wasn't hurt by it, and he didn't seem to be too invested because he was half facing away from them, looking towards the toilets. *Is he looking for me?* She felt herself peaking, and suddenly her head was swimming with Sam and all the emotions she couldn't feel whilst sober were bubbling away below the surface.

Sometimes, people can't bring themselves to say things out loud, no matter how brave they are. It's not because they are scared of the words themselves, but because they can't stand how they look written on someone else's face, reflecting back at them. If she said it just this once, would the words stay there, hanging in the air? Or would he take them greedily and never show them to her again?

The foam began to dissipate and his eyes met hers across the room. She wasn't sure if it was real if it was how she truly felt, but she felt it at that moment and that was good enough for her. So, she made the shapes with her mouth and took her time over each one, so she knew he would hear them.

"I. Love. You...I'm. In love. With you."

His face dropped just a small bit, but enough for her to notice and her heart went, her hopes dropping with it. He went to open his mouth, but she had already turned and left. She stumbled out of the club and looked left and right, the lights all blurring together, she wasn't sure where she should go. She was suddenly panicked that she was not far enough away from him like she could feel his pity tethered between them so she began to run, and she ran towards the sound of the sea.

She made it to the sand before the first tear fell down her cheek. Kneeling

CHAPTER 10

she dug her hands into the sand on either side of her until she felt the colder, damper sand underneath. She didn't cry, she just let the tears fall from her eyes. It was done. Sam had broken her. She had left all her feelings at his feet and he had stepped over them like they were nothing. Like she was a bath of water he had climbed into and made overflow. Then left her feeling half-emptied when he was done. In reality, she realised she had known this would happen and some part of her had even secretly hoped for it. Like a part of her wanted the pain of it.

The sand felt so good weighing on her hands and rubbing between her fingers. She lay back onto the sand and let the drugs take her away from her sadness. She rolled the grains of sand between her feet as slowly as she could manage, just to appreciate the feel of it.

She closed her eyes for a second, she was sure it had only been a second but it could easily have been longer. Time worked differently on ecstasy. Not sure if she had passed out or just lost her vision for a moment, the next thing she knew she felt a weight pressing down on top of her and suddenly she was frozen, her lungs were closing over. Calloused hands were roughly tugging on her clothes and she felt a tennis ball-sized lump in her throat and a pain inside her. Pounding against her, fingers digging into her forearms, sand scratching her skin.

She forced her eyes open but couldn't focus on anything, just a shadow, like the monster in the dark you always fear will find you when you are alone. Her adrenaline finally kicked in and her body seemed to surge into action, ahead of her mind. She pushed at the figure and brought her knee hard into what she hoped was his groin. The figure groaned and rolled off of her enough for her to pull herself backwards, digging the heels of her hands into the sand dragging herself out from under him. She threw herself onto her front and scrambled forward on all fours until she could push herself up onto just her feet. Every step felt difficult where the sand sunk away from her feet and made her push just that little harder.

Panting hard, tears were burning her eyes. She couldn't see in front of her, but she kept pushing forward until her feet hit the tarmac again and didn't dare look back. She told herself it wouldn't help, that it was too dark to see, but really, she was afraid. Afraid of what she would see and in her grief and fear, her brain screamed for Sam. All earlier thoughts had escaped her, dropped along the beach as she ran to safety. And she knew she needed to find him.

She wasn't sure how to get back to the club for a second, did she run straight? Did she turn at all? *Pounding against her, fingers digging into her forearms, sand scratching her skin.* Rubbing at her eyes she tried to calm herself. She looked up and realised she was only ten steps away from Bamboo. She had to find Sam. She muddled through two laps of the club before she gave up looking, gripping her phone in her hand in case he replied. At one point she mistook someone else for him, trying to spin around a stranger in a similar shirt.

```
Where are you?
```

She messaged him.

```
Need you
```

She messaged him again.

```
????
```

she sent, before going outside.

Heading back outside, she scanned the streets. Was he looking for her? She shouldn't have run away. Why won't he look at his phone? She thought she saw the back of him going down a side street, so she followed. She hoped it was him because if not she couldn't defend herself again tonight.

She was relieved when she saw it was him until she saw a woman drop to her knees in front of him and a new wave of pain hit her. Not that he was with someone else, but that when she needed him he was here, down some back alley getting his dick sucked. He caught her eye as she turned to leave, his shirt falling open revealing the anatomical heart tattooed on his chest but she was over thinking he had a heart at all, or that she could rely on him.

Ivy tried texting Agatha. She hadn't answered or even read it. She worked out the time difference in her head. It was about half four in the afternoon so she should have answered her.

Urgh – she could feel her body filling with a scream she couldn't quite let out. *Look at me. Typical daddy issues. He doesn't want me, so I obsess over him, as soon as something bad happens, I go running back to him – but he still doesn't want me.* So why did it feel like she had lost her safety net as well as her best friend?

Ivy felt like she had lost herself. She wanted to be protected and needed someone there. She felt so vulnerable and even more so when she realised she was no longer wearing her underwear. She put her hand up her skirt and the skin was tender and burned to the touch. *Pounding against her, fingers digging into her forearms, sand scratching her skin.* She felt sick. She felt disgusting. She needed to get back and wash this feeling away. Too scared to get in a taxi on her own now, she walked the main strip back making sure to stay in the bright light and crowds where people could see her.

The problem with pushing through the mass of people was how alone she felt watching them smiling and laughing and having fun but worse still every time someone bumped into her, which was a lot, she felt like throwing up. Every knock was a reminder of the rough hands gripping her moments ago. *Pounding against her, fingers digging into her forearms, sand scratching her skin.*

Stumbling back to the hotel she walked up the outside steps that lead to their room and felt grateful that people would think she had been drinking, not knowing that she was broken. She wasn't sure she was high anymore or even drunk. Trauma sobers you. Every step was a struggle, she just felt like a deadweight putting one foot in front of the other. Making it to the room she stuck her hand in her bra to find the key card when her phone started buzzing against her chest. She pulled it out and looked at the screen immediately hitting answer.

"Mum, this calls gonna cost a bomb, just text me yeah?" Ivy began, even though she was happy to hear her mum's voice right now, but she stopped when she heard her mum crying hysterically. She couldn't make out what she was saying. She was sobbing so hard. "Mum, slow down what is it?" she said her heart thumping a million miles a minute.

"She's gone, Agatha's gone,"

"Gone where?" Ivy asked.

"She, she... She took an overdose." Her mum managed to push out. "She's dead."

Suddenly Ivy couldn't hear anything her mum was saying. All she could hear was a tone in her ears and her heart breaking.

Part Two

"We understand death for the first time when he puts his hands upon one whom we love." – Madame de Stael

Chapter 11

She woke at the second beep of her alarm, her eyes snapping open. Hitting the off button, she stumbled out of the bed, kicking her sheets from her as she did. Drawing the blinds, she realised it was the first morning this week she could feel the warmth of the sun coming through the windows which meant spring had come back around. Brushing her teeth, Agatha stared at herself in the mirror and inspected her face for a moment. Her face was pretty, maybe not as pretty as her sister's but she had dark, round eyes and strong lashes which she had always loved and a small beauty mark above her pale, pink mouth.

She got dressed quickly, packed her work clothes in her gym bag and put her leathers on over the top of her workout clothes. She weaved in and out of the traffic to the gym that she joined because of how close it was to her office. Waving to the guy on reception, she swiped in. She didn't know his name, but he said hello every morning and it was now too late to ask. After a full hour on the treadmill this morning, she felt great, but she was a bit pushed for time to change and get to the office. She sat down with minutes to spare, throwing the bag with her gym kit, helmet and bike trousers under her desk.

"Ag, you'll never guess what I did last night." Melissa had started before her bum had even hit the seat.

"What did you do last night?" she asked, leaning down to turn her computer on.

"Joe messaged me."

Agatha pursed her lips together in a bid not to roll her eyes. "You didn't see him, did you?"

"I did. I couldn't help myself." Melissa replied.

"You know he's just going to ignore you again until he needs another one-nighter, right?" Agatha asked.

"I'm not stupid. But, maybe I'm OK with that."

Agatha raised her eyebrow at Melissa.

"OK well, maybe I'm not. But it's better than not seeing him at all." Melissa countered.

"As long as you're aware of the…situation," Agatha said, flipping her hand in the air to emphasise the last word. She knew how superior she sounded. Not that she had any reason to be. She hadn't had a boyfriend since she was about fourteen and wasn't interested in having one, but maybe if she was in Melissa's shoes, she would do the same.

"Anyway, I'll catch you at lunch. I've got to assist— she checked the system loaded on Agatha's screen over her shoulder —Toby with his urinary tract infection." she rolled her eyes and smiled.

The rest of the day went by in a blur of dogs, cats, budgies and even a tortoise. She loved her job, just getting to spend time with all the animals made her insides sing every weekday. She got on well with the veterinary nurse Melissa too, she wasn't her only friend, but she was probably one of her closest just down to how much time they spent together. Melissa could usually be found leaning over the reception desk talking to Agatha between patients and they had lunch together almost every day.

When the last patient flew out the door, Agatha pulled the roller shutter down, locked up and turned the lights off at the front of the surgery, before walking to the back-staff entrance with Melissa and a few of the vets. She had already stepped into her bike trousers and pulled on her jacket so only had to put her gym bag in her backbox and stick her helmet and gloves on. She waved goodbye to Melissa and rode home.

She cooked chicken parmigiana for dinner for the three of them. Her mum was catching up on some work and Ivy was in her room. She enjoyed cooking for her family, especially as they all sat around the table and talked as they ate it. It gave them a chance to catch up on each other's lives, which although they all lived together was more difficult than Agatha would like to admit.

CHAPTER 11

Since her dad had left when Agatha and Ivy were just kids, her mum had worked hard to support them on a single salary. Agatha never resented her mum for it but she would have preferred to have her around more. Ivy, on the other hand, had always been close with her until she went to university two years ago. She had moved out to live in campus halls, but she had dropped out in the summer so although she was around more, she was flitting about trying desperately to find herself.

When she had finished her dinner, Ivy took the plates and Agatha went upstairs to work on her poetry. She had been writing poetry for years. It seemed to be the one thing that centred her and gave her a chance to flex her creative muscles. She had stacks of notebooks all filled with a mixture of one-liners, snippets of poems, full pieces and doodles to match them. She pulled one out now and began adding phrases that she liked, her pen scratching the paper added to the sound of dishes being scraped downstairs.

When she couldn't keep her eyes open anymore, she packed all her writing bits up and piled them next to the bed and climbed under the covers. She drifted off within minutes.

* * *

She woke at the second beep of her alarm, her eyes snapping open. Hitting the off button, she stumbled out of the bed, kicking her sheets from her as she did. She wandered into the bathroom and brushed her teeth.

She got dressed quickly, packed her gym bag and put her leathers on. She weaved in and out of the traffic to the gym. She waved to the guy at reception and swiped in. She spent a full hour on the treadmill this morning and felt great for it, but she was a bit pushed for time to change and get to the office.

She sat down with minutes to spare, throwing the bag with her gym kit, helmet and bike trousers under her desk.

She spoke to Melissa for a few minutes and the day flew by again with fur and feathers and before she knew it, she was closing the front of the office up, waving goodbye to Melissa and riding home.

She cooked vegetable curry for dinner for the three of them.

Agatha, her mum and sister all sat around the table and talked as they ate it.

When she had finished her dinner, she went upstairs to work on her poetry. When she couldn't keep her eyes open anymore, she packed all her writing bits up, piled them next to the bed and climbed under the covers. She drifted off within minutes.

* * *

She woke at the second beep of her alarm, her eyes opening slowly. Hitting the off button, she stumbled out of the bed, kicking her sheets from her as she did. She wandered into the bathroom and brushed her teeth.

She got dressed slowly, packed her gym bag and put her leathers on over the top of her gym clothes. She weaved in and out of the traffic to the gym. She waved to the guy at reception and swiped in. She spent just under an hour on the treadmill this morning, but she didn't have the energy to run the whole time. She was still pushed for time to change and get to the office though.

She sat down with minutes to spare, throwing the bag with her gym kit, helmet and bike trousers under her desk.

She spoke to Melissa for a few minutes and the day flew by again with the only break from the usual being when she had to catch a parrot that had wandered out of the treatment area.

She closed the front of the office up, waved goodbye to Melissa and rode home.

She cooked jambalaya for dinner for the three of them.

Agatha, her mum and sister all sat around the table and Ivy and her mum talked as they ate, but Agatha wasn't really in a talking mood.

When she had finished her dinner, she went upstairs to work on her poetry. When she couldn't keep her eyes open anymore, she packed all her writing bits up, piled them next to the bed and climbed under the covers. She drifted off within minutes.

* * *

CHAPTER 11

She woke at the fifth beep of her alarm, her eyes opening slowly. Hitting the off button, she lay in bed for a while before eventually stumbling out, pulling the duvet with her as she did. She wandered into the bathroom and brushed her teeth.

She got dressed slowly and started packing her gym bag. She didn't feel like going to the gym this morning, but she knew she should. She weaved in and out of the traffic to the gym close to the office. She waved to the guy at reception and swiped in. She spent about ten minutes on the treadmill this morning, but she only walked it.

"You're a bit early today," Melissa asked as she sat down, throwing the bag with her gym kit, helmet and bike trousers under her desk. Agatha smiled in return.

The day passed by in a bit of a blur. Melissa did most of the talking at lunch and Agatha tried to concentrate on what she was saying but she felt removed from the conversation like she was sitting behind a pane of glass.

She closed the front of the office up, waved goodbye to Melissa and rode home.

She cooked fajitas for dinner for the three of them.

Agatha, her mum and sister all sat around the table and Agatha tried to listen as the words flew between them both.

When she had finished her dinner, she went upstairs to work on her poetry. But couldn't bring herself to write anything. She felt so tired. She started a poem three or four times before ripping the page out and screwing it into a ball. She fired it at her bin, but when it rebounded off the edge, she left it where it was.

She lay in bed trying to sleep but couldn't drift off. She wasn't sure what time she finally fell asleep, but she knew it was a restless one.

* * *

She almost slept through her alarm and had no motivation to go to the gym this morning. She hadn't been sleeping well and her body ached like she had been hit by a bus recently.

She pulled herself out of bed and went to the bathroom to brush her teeth and then threw on some work clothes. She pulled her leathers over the top and rode straight to work.

The first patient of the day was a golden retriever named Daisy and she was beautiful, Agatha thought. Daisy spent most of her time waiting with her head on Agatha's lap while Agatha smoothed her head patiently. Daisy's big brown eyes stared into hers and Agatha felt a moment of content. She was sad when Daisy had to leave.

"Where should we go for lunch?" Melissa said, appearing at her side with a clipboard she was ticking things off on.

"Can we just grab a meal deal? I've got a bit to catch up on here." Agatha said.

"Yeah, no problem — see you in an hour."

Agatha wasn't sure why she lied, she didn't have anything to do, but she felt like she needed to distance herself from human interaction right now.

She had dinner — her mum cooked this evening — and went straight to bed to stare at the back of her eyelids for a few hours. She was so tired.

* * *

She almost slept through her alarm again. It was becoming a habit. Just like her newfound lethargy. She really should cancel her gym membership because she hadn't been in months now. Just breathing felt laborious so the gym was too big a hill to climb. Maybe when she started sleeping better, she would feel motivated to go again.

She pulled herself out of bed and went to the bathroom to brush her teeth and then threw on some work clothes. She pulled her leathers over the top and rode straight to work.

"Where should we go for lunch?" Melissa said.

"Um...I've brought lunch in actually. Had loads of leftovers from last night, so had to use it up. But we'll go out again tomorrow" Agatha said.

"Yeah, sure. I'll grab something and meet you in the back room."

Agatha smiled back. She had no intention to eat or sit and talk with Melissa.

CHAPTER 11

Melissa was awesome but any social interaction felt like a drain on her already dwindling energy right now.

She had dinner - her mum cooked this evening - and went straight to bed to stare at the back of her eyelids for a few hours. She was so tired.

Her mind wandered while she led in bed and landed on a memory of getting lost at a theme park with Ivy. They stopped to watch one of the rides and when they turned around, their mum was gone. It felt like they were wandering around for hours when in reality, it probably wasn't that long until an announcement went over the speakers telling them to meet their mum at the information point. When they found the information point, she remembered her mum rushing to Ivy first before cuddling Agatha. Because *why wouldn't she choose Ivy first?*

Ivy didn't remember it, but that was the day after their dad left. He was supposed to go with them but when they woke up that morning he wasn't there. Ivy asked where daddy was and her mum just smiled as a response. Rachel put the girls on the waltzers and watched them spin from the railings. Ivy laughed and spun them around and Agatha watched her mum's face blur past, tears rolling down her face. She never saw Rachel cry after that, but Agatha always wondered if like her Dad, her mum was tempted to leave them, and then thought of how relieved she was to grab Ivy and Agatha knew if Rachel was to leave either of her children, it would be her.

* * *

She didn't feel like she woke up when her alarm went off, because to wake up, you have to have slept. She pulled herself out of bed and went to the bathroom to brush her teeth and then threw on some work clothes. She pulled her leathers over the top and rode straight to work.

It might have been down to how tired she was, but she felt like someone had turned the saturation down on her life. Everything looked and felt duller to her. But it was still winter, so it was supposed to be duller. Wasn't it? Maybe she had that SAD thing where you get really depressed during the winter, she thought.

"Lunch?" Melissa said.

"Um...I'm not feeling particularly hungry right now. Go on without me," Agatha said.

"No, come with — at least to get away from your screen for a bit. You can grab something to eat later?"

Agatha smiled back. "I'll be OK." Melissa sat on the edge of Agatha's desk and leaned close to her.

"Is something wrong Ag?" she asked in almost a whisper.

Yes. Me. I hate my life, I hate myself. I want to die. No, wait, I don't. I have no energy to hate anything. I just want to curl up into a little ball and hibernate for a while. Or forever maybe.

"No, no I'm fine," Agatha replied in her most reassuring tone. She even furrowed her eyebrows slightly to try and show how off base her question was. When Melissa didn't respond she added "I'm just...I'm just tired is all. I haven't been sleeping well lately. But it's no big deal."

"Oh really? How come?" Melissa asked.

"I don't know, I'm just struggling to sleep, and when I do, I can't seem to stay that way. Sorry, I didn't mean to worry you. You must think I am a terrible friend." *Because I am.*

"No, don't be silly! I was just concerned. You've been acting a bit off is all. Maybe you should go to the doctors? See if they can do anything to help you sleep. "

"Yeah. That's a good idea."

She skipped dinner. Both her mum and Ivy were out and she didn't feel like cooking for one. She went straight to bed to stare at the back of her eyelids for a few hours.

She replayed her conversation with Melissa over and over. She wouldn't understand, she asked what was wrong and nothing was wrong or maybe she was just wrong. She didn't know how to describe it. She was so tired. She was always tired lately. No one could understand, they would just think she was lazy or broken maybe. *I am.* She wasn't sure which would be worse.

* * *

CHAPTER 11

She lay in bed staring at the ceiling for almost an hour. She pulled herself out of bed and threw on some work clothes. She pulled her leathers over the top and rode straight to work.

Winter was finally starting to shrug its hold off of the world, but Agatha didn't feel it. She remembered a snow day when she was younger before Ivy was born. She had chickenpox, so she wasn't allowed outside. She remembered watching all the other kids outside playing and having fun through the window. Her breath fogging up the glass. She felt like that now. Like she was still behind that window, looking out at the world and not feeling the cold.

A car horn sounded behind her. The light she was stopped at had gone green and she hadn't noticed. She rode on.

* * *

She hadn't been going to work. She felt like an empty weight was stopping her from getting up in the morning. She had been calling in sick, but she couldn't do that for much longer without a doctor's note. The longer she was off, the worse she thought it would be when, *if*, she went back.

She didn't want to worry her mum, so she adjusted her bike cover after her mum left for work, so it at least looked like it had been used.

She managed to book a phone appointment with the doctor. She only mentioned the lack of sleep though and faked some flu symptoms to get a doctor's note. That should buy her another week at least. The doctor finally agreed to give her a weeks' worth of sleeping tablets and told her if she was really struggling, to take one at night.

She did take one that evening, and she did sleep, but she woke with such a sour taste in her mouth that didn't go away until the following evening, so she decided not to take anymore. She emailed her doctors' note to her boss and said she should be back next week.

Melissa tried calling a few times. Agatha sat there with her phone in her hand watching it ring and waited for it to stop.

```
Too ill to speak but will catch up later.
```

* * *

She hadn't left her bed for the last two weeks except to get her prescription and to eat or rather, push around her dinner. She hadn't bothered to keep up the facade she was going back to work. Her mum didn't seem to notice. She asked at dinner how her day was, and Agatha would respond with a made-up story of her day and her mum nodded and didn't ask her anything more about it.

Her boss had tried to get hold of her a few times and when she eventually answered he fired her. Which she could understand. Her job did require her to actually *be* there. Even Melissa was backing off. *Because she hates you.*

She thought back to a birthday party she had. Was she thirteen? Or fourteen? Maybe she was fifteen. She can remember inviting almost all the girls in her year to come to hers for a sleepover and only around ten had bothered to respond. But only three of those girls had turned up in the end - and one of them was Ivy. It was like she had been painted with a red X when her dad left that told everyone to stay back. The only people who didn't see it were her and maybe her sister, but even Ivy was beginning to drift now. She had been out more and more lately and didn't seem to have any time for Agatha at all.

She made dinner for her and her mum that night. She was getting really good at pretending, but it was a struggle. She felt like she was playing a part because if she didn't, no one would like the real her. *This is exhausting.*

* * *

When Ivy called her from the airport, she was searching the internet for drug overdoses.

"Hey!"

"What's up? You're bored of Thailand already?" Agatha said jokingly, but her attention was on her laptop. She didn't really think she was going to do it. She was just interested. *For zolpidem,* the sleeping tablet she had been prescribed, *the maximum daily dose is 10mg and the toxic dose begins at 70mg.*

"We haven't got there yet. Our flight's delayed, but even if it was on time, we're about thirteen hours away from being there." Ivy replied. *Scrolling through the forums though, it seemed like 70mg wasn't going to cut it.*

"Sounds great," Agatha replied, realising she had to say something.

"What, the delayed part or the thirteen-hour plane journey?" Ivy replied confused.

Agatha pulled her attention away from her laptop, "Oh, you're delayed? That sucks. What are you going to do?" *Maybe she should tell her? Maybe she should ask her to stay.*

"Drink," Sam said, sitting down next to her and handing her a pint of lager. They tapped their plastic glasses together and said cheers. *No, she wouldn't care. I would ruin it for her.*

"How was work?" Ivy asked.

"Work like." She lied. *You're already ruining it.* "I'm gonna go. Not all of us are on holiday. Some of us have real-life things to do." Agatha said smiling but she felt angry and didn't know why.

Ivy smiled back. "Yeah sure. I'll see you in a few weeks."

"Be safe," Agatha said, regretting her anger then hung up. *She would be better without me.*

She called the doctor again, but they said if she wanted more sleeping tablets, she had to see the doctor in person. She managed to drag herself there and convinced the doctor she was fine, just couldn't sleep. Yes, she had tried the natural remedies they spoke about last time. Yes, she was feeling well otherwise and just like that, she had another two weeks' worth of tablets. She even went to the reception after and booked a follow-up appointment for the beginning of May.

Her mum was asking her more questions than usual at dinner. Maybe because Ivy was gone, she needed to focus her attention somewhere else. *She doesn't really care.* She had been fairly irritable with her mum for the last few days. She didn't know why her mum was probing her so much when she didn't care anyway. *She feels like she has to because she's your mum.*

She had gone from having no appetite to starving all the time. She had had two helpings for dinner every night this week, which was very unlike her, but her mum didn't seem to mind, she hadn't adjusted the portion size to account for Ivy's absence.

* * *

Agatha didn't want to die, she just didn't want to feel this way anymore.

* * *

She told her mum she was fed up with her job and wanted to look elsewhere. In reality, she wasn't going to look at any other jobs because she was fed up with all of it, but her mum didn't question it. She just said she was glad she knew what she wanted out of life. *Yeah to end it.*

* * *

```
So, I did something...
```

Help me. I hate myself, I hate my life. I want to die. Please come home.
   Agatha started typing. *What?-* then deleted it.
   Come home- she tried again but deleted it again.

```
I slept with Sam
Several times actually
And now I think maybe, in the movie of me, it could have been the
best friend all along??
I don't know, maybe not, but with Sam, it's just easy
```

I want to die.

* * *

CHAPTER 11

She poured all the tablets onto the duvet. *It will be like going to sleep and never waking up again.* Her heart ached for it. She was just so tired of it. She took them all.

* * *

It wasn't like falling asleep. It was like being drunk to start with. *She thinks she might have texted Ivy. Maybe she should call her mum.* She didn't feel good.

* * *

Her stomach hurt. Her throat was so dry. *Had she called out to her mum? Too late now, she couldn't if she wanted to,* her throat felt swollen.

* * *

Shadows drifted across her vision and lights flashed from all angles. *Did she leave a note?*

Chapter 12

She threw up on the tiled mezzanine floor, collapsing in on herself she fell to a half-crouch. Balanced on the balls of her feet, her head hanging in front of her bent knees whilst she took a ragged breath. She wiped her hand across her mouth, smearing sick further across her face. The sound of ringing in her ears had left her disorientated. Her mum's voice began coming into focus again. She hadn't realised she was still on the other end of the phone or that it was still in her hand. Rachel was still talking, but Ivy couldn't make out the words.

"I'll...um...I'll...I'll call you back." said a voice that Ivy couldn't recognise as her own.

Turning to grasp the door handle and, still crouched and shaking, she pushed the key card into the slot. It flashed red. She tried again. It flashed red again. She stopped and took a deep rattling breath and closed her eyes. The air burned her throat in the path left by the vomit. She held the handle down and pushed the card into the slot more slowly and this time it went green. She almost fell into the room as the door flung inwards. She crawled inside, forcing the door shut behind herself, needing to protect herself from any more blows tonight.

She sat there on the other side of the door gasping for air in the dark. She hadn't the strength to pull herself up to reach the key card slot to turn the lights on. The room was lit only by the moon and artificial lights streaming blankly through the balcony doors, only partially lighting the room. And in this half-light, the room became a nightmare.

Innocent shadows began to take on sinister shapes around her and Ivy's head swam with thoughts of her sister. The bunched pillows on the bed morphed

CHAPTER 12

into the silhouette of Agatha's body, her arm hanging down towards the floor dripping blood onto the tiles. Ivy could hear the small splats it made as it landed. Her wide, blank eyes stared back at Ivy from an unnaturally crooked face.

She was sobbing so hard, it was painful. No longer able to breathe through her nose, she could only take large, hysterical gulps of air through her open mouth. Liquid spilt from her eyes, nose and mouth and she felt like she was drowning.

Ivy pulled herself across the floor towards the bed, digging her nails into the grout lines and attempted to throw herself at Agatha, only to find the apparition had gone and the bed was filled with pillows as before.

Burying her face in the mattress, she sobbed harder, making a guttural sound that ripped through her and into the muffled mattress. She stayed like that until she was forced to come up for air. Lifting her face, her bleary eyes adjusted to the half-light of the room. But it wasn't long before her eyes fell upon the chair in the corner of the room and instead of Sam's clothes piled high, she saw her sister slumped, twisted form. Eyes vacant and foam escaping the corner of her mouth.

Ivy pulled herself off of the bed, her body a dead weight, her fingers clawing into the mattress and then the tile edges when she hit the floor. Her feet were no longer working, her heavy body dragged behind her over to the chair. Pulling the pile to pieces, pulling the ghost to pieces she covered the floor with clothes until the chair was empty and Agatha sat there no longer. She beat it violently with her fists, hard enough to move it and knock the curtain tucked behind it. Her swollen gaze followed the movement and found another phantom in her sights. Agatha, hanging from the curtain rail limp and bloated, spinning softly as if caught by an evening breeze.

She tugged on the curtain. Unable to face her sister anymore. Her skin was burning with anger, hatred and shame so she dragged herself up and pummelled through the bathroom door. Into the shower cubicle, she slapped the water controls and pulled it around with her open palm and sat there under the lukewarm water to try and rinse the sin from her skin.

Angry and hurt from the events of the night. All she could think about was what would have happened, if she was at home with Agatha, if she hadn't told Sam she loved him. If she hadn't slept with him in the first place, she wouldn't be here right now. Then her mind went to the darkest thought of all. She thought about what was being done to her while her sister was dying.

Feeling sick again, she turned herself to throw up into the plughole. She watched it swirl down the drain and wished she could purge herself of the pain as easily as the contents of her stomach.

* * *

Ivy had a pretty good head start on Sam, but he thought he would be able to catch up to her along the way. Taking the stairs up to the mezzanine floor two at a time, he was pretty sure he had fucked it. He was an idiot, he had gotten scared and being an asshole felt easier than being vulnerable, but now he was even more scared. What he was sure of was that he had hurt her, and he had to deal with that, as much as he didn't want to. This wasn't something he could avoid indefinitely, he had to come back to the room at some point so he might as well get it over with.

He had made it to the hotel room door, narrowly avoiding the vomit which covered most of the tiles at his feet. For a moment he was horribly relieved at the sight and clarified his thoughts; *she must be reacting to the Molly.* He had added a pill to his drink, crushing it in his fingers and sprinkling it in to make it more palatable, but she took it from him. She had taken his drink and his dose along with it and part of him was *glad.* He knew he was a dick for thinking it, but if Ivy was fucked up then there was still a chance he hadn't ruined things between them at all. The thoughts began to connect across his mind. *She had probably said she loved me because she was high, she meant it like she always did.*

He was more eager to get inside now and see her. *This is starting to make sense. Ivy loves the world coming up on Molly, I'm so stupid to react the way I did. Plus, she probably — hopefully — won't remember the girl sucking me off at all.* Having perfectly rationalised the entire thing, he imagined them laughing about it when she sobered up, they could go back to how things were before.

Or at least, some version of it.

The truth was he did love Ivy but that was the scariest feeling of all. The only people he ever loved before had ignored him his whole life — *what if Ivy did the same?* But she wouldn't, she wasn't like his parents, he knew that, but it didn't stop him from still feeling like if he admitted how he felt she would see him clearly, as his parents did, as some sort of mistake and leave. He rubbed his head with the heel of his hand. *She won't,* he thought. *I better fix this first before I decide that.* He leant over the sick and pushed the key card into the slot. *Some poor, unsuspecting maid will have to clear that up tomorrow.*

He tripped over her phone on the way into the room, kicking it into one of the pillows that were scattered all over the floor. *Why is it so dark in here?* A picture flashed in his mind of Ivy crying in the dark, drunk and tripping on molly. He dropped his key into the slot on the wall and the lights flickered on around him.

The room was a mess. She had trashed the place. The bedding was all over the floor, as were his clothes, the beds pushed further towards the outside wall. As he tried to take in the full chaos of the room he realised he could hear the shower running in the bathroom.

Less than a week ago he had come into the room while she was showering, and they had slept together for the first time. He had a hollow feeling in his chest that this wouldn't quite end in the same way, as much as he might have wanted it to. He walked across the bedroom and over to the bathroom and stopped in his tracks once he reached the doorway and saw Ivy curled up on the floor of the shower her eyes closed.

His heart dropped into his stomach and he instinctively threw himself towards her. The water was freezing. She was still fully clothed, her dress was clinging to every inch of skin it could find, and Sam could see she wasn't wearing any underwear.

This thought was overridden quickly by guilt and then pain as he tried to lift her from the floor. She was a complete dead weight and wouldn't budge, so he reached further into the shower, turned the water off and tried again. She was cold to her bones and her skin was rough with goosebumps that grazed his skin as he lifted her. The tips of her fingers were wrinkled and white.

This time, he managed to lift her and he was grateful to see she seemed to be coming round as he scooped her up. He carefully placed her on the bed and struggling against the dampness of her, pulled her dress that had become a second skin, over her head, carefully unhooking her arms from the sleeves and wrapping her in the towel he had pulled from the small, plastic table he left it on this morning. Then wrapped her in the padded bedspread to try and dry her quicker.

She seemed to be more with it now so the drugs were hopefully wearing off *but if she wasn't loaded, then her behaviour could only be down to me*, he thought guiltily. A cold beat flashed across his chest. She could be concussed, she might have fallen, hit her head onto the shower floor. He checked her pupils by forcing her eyes open with a finger and thumb.

"Ivy, you in there? Can you tell me your full name?"

She mumbled faintly.

"What about my name V? Can you remember my name?"

She mumbled something he couldn't make out and started to cry. *Should I take her to the hospital?* If he went to a doctor, he could get in a lot of trouble for the drugs. He didn't know how the law worked over here but the police would probably be involved. Not that it mattered, he knew he would risk prison for Ivy.

Still holding her with one arm, he reached out and pulled the chair up to the bed, pushing the clothes out of the way with his feet and tried to listen to what Ivy was saying, but she wasn't responding to his questions. "What's that Ivy? Tell me again."

And when she mumbled, half-words caught between stiff breaths, he could make out the sentiment more than the words. She either didn't hear him asking her or she was ignoring him, but she carried on mumbling and the only words he heard clearly were 'Agatha', 'help' and 'dead'. *Maybe I should take her to the hospital.*

"She's dead, she's dead Sam, she's dead, she died, she died." Once she had said it once, she couldn't seem to stop and he could now see why she was in such a broken state. He didn't know how to react, no one around him had died before. Wiping his own tears with his arm, he felt even more selfish and foolish for thinking that everything revolved around him. That Ivy had been crying because of him and his negligible behaviour. He had been so wrapped up in their bubble, he thought they were untouchable from anything but themselves, but the outside always found a way to get in eventually. All thoughts of earlier that night left him.

He wondered whether he should call Rachel because she was probably in a similar state to Ivy, but he didn't know whether Ivy could handle that and truthfully, he didn't know what to say. Tears fell down his cheek as he robotically tried to warm Ivy by rubbing his hands up and down her arms over the layers he had put her in.

Why, Agatha? Why would you do this? He had loved her too, but she wasn't his sister, he didn't feel entitled to his own emotions when Ivy was so broken in front of him.

Without meaning to, he cast his thoughts back to a time he had argued with Ivy. They must have been about fifteen and Agatha, saviour that she was, told him what to say to make it up. She was always just there. She cared about everyone — What was that thing Rachel called her? A light ball or something — and that's exactly what she was. Sam felt a pang of pounding, personal guilt that the world was left with a black smudge of nothing like him but was denied the beacon that was Agatha.

The guilt was like an ever-growing lump in his throat when he thought about how much dimmer Ivy's light would be now and even more when he thought about what he was doing when Ivy must have found out that her sister was dead. *You were down some alley with a stranger when she needed you.*

He didn't know what to do but, as selfish as it was, he couldn't cope with a catatonic Ivy. Her pain was cutting, and it was too much for him to bear. Pulling back from Ivy for a moment, he propped his foot onto his opposite knee and carefully pulled his shoe off. Lifting the sole, he took the clear, plastic bag out and emptied the contents into his palm. He took one of the five small coloured pills, put it on his tongue and swallowed it down.

"V?" he shook her slightly to get her attention. "Ivy? Take it, Ivy," he said holding one of the pills out to her on the tip of his finger.

"No...no, no...more," she said between sobs.

"It will make it better V. It will take the pain away," he said gently, trying to make eye contact with her. *If just for tonight.*

* * *

She stared back into his eyes and saw in them the gesture for what it was. He meant this as a kindness, and if she was in her normal frame of mind, she would think him damaged, but right now she was feeling pretty damaged too, so she let him put the tiny pill on her tongue and she swallowed it. Relieved it didn't take long for the pill to swirl in her mind and add to whatever was left from her last dose. That rush of elation and love she had felt earlier had taken over her again. She had stopped crying, the tears were still in her, though she was almost unsure why she was crying in the first place as if she had woken from a dream that was slipping away. She knew the shape of it, but the details escaped her.

It was because of this, Ivy was almost happy when she saw her final ghost of the night because even though deep down she knew it wasn't real, she could pretend. *Even if it was just for tonight.* Agatha danced around the room in front of her. She watched her stop and drape herself around Sam's neck. Tutting at her with mock disapproval and shaking her head. Agatha licked from his neck to his ear, nibbling the lobe once she reached it.

Sam didn't react but Ivy was enthralled by her sister's actions. She leant forward on the bed, to get as close as she could to Agatha and as if someone else was doing it, she watched herself pull Sam on top of her and kissed him.

The faces blurred nightmarishly between Sam and Agatha's and her own and she bounced back between lust and love and heartbreak until she somehow finally spiralled into sleep.

Chapter 13

When she awoke the next morning, she remembered everything and something inside her had died. For the last few weeks, she had lived in a world between dreams and reality with Sam and last night reality had come and banged her front door down.

Ivy lay there, eyes open trying to count the pieces of her that were left. A piece had gone with Agatha. A piece had gone when she was — *Pounding against her, fingers digging into her forearms, sand scratching her skin* — she could barely even think of the word. *Raped.* A piece had gone when she saw Sam with someone else. She didn't know what was left of her now, but she couldn't stay here and be taunted by the pieces she had lost.

She looked over to Sam who was still sleeping, and she hated him for it. Hated him for all of it. As much as she wanted to, she couldn't blame him for Agatha, but she could certainly blame him for everything else.

Feeling a sudden urgency to get up, she left the bed and picked up her phone. Eleven missed calls from mum and two voicemails. She deleted the voicemails without listening to them. She could guess what they contained. She couldn't listen to her mum crying again without breaking down and she needed to stay in one piece, at least for now.

Typing a text to her mum:

```
Coming home. Can you sort my flight? X
```

before throwing her things into the suitcase, not concentrating on what she was putting in because, in all honesty, she didn't care, she didn't need any of it. None of her things would fill the empty hole that now resided in her chest.

Sam began to stir and looked at Ivy smiling dopily. She continued packing but watched his expression change out of the corner of her eye when realisation and the memory of last night washed over him. He got up, pulled a t-shirt and shorts on and started to pack his things up without a word passing between them. She stopped packing.

"Don't," Ivy said, glaring at him. He continued packing. "I said don't," she said more forcefully, and her voice almost gave way on itself. She closed her eyes in an effort to regain control.

"Don't be stupid V, I'm coming," he said matter of factly.

"I don't want you around me." She almost shouted back.

Sam stopped and looked at her. "Look, last night…last night was more than shit, but I'm still your best friend and I *will* be here for you. I loved her too." He said, realising this was the most open he had ever been, and he felt the slipperiness of vulnerability in his chest.

"Last night was shit? You're what's shit!" she barked quicker than she could stop herself. The look of injury in his eyes was horrible but as quick as she saw it, it was gone, his walls were up. She took a breath. "You can't be there for me Sam. You proved that last night. This — she gestured to the space between them — this is toxic and I need to go. I'm going home but you need to stay here." He opened his mouth to protest and she continued "We've paid for another two weeks so you might as well. I need some space. I think we both just need some space."

After what felt like forever Sam just nodded and walked out of the room and Ivy let go of the breath she didn't know she was holding. Relieved he had left, she couldn't cope with him standing there watching her pack and she didn't want the opportunity to change her mind. She needed to punish him even if that meant punishing herself too. She hated him for not being there when she needed him, even though she needed him now. Her phone beeped.

```
What's Sam's middle name and passport number?
```

CHAPTER 13

```
Don't worry about Sam just book me on.
```

Then, staring at the blinking bar for a moment, added

```
Sam's made his own arrangements x
```

* * *

Maybe he shouldn't have stormed off the way he did, but he couldn't stay after what she had said, no matter how true it was. In the smallest of moments, Ivy had just confirmed his deepest insecurities and fears about himself and it hurt more than he could even register right now.

He kicked an empty glass bottle as it crossed his path, smashing against the edge of the kerb. Ivy was supposed to be the other half of him, and they were supposed to be able to rely on each other in the most basic of ways. But now she was going home. She was getting as far away from him as she possibly could — the other side of the planet away — and here he was all alone.

Patting himself down he realised in the heat of it all he had forgotten everything; his wallet, key and phone. He found a few crumpled notes in his short which he unfurled with the pad of his thumb. It would be enough for a bottle of wine or two. He needed to numb himself and forget for a while. So that was what he did. He bought two bottles of party wine from a small newsagent type shop and walked to the beach. His feet sinking into the sand as he walked closer to the water. Watching the tide coming in and out, he sat there until the sun went down.

By the second bottle of wine, he had thoughts of walking into the sea and just going to sleep, but after what Agatha had done, he couldn't do that to Ivy too. No matter what she thought of him, or what he thought of himself, he knew he couldn't do that.

* * *

Ivy was two hours early for check-in, but she needed to get out of the room and put some much-needed space between her and Sam. She was worried he would come back and she would change her mind, apologise for being so cruel and beg him to come home with her, but she knew where that version of herself would end up and that was not somewhere, she needed to be. Her mum had sent through her new boarding pass to her phone and as she read it through, she saw she was able to collect a paper copy at the desk when she dropped her bag in. Now all she could do was wait.

Finding a small row of metal chairs that were welded together and into the floor, she sat down, pulled her case into a gap between seats and began scrolling through old photos and videos on her phone of her and Agatha. Her finger hovered over one, she remembered the night this video was taken. They were at some aunt or uncle's birthday party, laughing and sucking the helium out of the birthday balloons. The video was just them squeaking "I'm king of the world!" One after the other, over and over and crying with laughter at their high pitched voices.

She played it again, biting her nails while silent tears fell down her face and as soon as it finished, she skipped it back to the beginning and watched it again and again, lost in memory. By the time she next looked up, she saw that she could finally check her bag.

When she reached the desk, she went through the motions of *have you packed your bag yourself?* and *do you have any sharp objects in your hand luggage?* the *thank yous* and the rest like she was a real person and not the broken wreck she felt inside.

She passed through security easily and sat down at a deli on the other side and carried on watching videos and flicking through pictures. Someone came to clear the empty cups and rubbish that had been left behind, but she didn't notice, too engrossed in what she was doing. When she ran out of photos on her phone, she went through Agatha's Instagram account.

Ivy sat lost in memories of her sister until her phone flashed up a battery warning. Not ready to live in reality yet, she reluctantly got up and started looking for a socket to plug her charger in. Wandering around the terminal watching the other travellers, the other people going about their lives as if

CHAPTER 13

nothing had changed and nothing was amiss. She wished she could be one of those people but at the same time was angry that the world hadn't stopped around her.

Her sister was dead. She had done it to herself. She had left Ivy behind. Never even let Ivy in. Agatha chose to go and now nothing would ever be the same. Ivy wished she could tell herself she didn't know why, but she knew why. Her sister was always stretching herself for others and it had finally got to her. *Agatha decided she was never good enough and she could no longer stomach it.* But this is something Ivy would never admit to knowing out loud.

She found a socket not in use, on a pillar away from the duty-free but still fairly crowded with families and gap year students waiting in the same limbo she was in. She pulled her charger from her carry-on bag and, bending down, pushed the plug into the port. As she stood and tried to put the charger end into her phone, she dropped her phone face down onto the floor hearing a loud crunch sound as it landed. Picking it off the floor to see the screen had shattered felt like the last straw. She broke down. She cried so hard her chest ached with every breath, ignoring the stares and looks from other travellers, she just let herself cry.

When she had no tears left, she picked up her phone and charger and put them back into her bag and sat there staring at the TV screen until her gate was announced. Then sleepwalked to the plane, boarding with her paper pass that she was lucky to have, the one on her phone now useless.

She sat in her window seat and slept, only waking once in the sixteen-hour flight to find the kind person sitting next to her had put his jumper over her while she slept. She hadn't even registered his presence and she felt guilty for absently accepting the kindness. Thanking him and handing it back, she smiled gratefully, before asking him to move so she could get up to stretch her legs and go to the bathroom. She grabbed a can of coke from the steward station and returned to her seat, finished her coke and went back to sleep.

When she arrived at the airport her phone buzzed repeatedly in her back pocket, updating itself to the local settings. She pulled it out to read the notifications, before remembering her phone was next to useless. She went through the automated passport control and stared into the camera to avoid looking at her haggard, tired face on the screen. The glass barriers slid open and she continued through to the baggage claim. Her case was one of the first off, so she breezed through easily. On any other day, she would be grateful for the hassle-free journey, but she barely noticed today.

She walked to arrivals where she saw her mum waiting. Rachel's dark, soft skin seemed to have aged since Ivy saw her last, her near-black eyes were clouded with both fresh and old tears and her body sagged as if it was broken from the inside.

Rachel was a young fifty-five, looking forty on her better days. She had a wise face and the only lines around her face were from smiling. Her tight afro hair and dark complexion had been passed down to both her daughters, watered down somewhat by the generation gap and perfectly straight hair and pale skin of her ex-husband. In Rachel's eyes, that was all he contributed to her girls, she had raised them both practically by herself, which made it hurt so much more to lose her eldest.

Ivy wrapped her arms around her mum for a brief second and fought back the tears that had replenished inside her since she last cried.

"Come on, mum," Ivy tried to say while patting her back, but her voice cracked, and only part of the words came out.

She followed her mum to the car in silence, pulling her case alongside her and loaded it into the boot when they reached the car. Ivy climbed into the passenger's seat next to her mum and plugged her seat belt in. Her mum sat there clutching the steering wheel and the dam was broken again, they both broke down in tears.

Ivy unplugged her belt and reached over to her mum, pulling her into a tight hug. They sat there clutching each other for ages, their bodies shaking up and down and the occasional sob escaping their lips. The car became their silent bubble of pain.

They both eventually straightened up and they were out of tears again. Rachel said she didn't think she could drive anymore, so she and Ivy swapped seats and Ivy drove them home, holding her mum's hand most of the way. Stopping only to change gear, she squeezed it at regular intervals to make sure she still knew she was there. The only words between them were the occasional 'left here' or 'straight on' from Rachel.

When they finally pulled up to the house, they left the luggage in the car and both went straight up to bed. Ivy paused outside Agatha's room on the way to her own, but couldn't bring herself to look in.

Chapter 14

She wanted Agatha. Her Agatha. She wanted someone to know what she was thinking without saying it. To send her stupid pictures of herself looking like a thumb and get one back of Agatha sneezing. She wanted to find something missing in her drawers because her sister had taken it without asking. To use their stupid code words when they'd had enough at parties and wanted to escape again. She wanted to fight over the remote control and have whole conversations based entirely on Mean Girls quotes. She wanted her sister to help her with her homework. To gossip about boys with her and get up at 6 a.m. on a Saturday to watch cartoons with her. She wanted to climb into her bed and laugh until her mum came in and kicked her out, only for her to go back again when she was gone. She wanted to argue about who was putting the cutlery out for Christmas. She wanted her to curl her hair at the foot of her bed. She even wanted her to push her over or thump her like when they were kids. She wanted Agatha. She wanted her sister.

Chapter 15

The smell of her was starting to fade from her sheets, but Ivy wrapped herself in them, cocooning herself from the harsh reality that no longer held Agatha. Her notebooks piled high next to the bed would never be written in again. She couldn't cry anymore. She felt it in her throat, but her tears had long dried up. She slept.

Chapter 16

Ivy woke crying, laid across her mum's lap, head in her hands.

"Shhhhhhhhh, Ivy love. You're OK."

No, I'm not. Agatha is gone. She's not here anymore. She didn't want to be. Ivy thought it, but she couldn't make the words. All she could manage was a guttural cry while her mum cried silent tears of her own and stroked her hair, cupping her cheek in her other hand. They stayed like that for a long time. Until Ivy could no longer make a sound. Rachel got in bed beside Ivy and held her as they both slept, trying to dream.

Chapter 17

Ivy knew she couldn't wallow in her grief any longer. People expect you to start acting normal and carrying on at some point. *Oh, your sister died? Wasn't that like a week ago?* She had gotten out of bed, she had left the house, she had even gone to the shop for her mum at one point, but it was all so exhausting. Her grief was exhausting.

Her eyes flicked over to her phone, still broken on her bedside table. Still not ready to get it fixed, she was grateful for the disconnect. There would be countless people posting on social media as if they were Agatha's best friend and she didn't think she could cope with the *sorries*, the condolences and the good wishes.

It was also her way of avoiding Sam. Another thing she couldn't cope with: him trying to contact her or even not trying to contact her. She wasn't sure which was worse at this point. As broken as she was by Agatha's suicide her mind turned to Sam much more than she wanted it to and she felt a twinge of guilt every time her thoughts ran to him over her sister. It made her brain instinctively jump back like he was a sharp edge she was trying to avoid. She just had to keep moving, one breath after the last, no matter how painful. *Mum can't lose both of us.* Her thoughts turned to her dad and where he was now. *Had he heard? Did he care?* She doubted he even thought about them once after he left, he had discarded them all like a toy he had finished playing with *and look what that did to us.*

* * *

Sam had texted Ivy more than a few times and had even tried to call her despite the prospect of a large phone bill. *You're shit.* Her words flashed in his head every time he heard her voicemail. *This is toxic.* She wasn't just talking about the last few weeks. Although he knew just from how things had changed since they had started sleeping together, they couldn't be friends and lovers at the same time. He also knew that she thought he was toxic, that he would pull her apart if she let him. He knew that because it was exactly what he thought too.

Could he hold what she had said against her if it was the truth? He had waved the white flag, but she had never replied. As he palmed away tears, he told himself to be angry: angry at himself for getting too close, angry at her for leaving, being angry was easier than being hurt. *I'm not going to beg*, he told himself. If she wanted him, she knew where he was. *Exactly where she left me.* But the guilt was starting to eat away at him.

Spotting an inch of Thai wine in one of the bottles on his bedside, he poured it down his throat. He couldn't remember how to cope with life without altering it. He had been drinking since he was thirteen years old and he had his fine example of a mother to thank for that. Although, he was aware he had been drinking more recently and hadn't been saving his drug use to the weekends anymore either. It had been getting bad before Thailand but since Ivy left, he was almost in a total stupor, worried to sit with himself for too long in case it drove him crazy. He was self-aware enough to know that it wasn't a solution, but not enough to stop.

The problem was that he didn't care and without Ivy here to pull him back he had no reason to. Without her, no one saw a problem with a white, middle-classed bloke who drank because he was a bit sad. Most people had real problems to worry about. He hadn't realised before how much he relied on Ivy to be his anchor. Maybe if she stuck around he could care. If she stuck around could he do that for her?

He picked up his phone from the bedside table and finally worked up the courage to call Rachel. It was the right thing to do and he thought he could gently probe her to see where Ivy's head was at. Sitting on the edge of the bed he dialled the number.

"Hello?" Rachel answered on the fourth ring.

CHAPTER 17

"Rache — it's Sam," he said. When she didn't respond straight away, he carried on, uncomfortable with the silence. "I just wanted to call to say, I'm sorry and ask you how you are but that's a stupid question because your daughter's just die- passed away." *Shit, was it insensitive to say "died"?* He was rambling, but he couldn't stop himself. "I miss her too, by the way. And I miss Ivy. How is she?"

"Sam. It was nice of you to call," she said somewhat awkwardly, and Sam could tell she was fighting back tears. "Ivy is...as expected really. She is coping though, I think. Haven't you spoken to her?" she asked, sounding genuinely surprised.

He thought about how to respond for a moment and decided on the truth. "She isn't replying to my messages or anything. She asked for some space when she left, so I'm trying to give it to her."

"I see." was all she said. Then after a beat added "She has broken her phone though so I'm sure she's not trying to ignore you." she scuttled. "I think she *thinks* she wants space, but in all honesty, she could really do with a friend about now. When do you get home? Will you be here for the funeral?" she asked without thinking. "It's not until the end of May — apparently that was the earliest they could... I'm sure Ivy will let you know all the details when her phone is fixed," she added quickly.

"Yeah, I'm sure she will and don't worry — I'll be there," he said.

He hung up and threw the phone onto the bed next to him and hung his head in his hands, rubbing his temples and frowning hard. He needed to go out, he needed to wash Ivy away, scrub her from his mind. She was obviously doing the same to him. *But her sister is dead.* Should he go to her? Just fly home now and knock on her door, then she would have to speak to him. *But her sister is dead.* He kicked the small bedside table, knocking the old alarm clock onto the floor.

Even at the best of times, he struggled to cope with his emotions, that was what booze and drugs were for, but life had suddenly gotten very complicated and he could no longer decipher one feeling from another.

"Fuck this," he muttered under his breath and jumped up from the bed. It was the Full Moon Party tonight on Koh Phangan and he and Ivy had both been looking forward to going. It was going to be their ending with a bang, a goodbye to freedom. Why should he miss out just because she wasn't here? He picked up a short-sleeved shirt and pulled it on spraying a bit of aftershave on the collar before walking out the door.

Koh Phangan was one of the smaller islands and boats went back and forth every hour or so from the harbour at the edge of the beach. He read the small scribbled time table on the rickety jetty and looked up the strip which was unusually quiet this evening. That boded well for the party. He managed to hop on a ferry to the island just as the sun was beginning to set.

Except for that small sip of wine in the room, he hadn't drunk since this morning and his thoughts were too clear for his liking. So he bought a bottle of local whisky on the tiny boat. It wasn't like whisky at home, it was more of a sweet rum, but that didn't bother Sam, booze was booze and he planned on drinking so much tonight he couldn't taste it anymore.

The bottle was almost gone by the time he reached the port in Koh Phangan. As he climbed unsteadily off the boat he could already feel the vibrations of the sand around his feet from the throbbing bass of the music, but that could have been the whisky. He was immediately hit by the number of people amassed in every direction he looked. Almost all were tourists, but a few locals were also dotted around. He expected the island to be less touristy than Koh Samui, but hoards of people were filing in, collecting their wristbands to enter. Huge pillars built entirely of lost shoes stood at the gateway. It couldn't have been later than 10 p.m. but the beach was already littered with passed out people as well as a smattering of cups and cigarette packets. There were also several sandcastle buckets on the beach, which most of the drinks came in. He had already seen hundreds of them on his way down to the beach.

Sam weaved through the crowds aiming for a bar. He stopped at a short queue for the first one he could find, which was nothing more than a pop-up shack. All the drink stalls had large signs with the stallholders name written in marker as if it was an election campaign. Vote for Alex or Lydia or Jane, but they all have the same on offer. The beach went on for miles. It was hard to tell how many people were there. There were clusters of what looked like thousands of people near the music stages but once you moved away the crowd

CHAPTER 17

thinned and some people had a whole section of the beach to themselves.

"Oh my god, — Sam? That you?" a familiar voice with a slight American twang said to his right. It was Gemma. She was carrying a sandcastle bucket full of what looked like a blue cocktail, but it could have been the reflection of the bright green bucket, and a handful of plastic, striped straws.

"Hey Gemma, what's good?" he asked as if he wasn't particularly bothered about seeing her or anything, but he was glad for the familiar face. He didn't realise how isolated he had felt the last few weeks, drinking alone at the hotel.

"Where's Ivy? You guys should come hang with us," she replied, ignoring his question and actively looking around him for Ivy.

"She had to go, but I'm here, I'll come hang with you guys," Sam said, taking a straw from her bucket and taking a swig to make space to pour the end of his whisky into it.

"You're so naughty," she said with a flirty grin, smacking his arm softly but partially missing, spilling some of her drink. She was clearly already drunk. He wasn't sure if anyone had said that to him since he was a child but chalked it up as a weird American thing.

They stood and talked while they made their way through the queue and once Sam had bought two bottles of beer, she took his hand and walked him over to the rest of the group he met a few weeks ago. He thought he might feel awkward around them at first, but he was relieved to feel like he was meeting old friends.

They worked their way through the crowd, passing large flaming letters that spelt out FULL MOON PARTY HAADRIN KOH PHANGAN and four different stages. All of the music blended together to make one continuous bass line. "Look who I found by the bar," Gemma announced. Sam waved at them with the two fingers not wrapped around the neck of his bottles and tipped an imaginary hat. *OK, maybe I am a little drunk.*

"Sam-o!" Dom shouted and came bounding clumsily over patting him on the back as he hugged him with one arm.

"You alright Dom?" he replied as he locked eyes with Alice who was sitting on an overturned bucket on the sand with her long blonde hair falling over her shoulder, wavy and bouncy like a Californian beach babe.

"I mean, you don't call, you don't write…" she said sarcastically as she stood and walked over to him, planting a kiss on his lips.

"Hey Alice," he said.

"Travelling light tonight I see?" she said turning from him and taking a long drink from the bucket Gemma was carrying before looking up and staring directly at Sam. She noticed his look of confusion. She stopped drinking. "You seem to have lost someone. What did you do to the poor girl? Leave her behind on Koh Samui?" she asked, feigning innocence.

He wasn't sure how to answer, but within a few seconds she must have read the answer on his face because she then said, "Oh, I see." She raised her eyebrows and turned her back to him. "Not to worry, there are more friends where she came from." She turned her head so only her profile showed "Maybe not as fun as that one though." She smiled, relishing the moment,

She spoke as if she were on stage. The group seemed to stop their individual conversations to circle around her, absorbedly watching her perform. He should have found the whole charade crude, but Alice had a magnetic quality that drew you in and he could understand why the others were enthralled by her little show even though they all get front row seats every night.

"Stick with us Sammy-boy, we'll show you a good time." she smiled sweetly as if this was the only thing she had said on the matter. She took a small pill from Alex and stuck her tongue out so the tip almost touched her chin. She placed the pill on her tongue and leant forward offering it to Sam to take. He placed his tongue on hers and took the pill from it. Swallowing it down. That was the last point he remembered being in control of himself and it was bliss. His brain felt like it had a five-minute delay, like everything he was doing, he had already done and everything he thought he was going to do had been done by someone else. He remembered drinking more alcohol and taking more drugs. Running on autopilot, his hand kept putting the bottle to his mouth and he dutifully sucked whenever a straw was offered to him. He wandered off to the ocean at one point and Chad started pulling him out because he had gone too far in.

"I just need a piss mate." He heard himself saying.

Chad laughed, steadying himself by holding Sam's shoulders. "Yeah, that's cool pal. You can *have a piss* — he mimicked him in a false English accent — but do it here yeah?"

He realised that he was missing something in his drunken state, but the next thing he knew he was peeing into the sea and he felt much better. *Must be shark season, he had said to her.*

Thinking he couldn't remember ever drinking and taking this much was novel to him with all of his experience negotiating with reality. And he was unsure what time it was when he first began blacking out, but at one point he was walking towards one of the bars and the next he was on top of Alice, kissing her and groping her with people walking closely past them. They were having sex, but it wasn't Alice it was Gemma. He wasn't sure. He was fucked.

Stopping himself, he jumped up, did his shorts back up and walked quickly away. His head was spinning, and he was very hot. Sitting on the spot, several people almost fell over him. He could feel the heat from the flaming limbo and skipping rope attractions to his right and heard the crackle of the fire.

Why did he think limboing under fire was a good idea? He couldn't even remember getting up but he hadn't gone low enough under the beam, it burned. His chest was on fire, literally on fire. Someone threw some sand at him and someone else patted it out. He was sitting back down again with a bucket of ice. Where had his friends gone?

Sam woke up and Alex was throwing up next to him. Dom was patting his back and suddenly a strategic puke seemed like a great idea, but he must have dozed off again because he woke up to find Chad propping him up and talking to him. He didn't know how long he had been talking.

"You want a drink mate? I'm gonna get us a drink." Sam's mouth said, even though Sam's brain definitely didn't want another drink. A man was wandering with several buckets strung onto his arm and Sam decided he looked like he could do with a hand. "I'll have a bucket mate," he said.

"They're two for one." the man responded with a thick Thai accent.

"I'll have two buckets then," he replied and put his hand in his pocket to find some money. There weren't any notes in there. Had he been robbed? Luckily, he had several places for money and took two rolled-up notes from his sock. He wasn't sure how much money it was. He was way past seeing the numbers on the notes. "This enough mate?" he held the cash out and the man took it quickly and handed him two buckets.

"You need a friend," he said.

"She's gone. She left me," Sam replied.

"Don't drink both." the man said before walking on and Sam realised, he didn't mean anyone in particular.

"I'll be fine mate!" he called after him and took the drinks back to where he thought he had left Chad. He probably drank both buckets, in between sniffing what he thought was cocaine from strangers' hands and taking some pills even though he had no idea what they were, and the sun was rising, and the day was coming.

He woke with his arms around Gemma and Alex on either side of him. It was horrendously bright, and the party looked pretty gross in the light of the sun. Both Gemma and Alex looked worse for wear, so he probably did too. Pulling his arms out from under them and sat up. He was still high, but the alcohol felt like it was wearing off because the spinning had been replaced with a banging headache and the veins in his skin felt like they were shaking.

Somehow, he had made it into a taped-off section of the beach surrounded by a lot of dozing partygoers, so he guessed that was what these areas were for. The party was still going on around him, the music was still pumping out and the flames were still going strong on the limbo and skipping rope but the large flaming letters that spelt out FULL MOON PARTY HAADRIN KOH PHANGAN was dying, clouding the white-blue sky with thick, black smoke.

He looked up, his eyes finally beginning to adjust, to see Alice walking over to him across the disorderly beach, sucking on a lollipop and blocking the worst of the sun with her small frame. Sam saw Ivy's face instead of Alice's for a second and shook her out of his mind, blinking until Alice's face came back.

"Hey, Sammy. Have a nice nap?" she said between sucks. *Where did she get a lollipop from?* She held out a hand to him and he clasped it and pulled himself up.

"Those two gonna be ok?" he asked, gesturing to Gemma and Alex.

"Yeah, they just need to sleep it off," she said.

"OK well, I'm gonna head off then." Looking at her he decided she must not be wearing any makeup because she seemed to be the only girl on this beach who still looked the same as last night, without smudged, black circles under her eyes. In fact, she looked pretty beautiful, she had lost the bodysuit thing she was wearing last night and instead had a bikini top on but otherwise looked untouched by the chaos of the full moon.

"OK. There are boats over there." She pointed with the lollipop and then returned it to her mouth.

"But one just left so there won't be another for like forty-five minutes," she added.

"OK, how much is it?" He asked, searching his pockets.

"'Bout five-hundred baht," she said.

Did he spend everything last night? He briefly remembered thinking he had been robbed.

"Do you need five-hundred baht?" she asked, realising he was coming up short.

"Do you mind? I'll pay you back."

"It's like fifteen dollars honey, I ain't gonna starve," she replied and pulled a thin wad of notes from her bikini top and put one in his hand, then added another on top. "Just in case." she winked at him.

"When do you leave?" she asked and he looked, confused, to the small port. "Thailand, I mean," she added.

"The day after tomorrow," he replied.

"Tell her I said 'Hi' then." She kissed his cheek and went back to the party. He squinted his eyes at her as she disappeared back into the crowd, like a mirage.

Alice was a strange person, different from the others and obviously sexy, but she gave nothing away about herself and seemed to absorb information from everyone around her. She was good at reading situations, at reading *people* he thought and seemed to know exactly what the situation called for at any given moment. Sam thought he was harder to read than that, but Alice had him pegged.

Realising his feet weren't quite ready to work yet, he stumbled over to the port and waited for his ferry back, which arrived around forty minutes later, just as Alice had predicted. He wished she had given him a sick bag with the money though. The ride was so choppy, he managed to empty his stomach five or six times over by the time the journey was over, which he probably deserved for the shit he did last night.

    Between retches, he spent the ride hoping Ivy had tried to get a hold of him. If he hadn't left his phone in the room, he knew he would have spent the night constantly checking it. That's if he didn't lose it or worse, drunk call her. He doubted she had.

Chapter 18

Rachel did most of the planning, but Ivy made those plans line up with what her sister would have wanted. Of course, she knew funerals were for the living, not the dead, but if she could do it exactly as Agatha would want it, she could fool herself into thinking she was still there a little longer.

Ivy had never considered the cost of funerals before now. She overheard her mum on the phone to the bank about taking out a loan to cover it, which added to the twisting knots in her stomach. Of course, people didn't plan for funding their funerals in their twenties. She wouldn't ask her mum about it, because they never discussed money. So she took something off of her mum's plate and helped with the decisions.

She decided what colour the coffin should be. *White? Or oak? Or pine?* She decided on pink daisies and white carnations. *So many colours, so many types of flowers. Did you want to spell her name? Did you want "sister"? "Daughter"? A spray? Grass embellishments?* She chose the pub for the wake. *How many people are coming? What kind of food do you want for the buffet? Do you want a tab?* She chose the readings, opting for some of Agatha's poetry, it felt more like something she would want to hear than something someone else had written.

Her mum had gotten her phone screen replaced for her. She had woken up and the phone was on her bedside. Sam had messaged her, a few times actually and he had called her, but she couldn't bring herself to call him or message him back. She couldn't address the situations with him or talk about Agatha with him or even think about what she would say so she felt safe ignoring him.

She looked through Agatha's Facebook posts and, as she knew she would, she found hundreds of messages from people her sister had known. Photos of strangers with Agatha from school days and nights out, or even some edited photos of Agatha on her own with R.I.P. scrolled across the top of the image. The messages were about as expected too. *Heaven has gained an angel xoxo. R.I.P. Shining light. You will be missed. Another amazing person taken too soon. R.I.P.*

She had messages on her own Facebook wall too and private messages. Some asked when the funeral was, some wanted to offer their condolences and some just wanted to be close to the tragedy.

She kept wanting to call it an accident, she couldn't help but think of it that way, as something tragic that had happened to them. They didn't ask for it. *But Agatha did.* It didn't help that a week after the *incident,* a journalist called Ivy on her mobile asking about whether the doctors could have done more to save her sister and did she think the NHS failed them.

"But they prescribed her sleeping pills in a dose enough to kill. Did they not notice she was depressed?"

She didn't even know how the paper had got her number, but she saw the front page a week later outside the local Co-Op and her heart dropped into her feet. *Younger sister Ivy King was asked for comment but was too grief-stricken to speak.*

She considered vandalising them, or even buying them all and burning them but either way, it would not make her feel any better, so she walked into the shop, picked up some bread and cheese and paid. She was paranoid that anyone who looked at her knew who she was, *oh it's the sister. Poor girl. She should have known.* She got out as quickly as she could and stayed home for a few days after. When her mum suggested fish and chips for dinner, Ivy baulked at the thought. *Yesterday's news...*

Sam had texted her asking her when the funeral was. She stared at it for a while. He deserved to be there, he deserved some closure too, but she couldn't face seeing him, not yet at least. The longer she went without seeing him, the more she wanted him to stay away. She didn't know how she would feel confronted with his actual presence, especially right now. She could easily see herself overlooking everything that had happened and crawling into bed with him and the thought of it thrilled her but also horrified her that she valued herself so little.

* * *

He hadn't heard anything back from Ivy and by now he knew he probably wasn't going to. He had been home for almost a week but he didn't have to go back to work for another four days. He wondered whether he should just go over to her house. *And what bang on the door, tell her you love her?* He wasn't even sure that was true anymore.

He hadn't stopped drinking since he had come home, but he needed it. He was no longer on holiday, but he had lost his best friend and Agatha had died so he needed to numb himself somehow. He could see his mum noticed when she got home from work and saw him drinking a beer with four or five empty cans in the recycling bin, but she didn't say anything.

His dad had come into the living room with the paper and sat in the chair for twenty minutes before realising Sam was there. Sam opened another can and Richard almost physically jumped up to leave the room.

"Oh Sam, my boy. Didn't realise you were home,"

"I got home a week ago, Richard,"

"Well, yes — he cleared his throat — of course you did. How was um...how was...how was it?" he asked after a few minutes of silence.

"It was great," Sam replied, turning the TV onto the football, turning the volume down but keeping it loud enough so there was some background noise to the tension that sat between them.

"Good. That's good," he settled back into his chair and went back to his paper before making some excuse to leave and Sam turned the TV off. It wasn't long after his mum came and stood in the doorway holding a glass of wine in one hand and a pen and paper in the other.

"We're ordering in, so write what you want down and your father will call them up," she said, putting the paper down on the coffee table nearest him.

This was truly becoming a record day, both his parents had spoken to him and were even asking him to join them to eat. If he didn't know better he would think they missed him.

"Yeah, sure okay." he picked up the notepad and she left the room without telling him what they were supposed to be ordering.

He put down chips and battered sausage because that covered him if Richard ordered from the chippy or the Chinese down the road. If it was the Chinese he wouldn't have picked his usual anyway. He'd had enough noodles and rice for a while.

When it came it was from the chippy and they all sat in front of the TV eating it. His dad in the armchair by the window, his mum on the sofa nearest him and Sam on the sofa furthest away. The TV was too quiet for him to hear, not that he was interested in the show his mum had put on anyway. As usual, she had made them all use a plate and cutlery. Sam thought if they had ordered a chip shop tea at Ivy's they would all be squished up on the sofa eating it out of the paper with their fingers. They would be talking and laughing and the TV would just be in the background. Rachel would be asking them questions and Agatha would give him half her curry sauce. He wondered if one of the other Kings would order curry sauce now.

He reached for his phone and messaged Rachel.

```
When/where is the funeral? Guessing V hasn't fixed her phone yet.
```

A few minutes later he got a reply:

```
11 a.m. on 28th. Service is at Amber Valley Crematorium. See you there Sam.
```

He knew she would have had her phone fixed by now and even if she hadn't, she would know he had been trying to call and text her. It hurt knowing she didn't want him there, at her sister's funeral, but he knew he had some making up to do, even if he wasn't sure how yet. He would see her at the funeral, she couldn't avoid him then, as selfish as it was, he knew if he could push himself back into her life hard enough, she wouldn't push him back out.

CHAPTER 18

* * *

The day of the funeral arrived, and Ivy held it together much better than she realised she could. She had a minor breakdown in the morning when she couldn't find anything to wear. She hated everything she had, and nothing looked appropriate for the occasion. In the end, her mum picked a dress out for her, ironically the one she had planned on wearing originally, and she put it on.

By around 9.30 a.m., people had started arriving. Friends of her mum, some of her cousins, distant uncles and aunties Ivy hadn't seen since the last funeral. They all made quiet, small talk for a while in groups, huddled together in their small kitchen and hallway. Rachel busied herself making cups of tea for everyone and Ivy helped her to hand them out. She didn't want to sit down. She didn't want to get comfortable then have to get up again for the hearse. Eventually, the hearse arrived, and Ivy pulled back a corner of the net curtain in the living room to look at it.

She had made the right choice with the flowers, she thought, and the coffin looked nice even though it probably didn't matter seeing as it was going to be burned later. Her mum appeared behind her, gently placing a hand on her shoulder.

"Are you ready? Uncle Donald is driving us — I, uh, I don't feel up to it," she said. Ivy nodded, fresh tears sprang to her eyes looking at her mum's blotchy and swollen face. They hugged for a minute and everyone filed out of the room and began climbing into their cars.

They followed the hearse in silence, Donald drove them seamlessly and held a sad smile the whole journey which reflected back at Ivy in the rear-view mirror.

They followed the coffin into the crematorium to Good Riddance by Green Day, one of Agatha's favourites.

The service went smoothly, and they all filed out to look at the funeral flowers. What an odd thing to do, Ivy thought. To pay for these beautiful flowers to sit on top of your loved one, then to gather around them on the floor outside, while another service began in the room they had just left.

She was lost in thought when she felt familiar arms wrap around her chest from behind. She almost broke inside them. He had come and she was surprised to realise she was relieved he was there. She didn't know how much she had missed him after almost a whole month of silence.

She leaned further into him and reached up to clasp her hands around his arms and return his affection, but as she did, she smelled the sourness of alcohol on his breath. She was immediately thrown back to that moment in the club and then on the beach and that alley and she had to swallow the bile that had risen in her throat.

Luckily her Uncle Donald was walking over to her at that moment, so she pushed Sam's arms off of her and met Donald halfway. She wasn't forceful with Sam, but she had to keep moving or she would feel guilty. She knew he would be hurting too but she couldn't think about that right now.

"Can I have the car keys please?" she asked.

"Yeah, course you can, my love. I'll get your mum yeah? We'll start making our way to the pub." he answered a little surprise in his tone. He looked up at Sam and handed Ivy the keys.

She walked hurriedly to the car, falling slightly with every step as her heels dug into the gravel. She sat in the back of her mum's car and locked the doors behind her. How could she be so wrong to think he could be anything other than he is. She should have just left it alone. She never should have slept with him, if she hadn't maybe she would still have a friend right now instead of no one and she would never have been on that beach. She would have been OK that night. She was feeling increasingly sick now. If she wasn't on that beach in the first place would Agatha still be alive? The two traumas were starting to bleed together.

She was shaken from her thoughts by the crunch of gravel signalling her mum and Donald's approach. She unlocked the car and hoped that Sam wouldn't follow her to the wake, but she had a feeling he would.

She had a vodka and coke put in her hand as she arrived and spoke to a wave of people who knew her sister in some form or another. She made her way through the procession of colleagues and teachers and friends and family offering condolences in a daze.

CHAPTER 18

"Did you speak to that girl Melissa?" Her mum said. "She was nice."

Ivy smiled. Maybe she had but the faces were all blurring together.

She couldn't eat anything, even though she chose the food, so by the third vodka and coke, she was beginning to feel a bit fuzzy around the edges, but that was almost a comfort at this point. She thought for a moment about how her standards for herself differed from those she had for Sam. She was allowed to numb herself with booze but when he did the same, he was off-putting and destructive. It was then when her thoughts had drifted to him, that he appeared as if summoned. Her mum was sitting next to her, talking to someone on the other side of her but she looked up to see Sam when Ivy did.

"You should talk to him. I don't know what's happened, but he's your best friend," she said in Ivy's ear.

She debated what to do for a minute and she decided she was leaving. She called an Uber on her phone before walking outside to wait for it. Her mum had brought a few of Agatha's notebooks for guests to look through. Rachel was always very proud of Agatha's poetry and Ivy wondered if Agatha had realised that. She absently picked up the most recent notebook that was on the table in front of her but she needed something to do with her hands. She knew Sam would follow her but at least this way his time was limited to the four minutes it took her driver to arrive.

It was cold outside, and she had left her jacket in her mum's car. She folded her arms in front of herself and crossed her ankles while she looked at the end of the road for her car to come.

"I'm sorry," he said behind her.

"What about?" she replied coldly.

"Everything."

"Are you sorry because my sister is dead? Because I think everything else is pretty normal Sam Johnson behaviour." she meant every word she said but there was a part of her beating inside that wanted to fall into his arms again.

"Okay, I get it, you're punishing me. I'm an asshole and I fucked up, I deserve it. I'm sorry I got scared and ruined something great. I'm sorry because your sister's not here anymore and I am most sorry about that. But I'm here. I'm here because I think you need me," he said.

She could write a book of all the things she wished he would say, but so far, this was just the prologue and it wasn't enough. She wanted him to tell her that he would love her and that she was enough for him, but even if he said those words to her she wanted him to mean it but she knew that would never be the case.

"I don't need you, Sam. I don't need anything from you. I'm just over it, Sam. I'm over thinking I can trust you to be there for me. I'm over thinking you can be better than you are. I'm fine okay?"

"How is any of this fine V?"

Her car arrived.

"Ivy?" the driver said as she opened the door.

"Yeah," she said as she got into the car. She thought about telling Sam not to try contacting her anymore, but she didn't think she had the energy to. She didn't turn to look at him as the car drove away until they were just about to turn the corner. But he had already gone back inside.

As she travelled further from the pub and Sam, she opened Agatha's notebook and turned to the page that made her think of him.

You can make pretty poetry out of broken people, but broken people will always break good people and that is never pretty.

Part Three

"It doesn't interest me what you do for a living. I want to know what you ache for – and if you dare to dream of meeting your heart's longing. It doesn't interest me how old you are. I want to know if you will risk looking like a fool – for love – for your dreams – for the adventure of being alive." — Oriah Mountain Dreamer

Chapter 19

He didn't try to contact her again. Friendship over. Relationship… she didn't even know. Ivy tried to convince herself they had outgrown each other as friends sometimes do, but deep down she knew she couldn't look at him the same way anymore. Especially since he reminded her so much of her life with Agatha and more importantly of losing her. But it wasn't just that. Their fate was sealed before Agatha died. She knew from the moment she kissed him they wouldn't be able to go back. And once she had slept with him and let her feelings hinge on him, they wouldn't be able to go forward either. She wanted more than he could give and the rest was just filler. Overall, it was an apathetic goodbye to two of the best friends she had ever had and most of the life she had known.

It had been over two years since Agatha's funeral and Ivy still missed her every day, which was not something she saw changing any time soon, if ever. At least once a week she would do something or hear something or see something and want to tell her sister all about it. It used to be every day, so she knew time was beginning to heal her. The problem with that was that a part of her didn't want to be healed.

Ivy clung to her pain and carried it into everything she did. If they took the time to look, she was sure anyone could see that everything she did, she did for Agatha. For her sister, who wouldn't get to do it herself. And by doing so, she told herself the pain can only be good for her. It would drive her and push her where she needed to be. Push her to a point where she was living enough to make up for both her and Agatha.

It was because of Agatha she began working at the publishing house a few months ago as an editor's assistant. Her uncle Donald had gotten her an interview at Braitons with an editor friend of his. The pay wasn't great, as it was an entry-level position, but it meant she could spend a lot of her time reading and there was room to climb. The best part was that the job required her to have a degree, ideally in media or English, but she was able to negotiate at the interview. She fought hard and convinced her new boss not only that she was perfect for the job, but to give her the time off she needed to attend her classes for the final academic year of her business degree, arguing business was applicable in any field.

She had met with the course director and worked with her to arrange her classes to fit into her work scheduled study time and pick up any credits she was missing from her second year. And that September, when she first stepped onto campus, she saw uni through different eyes. It was surprising how grateful she was to be a part of student life again. She didn't realise how much she had missed it and the chance to work towards something, a goal to reach was motivating, and she knew Agatha would have wanted that for her.

She chose a local university and told her mum she had chosen to finish closer to home so she could fit it in easier around her work commitments, but really it was so she didn't have to leave her alone. At twenty-five, things that seemed unimportant before were beginning to slot into focus and she not only knew she could do well, but part of her wanted to, more than she wanted to be miserable.

She spent most of her free periods reading in the SU common room, drinking copious amounts of fancy coffees from the machine and it was here, whilst reading This Side of Paradise, she met Jessie.

"How do you spell 'necessary'?" she said a table away from her. Ivy looked up to see a dark-eyed, Latina woman with long dark waves covering her face as she wrote something down in her notebook. "Is it double *C* or double *S*? I can never remember," she said before looking up and into Ivy's eyes, confirming it was her she was speaking to.

"Double *S*," Ivy replied.

"Yeah, that looks right." She finished writing and closed the book, picking up all of her stuff and bringing it all so she could sit opposite Ivy. "I'm Jessie."

"Ivy."

"Wanna get something to eat Ivy? I mean, I've been here for like two hours and all I've seen you eat is the cream off the top of your coffee and I don't know about you but I need to eat at least every two hours or I can't be held responsible for my actions." Ivy stared at her dumbly for a second before she continued: "Plus, although looks can be deceiving, this is what is known as a 'canteen', a place where students and teachers alike come to fuel their bodies so I feel like we should be a part of that. Conform to the system as it were."

"Um, yeah? I mean, sure, let's get something to eat," Ivy replied, putting her books back into her bag.

"Great! I would have probably just bugged you until you agreed, so a yes off the bat is always good." They collected a tray each and joined the other students lined up to select their lunch from the steaming hot plates and bain maries behind sneeze guards. "OK, serious question," Jessie said. Ivy arched a brow. "Ketchup or mayo?"

"Definitely mayo," she replied.

"Nope. Mayo is disgusting. The correct answer was ketchup,"

"Hmm, ask me another and I'll try again," Ivy replied smiling.

"OK. Burgers or nuggets?" she said looking at the two options in front of her, as she tonged chips onto a plate.

"Both,"

"Good answer," Jessie laughed and added both to her plate.

"What's the best gift someone has ever given you?"

Ivy thought for a minute. "My Dad left when I was young and he was a sucky dad and all but I missed him. So my sister had found one of his old jumpers. It was full of holes and covered in paint splatters but it still smelled like him, so she kept hold of it until she could see how much I missed him and gave it to me,"

"Well, that puts my best gift to shame,"

"Why what was yours?"

"A slinky," she replied, smiling guiltily.

Ivy laughed. "You're a bit strange, aren't you?"

Jessie "Yeah — aren't you?" She was incredibly witty, and Ivy had never met anyone else who was so effortlessly smart. "So, what's your story Ivy?"

Ivy thought for a moment about how much to tell her, and although she felt immediately comfortable with her, she thought she was better off skipping to the highlights. "You know, dropped out of uni, fucked off to Thailand, came back to finish uni and now just trying to finish my degree and work at the same time."

"What do you do for work?"

"I'm at a publishing house — Braitons? I'm an editor's assistant so I do research, copy-editing and a whole bunch of reading. How about you, what do you do?"

"I'm doing my Masters in Civil Engineering and before you say it no that does not mean I am a maths nerd...actually, yes it does, but a cool one."

"That's not something I could even begin to comprehend, and maths was never my thing, give me a pile of books any day."

"Ew, you book nerd." she smiled at Ivy.

"Yes, but a cool one," Ivy replied, smiling back.

They sat down at one of the tables that had some free space. "What's that one about?" Jessie asked, gesturing to the book that Ivy had been reading.

"Trials and tribulations of entitled, white men in love."

"Sounds relatable," Jessie laughed.

It wasn't but that was the point. Reading felt like walking around in someone else's skin for a while and that was why Ivy read as often as she did. "It's giving me a deep sympathy for white men, they really do have it hard." They laughed. "It is good though. I've read a few of Fitzgerald's and this one is how he got his wife to marry him."

"Sounds like he was writing about his own entitled, white self,"

"They say write what you know," she shrugged.

"That looks good." A guy with dark curly hair and fair skin reached over Jessie's shoulder and took a chip off her plate, dipped it in the ketchup and ate it, before throwing his backpack onto the table and sitting next to Jessie. "Hey boo, where you been?" he smiled at her, taking another chip from her plate. Jessie pushed the plate towards him, so it was between them.

"Right here," she replied before turning back to Ivy. "This is Alden, by the way. Alden, this is Ivy. He's just some weirdo that follows me around a lot but he occasionally has something interesting to say so I don't mind so much." Jessie said.

"Oh, how you do honour me, Jess." he retorted with a grin before turning back to Ivy. "Truth is she wouldn't know what to do with herself without me — she would be a spinster by thirty"

"So, you two...?" Ivy asked.

"Oh god no, I mean there was that one time...but no, we're not," Jessie laughed. Ivy wasn't sure if this was a joke or not. The conversation bounced back and forward between the two of them all the while Ivy sat there trying to take it all in.

"Did you see Rochelle? She's still trying to get me to join the board game society," Alden said.

"I honestly couldn't think of anything more boring," Jessie replied.

"I don't mind a bit of Monopoly at Christmas, but every Thursday? I have better things to be doing,"

"No you don't. What did you do last Thursday?"

"Went out with you, you dingbat,"

"Oh, yeah. Forgot about that,"

"I know you, don't I?" Alden said interrupting the flow of conversation and squinting at Ivy.

"Yeah, I think we both went to the same school? But I don't think we've ever officially met," Ivy replied.

"Broomhill Park right? Did you know it's an academy now? I narrowly avoided ties and blazers by about a year. But you're a couple of years above me, so you were well in the clear. Loads of people here went to Broomhill." he looked at her notes that were sitting to the side of her lunch tray. "You're taking some business classes, then?" Alden said.

"Yeah, but not all of them, just strategic management and the critical enquiry project." She said reading from her notes.

"Let me see," he asked, turning her notebook towards himself. "Yup, I'm in the same classes — we have a strat. lecture in an hour. We can sit in the back and talk about boys."

"Ugh, you business types are all the same." Jessie moaned, mockingly raising a hand to her forehead in faux dramatics. "But that's cool, I have a much more interesting class on geotechnics to go to." She added sarcastically. Slinging her bag onto her shoulder.

"I'm not even going to pretend to know what that means." Ivy looked up as Jessie stood and grabbed her books.

"We'll catch you later though right?" Alden asked.

"Yeah, let's go for drinks. Give Ivy my number, will ya?"

"K, hon," he replied.

"Cool, peace out bitches," Jessie said in her best big man on campus voice holding up two fingers without a shred of irony.

"She really is the best but if you tell her I said that I will have to kill you," Alden said, mock conspiratorially after she left. Ivy smiled but winced at the word *kill* slightly. Even two years later, things like that caught her off guard and Alden's face softened a moment later when he must have realised. "I'm sorry by the way. About your sister." Ivy went to open her mouth, but he interrupted her. "I didn't know her or anything, but I heard. When a student dies it has its way of making it around the school, even if that person hasn't attended for years. You don't have to say anything either, I just wanted to say, I know and I'm sorry."

Sitting back she thought for the first time in her life she felt understood. Jessie, Alden, studying and working had all come together in a way that made her soul exhale and say *so this is who you are.* The trio didn't have a great deal in common, but they had developed such a strong bond over the first term that Ivy couldn't imagine another life without them, and she was glad that the huge gaping hole where a best friend should be was no longer so empty. And although this was a great weight lifted from her shoulders, she still held onto it, feeling like this was a betrayal to Agatha. That finding peace shouldn't be an option for her.

She often wondered what Sam was up to. As much as she didn't want to care, she did think about him. The way Jessie and Alden fell in sync with each other reminded her of what it was like to be with Sam but the difference was, neither of them expected more than the other could offer. Neither of them had the potential to be poisonous like Sam did and the more time she spent away from him the more she realised although she missed him, she was never in love with him like she had convinced herself she was. She had been infatuated with the idea of becoming lovers rather than holding a love built on the solid, firm foundation of their friendship.

He didn't update his social media very often, but she saw he was travelling again, this time it looked a little closer to home. He posted from Rome and Paris and Amsterdam. It looked like he was enjoying himself, but he always did. Even though a part of her wanted to be there with him, she was grateful for the physical distance between them. It made her feel safer as if she could reach out to him easier than if he was still living in the same city as her. In reality, she knew she could reach out to him anywhere really

What would he do? Would he come running? She thought. *Unlikely.* Even though she was aware of his flaws, Ivy still wondered if she had been unfair to him. She left him alone and unlike her, he didn't have his family to fall back on, but he should have fought harder for her.

Chapter 20

Ivy could tell the room was used to housing big events. The huge dome-shaped ceiling with cream, damask filigree held a delicate chandelier that lit the whole room with a yellow glow and gave the space an intimate feel that was a bit out of place for the business conference.

Most people were still in their business wear, although some had changed into their civilian clothes. She didn't mind attending these sort of events, because it meant getting out of the office and learning something new, plus she liked visiting London, even if it meant a two-hour train ride both ways and she wasn't going to see much more than the inside of the tube while she was there.

The talks were interesting and she had made a ton of notes to take back to work, but they were now at the portion of the day where you were supposed to "network over drinks with other like-minded individuals".

This was the part that Ivy hated. It's not that she wasn't good at talking to people. She was bubbly and interesting and could talk to anyone, but just because she was good at something didn't mean she had to like it and she wasn't going to go out of her way to speak to anyone today. She was the approachee, not the approacher.

She walked straight to the back of the room and picked up a glass of prosecco from one of the trays balancing on the bar there. As she turned, she turned straight into another body. Bumping into a woman, glasses colliding.

"Oh I'm sorry, I guess I crept up on you!" The stranger said, placing a hand on the top of Ivy's arm.

Ivy was staring at the front of her own shirt which had a small splash mark.

CHAPTER 20

"Don't worry about it. Are you ok?" She asked looking up and meeting her grey-green eyes for the first time. Her stomach did a small flip. She was beautiful.

"Yeah, I'm fundamentally clumsy so it was a case of *when* not *if* I ruined this shirt."

Ivy glanced down at the woman's chest to see she didn't get away as lightly as she did. She couldn't pull her eyes away from her. She tried to remember if she had ever seen someone so beautiful before. Her eyes were glittering and shifted from green to hazel depending on whether she turned her face to the light or shadow. Her long brown waves spilt down her shoulders and were pinned at either side of her face.

"I'm so self-absorbed, here — Ivy reached for another glass from the bar behind her — have a fresh one. Come on, let's go dry it out under the hand dryers in the ladies," she said softly in what she hoped was a friendly, faux conspiratory manner.

***

They caught the train home together that evening. They didn't stop talking the whole way home and although Ivy could feel something electric between them that made her heart race every time Thea spoke, at the same time, she felt completely at ease with her. She wouldn't usually have let her guard down so quickly, even though the few drinks she'd had at the event helped, but there was something about Thea Green. She came across as so sweet and charming that she could never judge you for saying the wrong thing but Ivy couldn't help but want to impress her nonetheless.

She had a face that was made for smiling and whenever she did she lit up everything around her so Ivy kept her laughing as much as she could. She was full of soft angles. Her cheekbones were killer and her collarbone that peaked out of her jacket looked sharp and sexy. There was a softness to her though, she felt warm and comforting while oozing sex appeal and she had Ivy hooked.

"My stop's the next one," Thea said and Ivy could hear the disappointment in her voice.

Ivy couldn't have said what they had been talking about for the last few hours but they had been so contained in their little bubble, the thought of Thea leaving sucked the warmth out of the compartment. Remembering herself quickly, she pulled back slightly, shifting to match the cold tone of disappointment.

"Oh, that's a shame. It was good to talk though," she said, immediately regretting how formal she had sounded. She didn't have time to smooth it over because Thea had already stood up and walked over to the door. "Why don't you come back to mine? It's only two more stops and I live just around the corner from the station." Ivy said, half shouting down the aisle. Her cheeks burned. She was now not only regretting that she had swung from cold to hot, but that she just put herself out on a limb in front of the entire five people sitting in the carriage around them.

"I can't — I have work in the morning," Thea said, hesitantly. Ivy couldn't work out if that was an honest excuse or she was trying to let her down gently. The train stopped.

"Right. I'll see ya then." Ivy said more quietly and watched Thea hold a hand up to wave before stepping off of the train and onto the dark platform. *There's your answer girly.*

Ivy began walking up the carriage, she didn't want to sit in the same carriage as the strangers who had seen her swing and miss so hard. Plus she would rather go to the quiet carriage and dissect where she had gone wrong in peace.

She had just reached the corridor carriage when she heard a loud knock from her right. Swivelling her head to find the source of the noise, she saw Thea standing there, on the other side of the train door. A man sitting on a small suitcase next to the door, pushed the button to open the door and Thea reached in and handed Ivy her phone.

"Your number," she said smiling hopefully and when Ivy didn't move she added "Put it in," as if she was hoping she hadn't misjudged the situation.

Ivy took the phone from her and added her number to the contacts before handing it back. Thea called her immediately and her phone buzzed in her hands.

"And now you have mine," Thea said with a smile before walking off. The

CHAPTER 20

door beeped and then slid shut.

"Sorry, I thought she was getting on." The man with the suitcase offered. Ivy just smiled at him and carried on walking unsure what else to do and found a new seat. Her heart was racing and she couldn't pull the smile from her face. Pulling her phone back out she saved Thea's number and stared at it in her address book. She thought about whether to text her or not. *Would that be too much seeing as I practically threw myself at her a few minutes ago? But what if she is waiting for me to text first?* Before she could make up her mind, Thea decided for her and her phone buzzed in her hand.

```
So just to be clear, I really like you, Ivy King.
```

Ivy bit her lip and smiled to herself, holding the phone close to her chest as if it was a secret to keep. She righted the phone to craft her response.

```
Just to be clear, I really like you too. You're a total babe Thea
Green.
```

She sent it before she could second guess herself. There was nothing like a screen and a few miles between them to make her feel bolder. She followed up with another message quickly.

```
So do you often pick up women on the train?
```

```
Ha, no not at all really. The last woman I picked up was on
Tinder. She asked me for pictures of my feet on like the second
message
```

135

I'm not saying I have a foot fetish or anything but I do like someone with nice feet

Oh, I sent the photos, don't worry I'm not a complete monster. I don't think anyone wants someone with bad feet, I think you're normal

So I'm guessing things didn't work out with feet girl?

I think it lasted a whole five messages -- she took the feet pictures and ran!

Lucky me then

They texted back and forth until Ivy got off the train. She walked home from the station pulling her coat around her to keep out the cold, all the while her cheeks were burning from the incessant smile on her face.

 Closing the door quietly, she used her phone to light her way through the house, reluctant to wake her mum as it was already 1 a.m. The kitchen light was shining through the window above the door though, so Ivy walked through to find her mum sitting at the kitchen table in her dressing gown, cradling a cup of tea. Her legs were crossed and her slipper on the crossed foot was hanging from it. There were photo albums stacked on the table.

 "How was the conference, love?" she looked up and she looked like she had been crying.

CHAPTER 20

"Yeah it was good, learned a lot and I met someone," Ivy said, her thoughts still consumed by Thea.

"A romantic someone?" Rachel asked, smiling warmly.

Ivy nodded, biting her lip as she smiled.

"Wanna tell me about them? Shall I make you a cup of tea?" her mum offered. Beginning to get up out of her chair.

"Not just yet. It still feels all shiny and new so I think I want to hold onto it a little longer if that's okay? Plus I am knackered and have to get up for work tomorrow, so I think I'm just gonna go to bed."

Her mum nodded understanding, sitting back in her chair. Ivy walked over and kissed her on the cheek.

"Night mum."

"Night my love. I am pleased for you," she said, giving her hand a small squeeze.

Ivy left her in the kitchen and walked upstairs to her bedroom, discarding her clothes as she made it to the bed and pulled a big t-shirt out of her bedside drawer and over her head before crashing down onto the pillow. She pulled her phone out and reread the messages that Thea had sent so far as she plugged it in.

The last one read:

```
Let me know when you're home.
```

```
I'm home   You still awake?
```

Ivy stared at the screen for a few seconds, waiting for the reply, when her phone began vibrating in her hand.

"Hey," she answered.

"Hey. I just wanted to hear your voice." Thea replied.

"Do you miss me yet?"

"I actually do," Ivy could hear the smile in her voice.

"So does that mean you will let me take you for dinner?"

"I thought you'd never ask."

Chapter 21

Life was much easier when he was travelling. It had only been a few months and he had already figured that out. He enjoyed the freedom of moving from place to place and not planting roots wherever he had chosen to stop. Of course, it wouldn't be this easy if his parents weren't funding it. Every month he had a lump sum deposited into his account with no questions asked. He wondered if it was easier for his parents to just set up a standing order and forget they even had a son. By the way, they acted when he came back from Thailand he knew that they weren't ready to deal with him and might never be, and with no Ivy, he didn't see much point in sticking around. Although he missed her, it had taken him almost two years to get to the point where he wasn't still pining after her.

He had lost count of the number of times he had woken up with a strange girl and no memory of the night before. But it was probably better that way. With all the women Europe had to offer, he couldn't believe he had let himself be hung up on Ivy all this time. Every woman he slept with convinced him he was one step further from her and their time together.

Sam knew he would have to get a job at some point but that day was not today, today was for living and drinking and fucking and whatever else took his fancy. It was surprisingly easy to find drugs in Europe but he never was one to look a gift horse in the mouth.

Lying back in the bed of his cheap room, he stared at the rumpled sheets next to him where the dark-haired, Italian girl from last night had left this morning. He could still see the indent in the space she had occupied for a short while.

The previous night, the night before the dark-haired Italian girl, he had slept on the street. He stumbled out of a bar at 2 a.m. and was shocked to find all the shops were closed. Including the CarreFour down the street from his hotel. There was a drunk, homeless man sitting outside on a broken cardboard box with "Spuma di Sciampagna" repeatedly written across it at varying angles. He had a small bottle of what smelled like a sour wine but it could have been the rough Italian's clothes. He asked to sit and drink with him in his limited Italian and his new companion scooted over to share the cardboard seat. They didn't speak much and mainly communicated in gestures, until the homeless man fell asleep, knocked out by the booze. Sam pulled the scratchy burlap sheet he was using for a blanket up over the man's shoulders and even though he was within ten yards of his hotel room he chose to sleep there.

When he woke, the homeless man had no idea who Sam was but the CarreFour was open, so he went inside and bought him a new bottle of wine along with some sandwiches and a multipack of crisps. He put a roll of Euros into his hand as he passed the carrier bag of food over and left him there on the street.

His neck still hurt from the concrete pillow as he rolled it side to side this morning. He stretched a little and grabbed his phone from the bedside table and scrolled through social media photos of people he knew back home. They were all moving on with their lives, growing up and having families, but he felt ambivalent towards them all, his highlight reel was better than most of that. Not that he remembered any of it, but he didn't envy any of them with their marriages and new jobs and two-point-four kids, but it did make him stop for a moment and think about the only person who he actually cared to keep tabs on.

He clicked into the search bar and started typing the letters I-V, but he changed his mind and deleted it. Then changed his mind again and typed I-V-Y before clicking onto her profile. He still followed her and she still followed him but they didn't communicate. He could see from her story updates that she had recently started back at uni. *Good for her. Looks like she's doing really well,* he thought. *Which does sting a little.* It's not like he wanted her to be miserable but it did make him think that she was probably right to get rid of him. He pushed it out of his mind, got out of bed and got ready for the day. What he was going to do with his time, he didn't know but that was half the fun.

It was a bright day and the sun was already on its way back down. The cobbled roads made way to modern, tarmac ones that were still wet where it had rained this morning, despite the warmth. He wove under canopies from small cafes and trattorias which provided a soundtrack of barista machines, clattering plates on surfaces and teaspoons clinking against saucers of coffee cups. The streets were fairly bare and the cafes were empty which seemed strange for a Saturday. Sam pulled his phone out of his pocket and with it a small bag of white powder, which he then carefully slid back. He was glad to know it was there, his fucked up self wasn't usually so considerate to leave himself a hangover treat.

Turning on his screen, he looked at the date. It was Tuesday. He wasn't sure where the weekend had gone. *That is the life of the leisurely unemployed traveller,* he thought. It did explain where everyone else was too, tucked up in their offices working away.

He liked Velletri. The slow pace it seemed to hold compared to its touristy neighbour Rome. The sense of community that was missing in Britain struck him as reassuring. Although he was miles away from his own friends and family he felt a warmth from watching them all come together and ceremoniously eat and drink into the late hours. How importance was placed on even the small rituals like an afternoon coffee. He reflected on this as he licked his finger and pushed it into the small baggie inside his left pocket, pushed it up his nose and sniffed.

* * *

Ivy stood awkwardly against the wall of one of the university toilet cubicles. The university had installed rows of these cubicles that had just enough space for a toilet and a sink in an effort to be progressive with gender-neutral toilets. But the addition of the sink meant that there was hardly enough room to shut the door unless you were already sitting down. She waited as Jessie pulled up her jeans and placed the pregnancy test on the edge of the sink. She flushed the toilet and lowered the seat so she could sit back down.

"So did you get his number?" Ivy asked. "I mean, in case it's...?"

Jessie closed her eyes and sighed hard. "No, it wasn't high on the priority list when he was inside me." she retorted, biting her cuticles.

"Right, yeah, I get it, but.." Ivy said. She wasn't doing great, she realised. She could tell Jessie was worried no matter how good she was at faking otherwise. It was hard to watch. She was used to Jessie being so strong and things never seemed to get to her, but Ivy realised it was stupid to think that a baby wouldn't change everything for Jessie and she had a right to be bat shit crazy let alone worried. "It's fine though. Either way. I mean, you only have, what, two months left of your degree? You've done most of your dissertation and you only have two exams to sit so you could do all that, with a...um, pregnant." Jessie looked up at her still biting the cuticle on her thumb. "And if not, you just go on as before...but maybe with a coil." Jessie laughed. *Good,* Ivy thought. *She can at least laugh.* She looked at her phone. "OK, it's been two minutes. We can look." Ivy said.

Jessie took her thumb out of her mouth and picked up the test and stared at it before handing it to Ivy. Ivy looked at the faint blue cross in the window of the stick and looked at Jessie to gauge her reaction.

"What's taking so long? Did someone fall in?" Alden banged on the door. Jessie took the test out of Ivy's hand and unlocked the door.

"Mazel Tov, it's a boy!" She said dropping the test into Alden's hand.

"Wait seriously?" He held the stick closer to his face before realising he probably should put something Jessie had peed on so close to his face. He pushed himself into the cubicle with them, leaning his back against the door and flipping the lock behind him.

"So this is that Jack guy, right?"

"Jack, John, Josh. Could be anyone for all I care. It was one night and we didn't swap numbers, just DNA." Jessie said.

"Well is this definitely right? Are you sure?" Alden asked.

"I mean, I could take another one but that would bring my total up to four positive pregnancy tests."

CHAPTER 21

"You're taking this pretty well seeing as you have to push a baby out of your downstairs in about nine months." Alden blurted.

Ivy swatted him in the stomach. "She doesn't have to keep it," Ivy said. "Whatever you choose to do we are in full support - right Al?"

"Right." he barked.

"Thanks, guys, but I have a class to get to in — she checked her phone — like fifteen minutes. So maybe we should decide my future later," she said and gave a weak smile before unlocking the door and sliding out of the cubicle through the gap between her friends.

Ivy and Alden looked at each other. Alden put the test into the sanitary bin and without saying anything, followed Ivy out a few minutes later.

"Haven't seen you much lately." Ivy looked at Alden hopefully as they walked towards the seated area down the corridor from them. He didn't look up from the floor and looked deep in thought. She wondered how much of his thoughts were on Jessie and whether the fact he was adopted had any bearing on these thoughts. "Classes are boring without you," she added, gently nudging him with her shoulder.

"What? Oh, yeah. I've missed a few, haven't I? Thanks for the notes by the way," he responded.

"It's fine. She'll be okay you know?"

"Yeah, yeah I know." He paused. "This will be really hard for her. More than most people I mean. How much has Jessie told you about her relationship with her mum?" he asked as they reached the sofa. She dropped the folders she was carrying onto the arm and swung her bag to the side as she sat. Alden dropped down opposite her.

"I know they don't get on, what more is there to know?" she replied.

"Let's just say seeing how her mum treats her, it makes me feel lucky to have my parents."

"She isn't alone in this though. She has us, we're her family too." she added, not sure what else to say. "So I take it things are going well at The Maple?" she said changing the subject.

"Good — great actually. The chef, Sean, turns out he used to teach at some fancy culinary school in France, he's sort of taken me under his wing as his protégé. So I've been running the pass some days and helping him to create the menu. It's pretty cool," he said, beginning to show some enthusiasm, his thought moving away from Jessie.

"Is that why you've been missing classes? To work?" she asked.

"Yeah, I mean sort of. I just think I'm doing well and uni just isn't high on the priority list anymore for me,"

Ivy arched an eyebrow. "That's fine, but just be warned that it isn't so easy to come back once you give up," she replied.

"Sorry, I don't mean to be flippant about it. I get you've worked hard to get back here and I'm flaking out with the finish line in sight which is shitty of me,"

"It's not shitty if you're sure it's what you want but you might as well just see the term through and then go off and be a big-time restauranteur or chef or whatever it is you want to do, don't you think?"

"Yeah, yeah you're right. Haven't we got a tutorial later?"

"Yeah — she checked her phone calendar — in like two hours, up on the fourth floor," she said.

"Cool, OK. Well let's grab something to eat and you can catch me up on what I should have done for this class."

***

Alden spent the next few nights at Jessie's to keep her company and they both stopped going to lectures. Ivy continued to share her notes with Alden and Jessie watched her classes online. Ivy checked in when she could but she couldn't be there for her like Alden could. She had her own life to deal with; completing her research project, working and still attending lectures.

A guilty feeling gnawed away at her stomach, she felt like she was letting her best friend down. Maybe a good friend would have skipped lectures to go see her, or at least for solidarity but she was at a different place in her life than Jessie was. Ivy didn't want to see Jessie fail, but this was the second time around for Ivy and she knew she couldn't flunk it again. Plus she was still in the honeymoon phase with Thea, things were going great for them but she still hadn't introduced her to her friends.

It was easy to tell herself it was the timing and Jessie had enough on her plate but she knew it was because she was scared. Scared it wouldn't last. Scared that her happiness was temporary. Losing her sister and losing Sam had changed her outlook on life and not for the better she realised. She knew it was ridiculous to be scared of life, waiting for the other shoe to drop, but it was always in the back of her mind whether she liked it or not.

She voiced her worries about Jessie with Thea. Thea was the most supportive and comforting person she knew. Ivy knew that no matter what, Jessie and Alden would always have her back, she knew they would fight tooth and nail for her, whether she wanted them to or not. But Thea, she knew, would make any sacrifice she needed to, to make her happy, which was an uneasy burden to bear if she thought about it too hard. Thea was selfless and Ivy didn't deserve her. It was strange to think these people had only been in her life for six months because on one hand, it felt like they had always been there and on the other, they weren't connected to Agatha in any way, they were a part of her life that belonged to her alone. Although it didn't replace the one she had lost, she had made a new family, one that kept her grounded in her life.

"As far as I'm aware, she hasn't made a decision about the baby yet," Ivy said.

"How far along is she?" Thea asked.

Ivy counted internally "She must be around nine weeks?"

"Well, that's still plenty of time, if she doesn't want to keep it,"

"Yeah, Alden has been working night shifts at The Maple, so he's been hanging out with her during the day,"

"Well that's good, she's not alone,"

"Yeah but I need to be there for her, just like Jessie would be if it was me,"

"So be there for her," Thea said reassuringly.

*　*　*

The bell rang and Ivy answered. Her mum had gone out for drinks with some of the other nurses from work so wouldn't be home until late, she hoped. She was glad to see her mum socialising again.

"How many times have I told you to just walk in?" she said walking back towards the kitchen.

"How many times have I told you that's creepy?" Jessie replied jokingly.

Jessie shut the door behind her as she stopped to wipe her feet on the doormat. A memory played out in Ivy's mind of Sam opening the door and running up the stairs as if it were his own home. He never knocked. She didn't think about him often, but when she did it was like a slap in the face. She turned to Jessie with a wide smile and took her coat.

"Hey, Rache!" Jessie shouted down the hall.

"She's out, it's just us tonight," Ivy responded as they walked toward the kitchen.

"Why Miss Ivy, if you wanted to be alone with me you only had to say!" she said fluttering her lashes with a hand to her chest, feigning modesty. "Something smells good - what's cooking?"

"It's paella. I know you love spicy, but I didn't know if they did — she pointed to Jessie's stomach — so it's mild and smoky, I hope that's OK?"

"Mm mild and smoky, that was my high school nickname, you know," Jessie said sitting at the table.

Since Agatha had died, Ivy had taken up the role of family chef. She began with the intention of minimising her sister's absence at home and never really stopped. She had been getting quite good at cooking but she still wasn't as instinctual at creating flavours like her sister was.

Ivy went back to the pan, stirring the stock while they talked about everything but the baby.

"So have you had any thought about whether you are going to go back to class?" Ivy asked.

"Yeah, I have actually. I spoke to the course leader — who is fine as hell by the way — and he said I haven't missed much. I just need to catch up on some reading and get my coursework in, when it's due next month, to be able to sit my exams."

"That's good then. Does it seem doable?"

CHAPTER 21

"Yeah, I'll be fine. I'm a genius — remember?"

Ivy smiled and filled two bowls before putting them on the kitchen table and collecting the knives and forks from the drawer and two cans of coke from the fridge. They sat down unceremoniously.

Jessie dove straight into the food, spooning a huge mouthful of rice into her mouth before putting her fork down and opening her can while she chewed.

"Good then?" Ivy asked.

"So good," she said, over the food in her mouth.

Ivy smiled.

"So when do I get to meet this new mystery woman?" Jessie asked.

"Who, Thea?" Ivy replied.

"Why? How many of these girls do you have on the go?" Jessie asked.

"Ha ha, I don't know when. Do you want to meet her?"

"Are you kidding? Of course, I do. She needs to know what she's getting herself in for," Jessie smiled.

"Hey, I am a catch I'll have you know," Ivy said, taking a sip of her coke.

"I know you are, but you're friends with me so there has to be something wrong with you," she smiled sweetly.

When they were finished, the two lay out on the sofa after dinner and watched a murder documentary. Jessie cradled a bowl of popcorn, occasionally throwing it at the TV in annoyance.

"How do they not know he did it?!"

"I don't know but stop hogging the popcorn." Ivy reached over to take a handful when her phone beeped. It was a text from Thea.

```
Hey, Ivy King, can I see you tonight? X
```

```
Soz Thea Green, no can do. Jessie's here - I'm helping her deal x
```

147

```
Want some help? x
```

```
Nah, I don't want the first time you meet to be when she's in this
weird place x
```

```
Totally get it. Have your girl time. Hope she's OK x
```

```
LY x
```

She smiled at how casually she could type that and even though a three-letter text wasn't the stuff of big romance, it felt just as serious. It wasn't much later when there was a rustling by the door. Ivy got up, expecting it to be her mum searching for her key even though she wasn't supposed to be back this soon. But when she opened the door, she saw Thea stooped down.

"Busted. I'm not stopping, I don't want to intrude but thought you guys might need this." she held out a bottle of non-alcoholic wine. "And this." she held out a tub of ice cream with a packet of cookie dough.

"New friend, who dis?" Jessie appeared beside her before Ivy had the chance to open her mouth.

"This is Thea."

Jessie made eyes at Ivy and said "Don't let me interrupt you two." she made to leave.

"Actually it was me interrupting, I just wanted to drop some things off for you guys." Thea held the treats up.

Jessie looked at what Thea was holding and almost jumping on her, hugged Thea. "I love you," she said in Thea's ear, loud enough for Ivy to hear before pulling away and saying: "She's a keeper." with a fake whisper and a wink to

CHAPTER 21

Ivy. She took the bottle from Thea and walked back inside. "Good to meet you, Thea," she shouted as she walked back to the living room without turning.

Thea laughed. "That's good, right? I guess that means she likes me?"

"Trust me, you would know if she didn't like you," Ivy smiled. "Thank you for doing this, you really didn't have to," she added as Thea handed over a pack of cookie dough and the tub of ice cream.

"I didn't know what you guys would like so I thought, can't go wrong with cookie dough and ice cream, right?"

"Right," Ivy echoed.

"Right," Thea repeated before smiling a wide toothy smile. "So I'm gonna go. Enjoy the treats and have a great evening and I'll see you...when I see you." Ivy loved how adorably awkward they still were together.

"Yeah, I'll um, I'll give you a call tomorrow?"

"Great."

"Cool." Ivy leant down and kissed her, lingering for a few seconds to feel the warmth of Thea's skin on her face before pulling back. Thea's smile widened and she half waved as she walked away towards her car. Ivy closed the door and smiled to herself as she walked back to the living room.

"Damn she's hot, well done," Jessie said and Ivy rolled her eyes and smiled. "Ivy and Thea, sitting in a tree, doing things they shouldn't be," Jessie sang at her as she passed her a glass of wine.

"Did I mention you're an asshole?" Ivy said but her smile only got bigger.

"Not tonight. Maybe you were thinking of Thea," she half-sung her name. Ivy sat on the sofa and picked up a cushion, ready to throw it at Jessie. "Oh - oh my, you wouldn't hit a pregnant woman would you?" she raised her hand to her forehead and used her best southern country belle voice.

Ivy threw the pillow but missed as Jessie ducked. "Pretty spry for a pregnant woman." and Jessie's smile fell a little. It was almost imperceptible.

"Tell me a secret," Ivy said lying back on the sofa, resting her head next to Jessie's.

Jessie thought for a moment before saying "I really love pizza," in a serious tone.

"No, a real secret. Something I don't know. Deeper than pizza,"

"Deeper than pizza. OK. I once stole a Barbie from the supermarket, because she was prettier than mine. The one I had at home was one of Barbie's friends. She was brown-skinned and had wavy brown hair and she looked like me, but all of the girls at school had Barbie Barbie. You know *white* Barbie. So I stole her. Like if I had the same Barbie, I wouldn't feel so *other*."

"Do you still feel other?" Ivy asked, turning her head to look at her.

"No. I mean, not in a bad way anyway."

And how do you feel about the baby?" Ivy said. Thinking now was as good a time as any to ask.

"I—" She was interrupted by her ringtone. She stooped to pick it up from her bag but put it back when she saw who was calling. Ivy couldn't help but look at the screen over her shoulder. MUM lit up the screen.

"Have you told her? You know, about the baby?" Ivy asked, gently.

"No, that would involve speaking to her," Jessie responded.

"Maybe that's not necessarily a bad thing?"

"She's not like your mum. She's...toxic. You wouldn't understand. You're mum didn't always put you down, didn't make you feel shit about how you looked, how you dressed, your ability to accomplish anything or who you were as a person,"

Ivy thought about Sam's mum Vicky and realised there are one hundred different ways you can damage your children. "You won't be like that you know?"

"What do you mean?"

"I mean, if you were thinking about not — you are not going to become her... You would be an amazing mum."

"You think so?" Jessie looked at her and then put a hand softly on her stomach. "When I found out, I...I bought a bottle of vodka, hoping it would... I think I was trying to prove to myself that I was as bad as her, you know? I opened it and went to drink it but I couldn't."

The vulnerability on her face hit Ivy's chest. She wrapped her arms around her tightly. Jessie buried her face in Ivy's hair and squeezed her back. She could feel tears threatening so pulled back and went to the kitchen to grab a spoon for the ice cream that was beginning to melt on the floor. Jessie sat at Ivy's feet, eating the ice cream while Ivy braided her hair and occasionally took bites of the ice cream that Jessie offered her.

Jessie wasn't intending to stay over but she fell asleep on the sofa, still clutching the spoon. Ivy took it from her and spread the blanket over her friend before going to bed herself.

Chapter 22

Ivy rummaged through Thea's drawers looking for a blouse to wear to work. She had run out of clothes but luckily Thea was a similar size to her if a bit on the smaller side.

"You know, you could just move in right?" Thea said behind her shoulder.

"That would be too easy. Plus I like wearing your clothes." Ivy said, buttoning up the cream blouse she had found. She turned to Thea, who did the pussy-bow up on her collar for her.

"I'm serious, you basically live here anyway. When was the last time you went home?" Ivy thought about it for a moment. It had been a while, almost the whole four months they had been together, but she didn't know if she was ready to move in yet and it would mean leaving her mum alone. "We're paying two lots of rent. I know your mum doesn't ask for much but it's money we could put towards something else. Like a deposit on a house." Thea looked up at Ivy hopefully.

Ivy looked around the one-bedroom flat. It was smaller and more out of the way, but it was cosier and she liked that it was just the two of them in the tiny space. "I'll speak to my mum about it. I don't know if she's ready to be on her own yet." Ivy said, kissing Thea on the cheek. She made to leave and walked towards the door, sliding her feet into her pumps. Thea seemed to consider this.

"She is a grown woman Ivy and I'm sure she wants you to have your independence," Thea said from the bedroom doorway in a small voice.

Ivy looked back at her. "I know. I just don't want to...I just want her to be OK." she said.

CHAPTER 22

Thea smiled at her, a half-smile.

"I'll see you when I get home, I love you Thea Green."

"Love you too, Ivy King," she replied, noticing how she had said the word *home*.

Her mum had taken it better than she had expected. She almost insisted Ivy move out. Ivy followed her mum upstairs and watched as she lingered in the doorway of Agatha's room.

"I need to downsize anyway, this house is built for four and I haven't touched a thing in here in three years." Ivy reached out and squeezed her mum's hand. "It's time we move on," Rachel said smiling but tears prickled in her eyes.

Ivy knew she was right. "I have been moving on." She replied. Her mum didn't respond. "I have a girlfriend, a job, almost a degree, new friends. How much more moved on can I be?" Ivy asked quietly, not sure if she was asking her mum for validation or permission because she wasn't sure if that all added up to everything she had lost.

"Yes you have and I'm so proud of you love, so, so proud. But I think you've just moved on in the ways that others could see. Not so much on the inside." Her mum rubbed her arm comfortingly. "It's not just you. I need to do the same and moving on doesn't mean forgetting,"

"I know," Ivy smiled tightly.

"I'm not sure if I've said it before, but I wouldn't have gotten through it without you." Rachel said, tucking Ivy's hair behind her ear. Ivy was so grateful to have her mum because she knew she wouldn't have either.

"How is Jessie doing?" Rachel asked.

"She's good. She told her mum about the baby the other day,"

"Does that mean she's decided to...?"

"Yeah, she has. It will be tough with her finals and doing it on her own but she will be a fantastic mum,"

"I agree. But she won't be alone, she has you," her mum said smiling. "Now, what do you need to take to your new home?"

"Oh, absolutely everything," she replied.

She packed up as much of her stuff as she could that evening and took it over to Thea's — she took it *home*, and Ivy knew she had made the right decision a few weeks later.

*　*　*

Ivy rubbed her eyes with the heels of her hands. She and Thea had pulled an all-nighter to complete her final project.

"Oh God, it's done," Ivy said, closing the laptop and stretching her back, arms reaching to the ceiling. "What time is it?" She asked, feeling a little disorientated by how tired she was.

Thea checked her phone, "A little after three." she yawned.

"Are you sure you don't wanna check through it one more time?" She asked over her yawn.

"No...but maybe I should." Ivy stretched her arms in the air, closed her eyes and stretched her neck from side to side. "But I'll do it tomorrow with fresh eyes. These no longer work," she said, putting the laptop to one side.

"Good idea", Thea said and kissed both of Ivy's closed eyelids, before getting up and walking to the bedroom. Ivy followed shortly after, the outside world was already beginning to shine through. Ivy rubbed her eye as she watched Thea take her trousers off, pull her vest over her head and climb into bed. She kicked her own tracksuit bottoms off and got under the duvet with her.

Although they were both exhausted, they stayed up and talked. They talked about everything. About friendships, about family, about life, and Ivy felt comfortable enough to talk about Agatha. She had already told Thea her sister had taken her own life, she hadn't given her all the details, mainly because it was too painful. Thea never pressed her for more, but tonight, she told Thea more of the story, about how she was in Thailand when it happened and the call from her mum, the calls from the press and rubberneckers, but she brushed over the Sam of it all. She had told her before that they were friends and they fell out on that trip but that was all she needed to know for now. Not to be deceitful or because she didn't trust Thea, but more because a little voice inside of her told her to hold this back. Almost as if, she was protecting her own interests. Even though she knew the chances of seeing him were somewhat minute, she didn't want to admit to herself that she still felt something for him, which she knew she would have to if she told Thea.

"So I came home the next day. Feeling guilty as hell I wasn't there of course but more because I didn't pick up that something was wrong with her. Well that's not true, I knew she struggled after dad left, we both did and, I mean I called her at the airport and she sounded off you know? but I just ignored it and carried on with my own drama — if you can even call it that."

She took a breath before continuing. Lying on her back she stared straight up at where she knew the ceiling to be. Thea was wrapped around her, so in an attempt to bare herself further she shifted herself to face her and wrap her limbs around her warm body.

"I play out — she cleared her throat as her words began to catch. I play out all these different scenarios, where I don't go away, where I pay attention to the signs, where I save her."

Thea squeezed her hand and opened her mouth to speak, but she closed it again and didn't say anything for a while. until she eventually said: "I was popular in high school, not to be up myself, but I was definitely part of the in-crowd. I was dating one of the most popular guys in school." she swallowed. "'Cause I hadn't come out yet and he seemed nice but I wasn't really into him, I just wanted everyone else to think I was. But he wasn't...he took me to this house party one night, loads of people from school were there. We were drinking but, I don't know, I think maybe he spiked me or something, because I don't remember going upstairs." A tear fell down her cheek, closely followed by another. Ivy looked at her as if to say, "you don't have to tell me" and hoped there was enough light in the room for Thea to see. Thea nodded at her and continued. "There were photos, they got sent around the whole school. My mum went to the headteacher, told her she would involve the police but I didn't want it to get worse so I told her it had stopped and I didn't tell her that he..." she swallowed again and wiped the tears brimming at her eye with a finger. "Everyone called me a slut, they said I wanted it and I couldn't say that I didn't, that I don't even like boys because it was bad enough as it was, you know?" Ivy used the pad of her thumb to wipe the tears from Thea's cheek and tucked her hair behind her ear. She didn't want to speak, she knew how brave this woman was for saying this out loud and she was offering her vulnerable self up in exchange for Ivy's honesty. "I lost all my so-called friends, the guy obviously dumped me like I was the..." she took a deep rattly breath. "I was so badly bullied I felt like I had no control over my life so I stopped eating. My councillor said I was punishing myself and I was using eating as a way to self-harm. She's probably right but I just thought this is something I can control. I decide how much I eat, I decide how I look. The thing that upset me most, the thing that really got to me, was that no one noticed I had a problem. Actually, it was the opposite, people praised me for dropping the weight, for dropping it so quickly, so 'easily'. It took me a long time to realise that people weren't psychic, you know? I had to take some responsibility, I was good at hiding it and I didn't want people to know there was a problem so they didn't see one." She turned to Ivy and held her gaze. "What I'm getting at is you need to stop blaming yourself for Agatha's death. You couldn't have known what she was going to do, and even though it was awful and painful that she took her life, if you could have helped her, Agatha would have needed to let you in first." Tears flowed freely down Ivy's face and Thea pulled her close to her, letting her own tears fall against Ivy's hairline. "This story does have a happy ending though. I realise it doesn't sound like it, but it does. I went to university, I came out to my friends and family and met a nice girl — not you but I'll get to that. But best of all, I realised that it was not my fault and I got on with my life. And then I met you."

She smiled and leant down, kissing her lips softly and Ivy, who was completely present all night suddenly wasn't. She immediately went back to that beach in Thailand. She could feel the biggest part of the story she left out, *pounding against her, fingers digging into her forearms, sand scratching her skin,* struggling inside of her like it was a living breathing thing trying to claw up her throat. The heavy beast pressing on her, pinning her down *pounding against her, fingers digging into her forearms, sand scratching her skin.* She pushed it back down inside again. If she acknowledged this part she would well and truly give it life and she didn't think she could handle that. If she kept it to herself then maybe she could kid herself it almost didn't happen.

Thea had offered Ivy this vulnerability to show her that she should not blame herself for what happened, but Ivy still wasn't ready to walk down that path.

CHAPTER 22

She still clutched onto her sister's ghost to remind herself of the part she played in her death.

Deep down, Ivy knew this wasn't how to deal with her trauma, but looking at her girlfriend's face, Ivy could see how much Thea loved her to tell her this truth. It made her feel selfish to want to tell Thea her own. *I will take what he did to me to my grave s*he promised herself.

She looked into Thea's eyes and knew she was reliving her worst days too, and she thought that every woman must have a variation of this same story. Every woman who lives in this broken world, who lives in the tears that she felt splash her cheeks. The tears that were not her own. They felt primaeval. She cried not only for herself, not only for the woman she loved but for her gender. Women who have always been subject to this cruel taking of power.

Women who are so much softer than men, but so completely full of strength. Ivy felt so safe with Thea. Safer than she ever had done before, with any man — even Sam. Thea made her feel whole, she wasn't a replacement for her absent father or a point to prove, she wasn't there to fill the void left by her sister, Thea was entirely herself, a whole person that made it safe for Ivy to be the same.

They led there, entwined with each other until the sun rose and the light streamed through the gap in the curtains, warming their faces and highlighting the specks of dust floating in the air. And eventually, they slept.

Chapter 23

"Ivy King, first-class honours." As she took those steps across the stage, she could feel the pride and positivity radiating from everyone in the cathedral. She shook hands with the university head and walked into the crowd beaming. She locked eyes with both her mum and Thea who were whooping and clapping louder than anyone else in the crowd and although she was grateful for both of them, she wished Agatha were here.

"To my brilliant daughter," Rachel said, holding her glass in the air. Ivy and Thea clinked their glasses against hers.

"I'm so proud of you," Thea said. Ivy smiled and squeezed her hand.

Rachel stayed to take some photos with Ivy in her cap and gown and some of her and Thea together before leaving. She kissed her cheek and rubbed her hand up and down her back.

"She would be proud of you too," she said into her ear. Ivy nodded against her hair. Rachel pulled back and tucked Ivy's hair behind her ear. "You are so much like her, you know? So full of contradictions. The way she saw herself so misaligned with who she really was. I hope you realise how loved you are." Ivy smiled and nodded again.

Rachel reached over to hug Thea "Bye Rache," she said and kissed her cheek.

"Are you sure you don't want to stay?" Ivy said.

"No, you don't want your mum tagging along. Go, have fun, have some drinks, be wild," and she left.

"So what should we do now?" Ivy asked. She checked her watch and it was nearly five o'clock.

"Why don't you hand your gown back and we can go grab something to eat?

CHAPTER 23

Maybe pizza?"

"I knew there was a reason I kept you around." Ivy laughed and kissed Thea before walking to the gown station. She felt a little sad at returning her gown, but she had worn it as long as she possibly could and it was time to leave.

It was a warm summer day and Ivy's dress floated in the slight breeze in the air. She looked around to all the graduating students, tossing their caps in the air, posing for photos and thought back to Agatha's graduation. Different city, different King but the atmosphere was the same. Except, for Ivy today was permeated by her loss. She remembered she and Agatha had argued in the car on the way, she couldn't remember what it was about but felt a stab of pain at the recollection all the same.

She and Thea walked slowly to a nearby pizza place and ate together. Thea picked up the bill despite Ivy's protestations and handed her card to the waitress.

"Shall we grab a drink before we go home?" Thea asked.

Ivy checked the time. "I mean, we both have work tomorrow," she said. The receipt spewed out of the machine and the two women stood to leave.

"Come on, just one drink? I want to celebrate you," she replied, tugging gently on her hand.

"OK, let's grab a drink," Ivy said, smiling. She had to admit, she was loving the attention.

Thea pulled her into a bar at random and Ivy was thrilled to find Jessie and Alden, sitting on a table near the door with balloons and a bouquet.

"That's my girl!" Jessie shouted across the room pointing at Ivy.

"Happy graduation baby girl!" Alden shouted as she ran to both of them and hugged them.

"I love you guys so much," Ivy said, before pulling back and bending down to hug Jessie's stomach. "All three of you!" She was almost five months gone and had the clear outlines of a bump pressing through her dress.

"Four, I hope," Thea said behind her.

"Of course, goes without saying." Ivy kissed her.

"Enough of this soppy shit let's drink!" Jessie shouted, popping the cork on a bottle of prosecco. All three of them looked at her confusedly as the bubble dribbled down the side of the bottle in her hand. "What? I have sparkling apple juice but it's fun to freak strangers out."

Alden took the bottle away from Jessie and poured it into three of the glasses that had been placed on the table in front of them. "To our favourite book nerd," Alden said as they clinked glasses and drank.

They stayed late into the night. Ivy and Thea spent a lot of the evening dancing to the eighties tunes that the DJ had taken to playing. Before bounding back over to their table for a refreshment break.

"They are just so cute," Jessie said to Alden for both the women's benefit.

Thea smiled and kissed Ivy's cheek.

"I know. What assholes," Alden replied and they all laughed.

"So, I have to ask: are you OK with not graduating today?" Jessie asked.

"Yeah, I really am you know," he smiled and continued. "I'm doing so well at the restaurant and I've learned enough about the practicalities of running a business to know the theory they teach was just that: theoretical."

"Don't get me wrong, I am super proud of you." Ivy reached out and took his hand "but you didn't have much left to do, so just don't want you to regret not finishing it," she said, thinking of her own experience.

"I know, and maybe I will go back one day like you did, but right now, this seemed like an opportunity that was too good to miss," he replied.

"What sort of percentage ownership is he offering?" Thea asked, sipping from her glass.

"thirty-five per cent right now, but he is looking to retire next year, so I will have the option to buy him out next year effectively."

"That's amazing! Have you signed the contracts?"

"Not yet. I've forwarded them to my Dad's friend who is a solicitor — he mostly deals in family law but he knows enough to check I'm getting a good deal."

"The benefit of wealthy 'rents ey?" Jessie said, trying not to sound bitter. "Sounds like you have it all figured out," she necked her apple juice.

"I wouldn't go that far, but I'm excited, yeah. Who would have known seven/eight months ago, I would be a restaurant owner, you would be having a baby and we would have not one but two new best friends," he said, refilling

CHAPTER 23

both of their glasses.

"I know, so much has changed so quickly," Jessie said.

"But it's good change right?" Ivy asked.

"Yeah, it's definitely good change, a bit scary, but good," she agreed and smiled.

"OK, enough of the grown-up stuff, you guys have to come dance with us," Ivy said, downing her drink before pulling Alden's arm and bringing them both onto the dancefloor to join them.

* * *

When Ivy and Thea got home, Ivy found a parcel waiting for her. She picked it up from the front door mat and unlocked the door before walking inside. Thea was a few minutes behind her, paying the taxi. It was addressed to her mum's house so she must have dropped it in on her way back home.

She set the brown box down on the kitchen side and stared at it whilst pulling her heels off her feet. She wasn't expecting anything and tried to think of who would have her mum's address. It could be from her dad. If it was him, that meant he could have reached out at any time after Agatha's death and that was a bit of a kick in the teeth. She debated what she would do with it if it was from him, before deciding just to open it and find out. She pulled the brown parcel paper off before screwing it into a ball and throwing it into the bin beside her.

There was a square white envelope with just the letter "V" written on it, along with a bottle of champagne and a small, silver jewellery box.

She recognised the handwriting straight away and laughed at herself for being so foolish. It wasn't from her dad but it was from someone equally as unlikely. Not in a million years did she think it would be a gift from Sam. She hadn't seen him since the funeral.

She lifted the lid of the square box to find a silver necklace inside, strung onto a faux velvet cushion. It had a silver bar bent to a point in the middle to form the shape of a V. She pulled it out of the box and ran her thumb across it. *Boy's got taste.* She caught herself thinking. Not sure if it was supposed to mean something, if it was supposed to be a reinforcement of the nickname he always called her or if it was just something pretty.

She put the necklace down and opened the envelope. There was a congratulations card inside. She opened the card and a small torn piece of paper fell to the floor. She bent to pick it up, keeping her eyes fixed on the card on her way down. It was blank except for a large hand-drawn "X".

"What you got there, Ivy King," Thea said, walking into the kitchen.

"Just a gift," she replied, instinctively putting the torn page in her jacket pocket, before turning and smiling at her.

"Who's it from?"

"My mum," she replied quickly. She wasn't sure why she lied but she still wasn't ready to let Thea in on that side of her mind yet. The side where Sam still existed and fucked with her head on occasion. Despite not speaking to him for so long, she still thought about him. Sometimes wondering what he would think of her life now or where he would fit into it if he could. She dreamed about him often, that they were friends again, that whatever had happened between them was over like her subconscious was racked with a guilt she didn't have in waking life. She knew she was right to part ways with him even if she still thought about what life would be like if she hadn't.

"That was nice of her," Thea said, breaking Ivy from her thoughts. "Didn't she already get you your watch?" she gently reached over and tilted the necklace to the light. "Very pretty though," she said.

"Yeah…it is," Ivy replied quietly. She changed the subject quickly and with it her mood. "Come on, let's pop this sucker," she said, grabbing the bottle.

"Really? We have to be in work in — Thea grabbed Ivy's wrist and read the time from her new watch — seven and a bit hours"

"Fuck it. You only graduate once," Ivy said and popped the cork.

"Unless you're Jessie," Thea added.

"Unless you're Jessie," Ivy agreed.

They finished the bottle before going to bed and having tipsy sex. Thea rolled over and fell asleep immediately and when Ivy heard her breaths growing longer and deeper, she reached to her jacket on the floor and pulled the crumpled note out of the pocket she had stuffed it in.

It looked like a page from a book that read:

At each of the four corners of a square, two perpendicular lines meet to form a right angle. <u>the sharper the corner, the brighter it appears</u>. And the brighter a corner appears, the harder it is to look at.

He had underlined part of the extract.

Ivy didn't think he had it in him. She suddenly felt a deep love for him and the effort he had gone to give her this gift but the feeling was short-lived and quickly replaced with anger at how easily he could still play with her emotions. Looking at her beautiful girlfriend sleeping peacefully next to her, she knew that it was strange to hide this part of her past, but some parts of Ivy still belonged to that time with Sam. There was no point in upsetting her relationship by making Thea feel insecure. She loved her. The last thing she wanted was to hurt her. *Then why don't you throw it away?* Ivy didn't need Sam's gifts or his words or his lazy attempt at a peace offering, but still, she slid the torn page into a book on her bedside table. She knew it could come back to bite her later but, she did it anyway before rolling over and drifting off to sleep.

Chapter 24

Jessie had finished her Masters, the last of her studies for a while, and now Autumn had rolled back around, instead of shopping for books for her PHD, she found herself shopping for baby clothes.

"Is this not the cutest dang outfit you ever saw," Ivy said, holding up a tiny all in one suit with a matching bow tie.

Jessie looked over and smiled. "You know she's a girl," Jessie said, turning back to the rack she was sifting through.

"Since when can a girl not rock a badass suit?" Ivy asked, putting it back.

"When you have to keep telling everyone she's a girl because she is bald and boy looking for the first six months," Jessie replied with fake annoyance.

"This one, this one is cute," Ivy said, holding up a tiny tutu with glittery pink tights.

"Too much the other way. You were closer with the suit," Jessie laughed. "Come on, let's not keep Al and Thea waiting too long," She said as she took a pile of clothes to the counter. Ivy noticed the tutu and tights had made their way into the pile and grinned.

She glimpsed Alden and Thea through the door to The Maple; they had a small booth and four glasses of pink smoothie were in the centre of the table. She held the door for Jessie with one hand with three big bags looped around the other. Thea walked quickly over to help.

"Mind out, beached whale coming through," Jessie said, making both women laugh as she waddled in theatrically.

"You are not that pregnant Jess. You just look like you had a lot of pasta for lunch...and last night...and the night before." Alden responded, holding out her smoothie, the contents had started to separate.

"Boy you need to watch what you're saying, no jury is going to send a pregnant woman to prison," she said, flipping her hair off her shoulder in Alden's direction.

"How are you feeling Jessie?" Thea asked.

"Gassy, large but pretty good actually. I didn't think it would go this well. I mean she's starting to get in the way a bit. I haven't seen my foof in about two months."

The group laughed.

"I'm not sure I need to hear about your foof babe," Alden said.

"She asked."

"What about your exams?" Alden asked, waving to the chef in the kitchen before turning his attention back to the conversation.

"They went good. I get the results next month and all being well, I graduate on the third of November."

"Wow, cutting it a bit fine, aren't you? Aren't you due on the eighth?"

"Yep, it will be a slow but majestic waddle across the stage. Which reminds me, my parents want to come," she said, picking up the menu.

"They do? Have the pumpkin risotto, you'll love it," Alden said.

"They do. My mum has been really supportive these last few months, surprisingly."

"Why wouldn't she be? What have I missed?" Thea asked.

"We didn't have the best of relationships growing up, but she seems to be really trying now. She's excited to be a grandma, which I didn't expect, but let's see how things go when she arrives," Jessie said, rubbing her stomach. "God, she is right on my bladder. Pregnancy is a blast."

"At least you only have a few more weeks until we get to meet her," Thea added.

"I know, can't wait."

"Neither can we! I promise I will be the best auntie this little thing has ever seen!"

"Well she hasn't seen anything yet so I'm sure you will be," Alden said, smirking.

When Thea and Ivy arrived home that evening, they finalised Jessie's baby shower plans before starting dinner.

Ivy ran up to have a quick shower, carrying bags around all day had made her feel sticky and warm. She changed into a baseball top and jersey shorts and was pulling a brush through her hair when she came downstairs. Thea was cooking some sort of pasta dish in the kitchen and the light was shining through the window, highlighting the angles of her face. Ivy stood and watched her for a minute, just thinking how lucky she was. She put the brush down on the side and walked up to Thea, wrapping her arms around her waist and propping her chin on her neck. She kissed her shoulder.

"Smells good. Anything I can do?" she asked.

"Tell me if the pasta's cooked," Thea said as she picked a piece off of the spoon and blew on it to cool it. She held it over her shoulder for Ivy to bite.

"Perfect," she said, kissing her cheek. "Like you." She unthreaded herself from Thea, took some bowls out of the cupboard and put them on the side for Thea to serve up.

"What are your thoughts on kids?" Thea asked, trying to sound casual as she spooned the food into the bowls.

"They are small and have lots of energy," Ivy replied sarcastically.

"You know what I mean," she laughed. "I guess we should have talked about this before, but do you want kids? Do you see us having them?"

"Yeah, I guess. I mean, I haven't thought about it, to be honest. Well, I have but in a very abstract sense you know?" she said opening the cutlery drawer and taking some forks out. "Do you want kids?" Ivy turned to her.

"Yeah, I do. I really want them actually. I know there are options. We could adopt. I know there are loads of kids who need a family but if I'm honest, I want one of our own. In fact, I've been thinking about how much I would love to be pregnant. Watching Jessie has made me super broody," Thea said.

"You're crazy - you want to *not be able to see your foof for two months?*" They both laughed.

"I know it's not all glow and tummy flutters but I think it's amazing to grow an actual human being inside you and give your body over to something that powerful."

CHAPTER 24

"You are the cutest person ever," Ivy said with a mouth full of pasta. She swallowed. "And you would make the world's greatest mum," she added.

Thea smiled at her.

Ivy imagined them both as mums and wondered what it would be like. She was truthful when she told Thea she hadn't given children too much thought but she was glad they were on the cards, even if it wasn't in the near future. She didn't feel like she had done everything had wanted to yet, just the two of them.

There was also a level of guilt that kids were something that Agatha would never have. Ivy didn't remember her ever saying whether she wanted them or not. It was one of those things that seemed unimportant until it either did or didn't happen, but now she would never know which path her sister would have chosen. *Would Agatha have wanted them for me? Am I taking something from her if I do want them?* These were the questions that Ivy knew she would never find the answers to, so she just had to do the best she could or she would never live her life at all, and Agatha definitely would not want that.

Jessie went into labour three weeks later and gave birth to Freya who was six pounds and nine ounces and Ivy had never seen anything so beautiful.

* * *

When they had finally saved enough for the deposit, Ivy and Thea bought a house together. Thea's only stipulation was it had a big garden and better parking than what they had to put up with at their flat. Other than that, she wasn't particularly fussy about where they lived.

Ivy, on the other hand, wanted to make sure they had bigger rooms than they had in the flat. Even though it held some amazing memories and it had been their own cosy love shack for over three years, Ivy thought it was time for a change and an upgrade at that.

They viewed what felt like a hundred properties together before realising if they wanted the space they were looking for, and the big garden they would have to move further out of the city.

They settled on a house that was part of an older estate and had spacious rooms but lower ceilings than either of them were used to. It was rented before, so everything was white and clean when they moved in, which Ivy loved, knowing they would be able to put their stamp on the place.

Their rent was paid up to the end of December, so the plan was to spend the next month gradually moving their things over and decorating. But Ivy couldn't wait to live in their new home, so they took the mattress with them first and slept there the day they collected the keys.

Ivy spent the whole of the next day painting their bedroom with a striking gold paint on the wall their bed would sit against, creating the illusion of a headboard, leaving the other walls stark and white. She sat on the floor smiling up at it while it dried. Thea came home with bags full of accessories and cushions a few hours later and found Ivy sat watching the wall.

"We need to get you out of the house if you're going to start sitting here watching paint dry," she said before dropping the bags and joining her on the floor.

"Do you like it?" Ivy said.

"I love it," Thea replied, kissing her cheek and burying her head in her neck.

They ordered pizza for dinner and sat on the floor in the living room eating it quietly but content. Just looking at Thea made Ivy smile and Thea couldn't help but smile back.

They didn't have any electricity yet, so Thea had bought dozens of candles at the shop earlier that day and filled the rooms with them. By late evening the flickering orange glow added a comforting rosiness to the house.

They had sex there on the living room floor, amongst the candles and boxes, with no curtains yet hung, christening the place they would now call home.

Thea trailed kisses down her stomach, bending Ivy at the knee and anchoring herself to her by hooking her arm around her shin, she buried her head in her. Ivy dug her fingers into her girlfriend's hair, tugging comfortably to get a grip on the physical plane for a while. Thea excited every nerve that lived there and made her orgasm with ease in a way that only a lover could.

Thea shifted so she was on top of Ivy, who began gripping the back of her neck, wanting to consume her. Ivy wove her mouth into Thea's, unsure of what was tongue and what was lips in lightheaded passion as she drove her knee into Thea's pelvis and gently rocked her to orgasm.

They were face to face, still naked on the floor, but Thea had pulled a blanket from one of the boxes to drape over them, more for comfort than warmth as the heat still emanated from the dying candles.

"When did you know?" Thea asked, her fingers drawing small circles on her lover's shoulder. Ivy loved the little freckles on the tops of her ears.

"When did I know? What, that I was a Power Ranger?"

Thea closed her eyes and smiled. "Do you know what? I think I liked you better when you were between my legs."

They laughed and Ivy poked her side, tickling her.

Ivy thought for a moment before replying "When I was around nine or ten. I was watching Buffy. I was obsessed with Buffy — she smiled at the reminiscence — and I was in love with Willow."

"You clearly have a thing for the cute lesbian, huh?" Thea jibed.

"Oh, no doubt," she smiled. "I mean it still took me a while to figure it out, you know? I couldn't tell if I wanted her or if I just wanted to *be* her? I figured, since I liked guys, that was it, I was straight or whatever. It took me time to realise it was okay to be attracted to girls too and that it didn't have to be one or the other. How about you?"

Thea sighed, "Rebecca Miller. We were five and we held hands under our desks for the whole afternoon".

"Wow, do I need to keep my eye out for Rebecca Miller? I mean, it sounds like you guys were serious."

"Oh yeah, I'd drop you for her in a heartbeat."

"Oh really?" She replied in mock annoyance and pulled her close to kiss her, both smiling against each other's mouths.

"Rebecca who?" Thea eventually said and they both laughed.

* * *

The next morning, they built the bed together, before deciding to divide and conquer. Ivy continued to unpack upstairs while Thea unpacked the study downstairs. Thea unwrapped a photo of the two of them at Freya's christening and positioned it on the sideboard beneath the window. She thought about how happy she looked in the photo, before remembering a time when she used to hate all photos of herself. She used to flip all her photos over when she lived with her parents. It was a part of the self-hatred that came along with her eating disorder. Her mum used to tell her off, not realising it was a symptom of a much larger problem. She didn't hold it against her though. Sometimes it's hard to see what you aren't looking for. The thing she was truly grateful for, was that both her parents noticed when her illness had gotten out of control, long before she ever would have.

She thought back to when she came home from uni for the summer break. Her dad barely recognised her as she dragged her frail frame through the door. She looked down at her wrist and made a circle around it with the index finger and thumb of her other hand. The tips just barely touched now, but that used to be the way she gauges how much she could allow herself to eat in one day; by how much space there was between her wrist and her fingers.

Casting her eyes around the room, realising if it hadn't been for her parents, she would never have gone to the E.D. rehabilitation centre. She would have never got better and she would never be who she was today. Just filling her new home with photos of her and her girlfriend, photos of them happy, showed Thea just how far she had come since then.

Moving to the next box, she continued unpacking. She was emptying a box of books and stacking them on the bookcase, arranging them by colour when a small piece of paper fell out of the book she was holding.

She bent down to pick it up and saw it was part of a page torn from what Thea could only assume was a textbook. A part of it was underlined but it didn't make any sense to her. Scanning the handful of books, none of them seemed to match the page she held. She tucked it back into the last book she had shelved, which happened to be Ivy's, and carried on stacking the others.

Should I ask Ivy about it? It could be private or it could be nothing, a piece from a school book that had accidentally gotten mixed in with her other books. Perhaps it was a makeshift bookmark or maybe an old love letter from a schoolyard crush, it could even be something of Agatha's. She pushed it out of her head.

CHAPTER 24

"Do you know what Thee, it is none of your business," she muttered to herself before continuing with unpacking. Ivy had never given her reason to doubt her and she trusted that if she wanted her to know, she would tell her. Which in itself probably meant it was nothing.

***

It took them only two weeks to unpack and decorate and when they were done they celebrated by meeting Jessie, Freya and Alden at his now fully owned restaurant, The Maple, for lunch. Jessie dropped Freya to her parents on the way back from the restaurant, at her *Abuela & Nino's house* so all the adults could go back to Ivy and Thea's to watch a Hunger Games marathon.

Ivy saw them at Jessie's house a few weeks ago and if it wasn't for how Jessie was still slightly standoffish with her mother, you would have thought they were always a happy family. It seemed she was a much better *abuela* than mum. But Ivy was glad that Jessie's parents were able to help her with Freya. She had been working long hours, consulting on some huge developments which she enjoyed and paid her well, but did leave her grappling for childcare at times.

By 2 a.m., the others had all fallen asleep, but Ivy put on the final film anyway. She looked over at her friends. Both Jessie and Alden were slumped in different awkward positions in the two chairs, Jessie with her legs over the arm of hers and Alden with his arms folded across his chest, his feet dangling off the edge. Thea was laid out across the sofa, cuddled up to Ivy, head in her lap.

They all looked so peaceful, but Ivy couldn't join them in sleep. She stroked Thea's face, sweeping her hand into her messy hair over and over. Watching as Katniss saw her sister die, Ivy couldn't help but think of Agatha. Catching herself off guard, she also thought of Sam. She pulled her phone out of her back pocket, being careful not to wake Thea and searched his name on Instagram. She just wanted to see a picture of him, she rationalised. They still followed each other, but she muted him a while back. After seeing another photo of him travelling, living his life, she decided she no longer wanted to see it, in stark contrast with how she felt now.

She scrolled through his photos and saw one of the most recent ones was of him on a beach, his arms around a stunning blonde with bright blue eyes in a bikini. *Is this his type now? Has it always been?* She couldn't help but notice this woman was the polar opposite of herself. Blonde where she was dark, pale where she was brown, slim where she was shapely. She could easily be a model which, although irrational, felt like a kick in the gut. She knew this woman's beauty didn't dim her own and she was happy and in a committed relationship so it shouldn't affect her, but it did.

Chapter 25

Sam never went in for that 'New Year, New Me' bit. Every January, usually on Facebook, he saw people posting paragraphs about how they are "going to be a better person this", or "their New Year's resolution that", but he knew better. There was no 'new you' he was never going to be 'Better Sam' he was going to be the same asshole he was last year and the year before that. He thought that until he met Ellie.

He met her in a coffee shop when he picked up her coffee order by mistake. Her eyes were icy blue and her long, straight blonde hair tumbled around her shoulders. There was an air of coolness around her, but when she smiled it rippled out from her mouth, melting any chilliness that had been there before.

Of course, Sam had seen beautiful women before, he had been with a lot of beautiful women. Ivy was most definitely beautiful, but the two women weren't comparable. Ellie was the kind of beautiful, that sparkled, brightly, like a diamond worn around your neck. A statement piece you only wore on special occasions and attracted every eye in the room. She was completely and utterly out of Sam's league, but she chose him anyway.

They had been together nine months when Sam first posted a photo of them together on Instagram and had been staying in her apartment in Porto for the past two months. He never thought he would be the type to settle down. In the back of his mind, he figured it would be Ivy if he did. She was the only one he thought could stand to be around him for prolonged periods, but Ellie was no second best.

Ellie challenged him daily with her fiery attitude and quick wit and it had been over a month before he realised he hadn't used any drugs since he met her. Even though she told him early on she was anti-drugs, that wasn't why he had stopped, he had realised he didn't need them. He didn't need to feed the hole inside himself anymore, maybe ever again and he had Ellie to thank for it. Despite her ambition for herself, she never seemed to push Sam. Never tried to make him be anything more than himself, which ironically, meant he wanted to do better, to be a better person for her.

He loved her. He genuinely loved her and he hadn't looked away since the moment he laid eyes on her, but that didn't stop him from holding a small part of himself back from her. He remembered a long-ago conversation between him and Ivy. *No one gives themselves over one hundred per cent.* Some things you keep to yourself because no matter who they are or how much they love you, no one could take that last bit, the last ten per cent, that small seed of the real you that you swallow down. *Ivy saw it,* a small voice offered up in contradiction. Of course, they agreed that they would be the exception to the rule. They would always give each other one hundred per cent, no matter what. *But look at how that worked out? She couldn't take it, better to keep it inside.*

He still thought of Ivy on her birthday and even sent her a graduation gift. He couldn't help it. One day he saw the simple V-shaped pendant in a shop window and remembered a long-ago conversation about corners.

When he took Ellie back home to spend Christmas with his parents he was convinced he would run into her. He saw her in every face that walked by, but it was never her. He made sure to catch up with his old friend George while he was home. They met at the pub on Christmas Eve and drank and laughed until it was past midnight.

"Merry Christmas bud!" George said drunkenly, hugging Sam.

Sam clasped his shoulder. "Merry Christmas, mate," he said, taking a draw on his cigarette. Ellie was sitting inside talking to George's sister Clara and her friends. They could see them through the pub window from where they sat.

"She's a keeper, that one there,"

"Yeah, I know."

George squinted at him, seeming to turn something around in his mind before voicing it. "And Ivy?"

"What about her?" Sam said, still watching Ellie through the window. She felt his gaze and waved at him, the other girls turning to see who she was waving at. Sam held his cigarette hand up in acknowledgement.

"I saw her a few weeks ago. She was shopping in Tesco." Sam looked up at him.

"Is she okay?"

"Yeah, she's good. She was with someone, a woman. She seemed nice. Real pretty," George replied.

Sam took another drag on his cigarette. "Did she look happy?"

"Yeah, I mean, she was leant over the trolley smiling and kissing her when I saw her, so I would say so," George stubbed his cigarette out on the corner of the bench and lit another. "What happened?" he asked when Sam didn't say anything.

Sam shook his head in a small way.

"Come on buddy, you were basically the same person and suddenly her sister dies and you fuck off travelling."

"It's not like that."

"What is it like then? Look, I'm not judging, and she was only my mate because we had you in common, but it's... it's I don't know, it's just weird."

"There isn't much to say. We had a fight, a big one I guess. We're not friends anymore," he said and George was silent. He patted him on the back and stood up to go back in. "Don't mention her to Ellie will you?" Sam asked standing and tugging George back slightly.

"I wasn't going to," George said. They headed back inside.

"There you are, we didn't think you were ever coming back," George's sister, Clara said.

Ellie leant over and kissed Sam's cheek. "Your skin is freezing. Go grab yourself a drink to warm you up," she said.

"What are you having? It's my round anyways — George, Clara, drink?" He looked over to the other girls around their table. They were Clara's friends but he recognised them from being a few years below him and George. He asked them but they both politely shook their heads which he was grateful for. He took the others' orders and went over to the bar. He looked over his shoulder and saw Ellie laughing with George. He really should have kept up with George more while he was away, he was a good friend. He made a mental note to keep in touch with him more when they went back to Porto.

He took the drinks back to the table and handed them out.

"These are going to have to be our last babe, I promised your mum we would be up at a reasonable time in the morning and not be too hungover," Ellie said.

"Vicky knows that's about as likely as the fucking Ganges parting El, don't worry about it," George laughed.

"I do worry about it, George. His parents love me," she said.

"They do, they really do," Sam added.

"And I don't want to get in their bad books, not yet anyway," she smiled up at Sam. He leant his head down and kissed her.

"You heard the lady, this is our last one," he said to a small chorus of good-humoured grumbles.

Chapter 26

"I'm home!" Ivy shouted out as she closed the door. She dumped her bag on the floor and unwrapped her jacket from her shoulders and hung it up. She looked up to see Thea descend the stairs. *She always looked so beautiful.* She stopped short of the last few steps and leaned over the bannister to kiss Ivy.

"Hey, Ivy King,"

"Hey, Thea Green," Ivy replied, returning the kiss.

"How was it?"

"Yeah good, I think it went OK."

"Do you think you got the promotion then?" Thea asked.

"I mean, I'd like to think I got it but we'll see, I suppose," Ivy said, noticing the stack of letters on the side table.

"You will have got it. You've been there, what four years now? You deserve that role,"

"Five. I guess we will find out if I do next week," she replied as she kicked her shoes off.

"That from today?" Ivy said, looking back at the pile of post.

"It was there when I got home. Your mum must have put it through the letterbox at some point today," she said following Ivy's eye line.

Ivy picked the small stack up and began sifting through. Most of it was junk. One letter was from the opticians saying she was due an eye test soon. Another was a bank statement from an account she didn't realise she still had, reminding her it still had zero pounds and zero pence in it.

Thea, still standing on the stairs, continued down and past her into the kitchen. "What do you fancy for dinner? We probably need to go to the shop at some point, 'cause we don't have much but I can make fajitas or something?" she called behind her.

Ivy dropped something out of the pile that was smaller than the rest of the enveloped letters she held in her hand. Bending down to pick it up, she flipped it over in her hand.

It was a postcard. It had a stylized drawing of some coloured houses on a waterfront with the word "PORTO" written in white text in the blue sky.

"Saw this and thought of home.

Hope you're good.

SJ"

"What do you think?" Thea was almost behind her suddenly, drying her hands on a tea towel.

Um...yeah sounds good." Ivy replied and slowly rose.

"What you got?" Thea asked innocently.

"Postcard. It's from a friend — uh old friend. A school friend actually." Ivy replied.

She knew that the postcard was completely innocent looking from the outside but it was completely out of the blue. She tried to act like it was as unimportant as it looked but inside she was internally dissecting it.

Ivy could see why this particular card would have stood out to him. The houses looked similar to the ones on the harbourside in the city centre that has almost become synonymous with their hometown. She pictured him walking past a kiosk on a warm, sunny day wearing a light t-shirt with board shorts and flip flops and thinking of her. She imagined Portugal to paint everything with an orange hue and the bright blues and pinks and greens would stand out against the glow.

"That's cute. They even remembered your mum's address." Thea said smiling and walking back to the kitchen.

"Uh, yeah he probably Google Mapped it," she replied somewhat distractedly.

Following Thea into the kitchen, she put the card on the side with the rest of the post and went to the fridge. She pulled a bottle of wine out of the fridge

CHAPTER 26

and poured her and Thea a glass each, hers slightly larger than Thea's, but she balanced them out by taking a massive gulp from the top before handing Thea her glass.

"So who's this friend?" Thea asked as she chopped the vegetables.

Thea's tone sounded casual but Ivy had a nagging voice in her head saying *maybe she is worried about it. Is she jealous?* She knew that she just felt guilty. Guilty that when she turned the card over she felt a small flutter in her stomach that she didn't realise was still there. *Am I excited about this? Do I want to hear from him?*

"Just a friend really. Well not so much anymore, we kind of drifted apart after Agatha..." It had been over seven years and Ivy still struggled to say the word. *Died.* She took another glug of her wine.

"Why don't you get back in touch with...?"

"Sam," she mumbled into her glass so the word echoed slightly. "I don't know. I mean, I have friends, one more would just be a hassle," she said, trying to sound lighthearted.

"Well, he's making an effort. Maybe he misses you," Thea added.

Does he? "Yeah, I guess," Ivy replied.

"Pass me the pan, would you?" Thea asked, changing the subject. She didn't mention it again but Ivy noticed later that evening that Thea had put the postcard up on the fridge.

She thought about what Thea had said. Maybe he did miss her. Maybe she missed him too. She felt unsettled at that thought. Although she hadn't entirely forgiven him, the more time that passed, the less she hated him.

Even though she looked present from the outside, her body had taken over while her mind was absent, ticking over somewhere far away from herself the rest of the week. Somewhere in Porto amongst the coloured houses.

* * *

"To our super amazing, very successful *multi*-business owner," Ivy said, raising her glass towards the others, straining her voice over the music.

"What?" Jessie shouted back.

"To Alden!" Ivy shouted again, leaning in.

"To Alden!" Jessie mirrored.

"To Me!" Alden joined in. "You'll have to come to the grand opening, the new chef is amazing,"

"Better than you?" Jessie asked.

"Better than me. At least he better be for what I'm paying him!" they laughed.

Ivy was so proud of Alden. Even though she was worried when he initially dropped out of uni, it was clearly the best decision for him. The Maple was now one of the city's top restaurants and now brought in more than three times the amount of customers than before he bought it. She was glad to see him investing some of the profits, along with some extra capital from his parents into The Oak, a new restaurant on the other side of town. It warmed her to know that while not everyone walked the same path, it didn't mean it was the wrong one.

The group spent the next few hours dancing together until Ivy looked up and realised some poor eighteen-year-old was trying to dance with her. She smiled and shook her head before walking off the dance floor. Jessie and Alden close behind.

"OK, I'm leaving. We're at least five years older than anyone here," she shouted over the music.

"That's not true," Jessie shouted back. Whipping her head round to the left, she gestured at a group of forty-something men tapping their feet at the side of the dance floor, eyeing up the barely legal teenagers dancing in front of them. "They're way older than us," Jessie shouted, smiling.

"OK, now I'm definitely leaving," Ivy laughed and threw her watered-down vodka and coke back before putting the plastic cup on the edge of the bar. Jessie rolled her eyes at Alden and they did the same. The music was still in their ears as they left. The drunk hubbub of people spilt out onto the streets around them.

"Go get in the queue for cheesy chips. I'll be back," Jessie said to Alden, waving him off in the direction of the small burger shop down the road and she walked Ivy towards the taxi rank.

CHAPTER 26

"Sure you don't want to stay at mine? We could all go home together. Like the old days when I wasn't a mum and we were still full of youth," Jessie asked.

Ivy smiled and shook her head slightly. "You are the very definition of youth, but I'm good. I miss my woman," she bumped her hip against her friend. *Is this what modern loneliness is? Feeling cut off from it all when you're with people who love you?*

"Fine, leave us," Jessie said, kissing her cheek.

"Don't you go waking my goddaughter up when you get back either," she said as she put her arm around Jessie's shoulders and pulled her in for a hug.

"Don't worry, that girl wouldn't wake for an air raid," Jessie said, rolling her eyes and hugging her back. "Are you guys still OK to have her next weekend?"

"Of course, we can't wait," Ivy said, making a mental note to get Freya her favourite snacks for their sleepover.

"Love ya," Jessie walked over to join Alden fluttering her fingers, to wave behind her as she left.

Ivy turned and jumped into one of the taxis parked outside the club. The door shut behind her and with it the outside world. She told the driver her address and leant her forehead against the window. It was cold but she didn't mind. Her head was beginning to spin and she realised that last vodka was kicking in and about to tip her over the line of merry and it was then when she watched the blur of streetlamps swish past her face did she think of Sam. She didn't understand why her life had changed around her but part of her was stuck in Thailand. Creeping up on her, usually, when she was drunk and usually alone, this loneliness hit her and the only person she could think would understand, was Sam.

"Do you have someone?" she asked the driver, surprising herself.

"I've been married twenty-three years if that's what you mean,"

She thought about it for a second, to decide where she was going with this. "What would you do if you thought you were over someone, someone else and they popped back into your life. Someone you thought you had closure with."

"Well I love my wife," he replied as if this answered the question.

"Yeah, you do. You love your wife, but this person is just kind of hanging around in your mind. I mean, you're not sure why because your wife is better than them. In every way. You love your wife more, but there is something still hanging on with the other person that..." she trailed off. She didn't know the end of that sentence "Sorry, I'm rambling. You must get a lot of drunk people rambling in your cab," she smiled.

It was silent for a moment, but he replied: "If that was the case, if I was in that situation, I would say, the absence of closure does not a connection make. You can drive yourself crazy with 'what ifs' but sometimes you have to just let yourself be happy."

She sat up, taking her head away from the window and blinked a few times. "That's some good advice," she said eventually and smiled at the driver. They didn't talk for the rest of the journey. When Ivy got out she handed the driver an extra fiver, before stumbling back to her front door.

She took a few breaths at the door before opening it. The fresh air was helping to clear her head a little. *The driver is right: let yourself be happy.* She told herself before putting her key into the door and stepping inside the place that held her happiness.

Chapter 27

He threw his keys on the sideboard as he walked in the door of their small apartment.

"Hey, you're home early," Ellie said as he walked into the kitchen.

"The bar was dead, so Paul said I could chip off early," he replied, walking to the fridge and pulling a beer out. Sam wasn't looking for love when he found Ellie, but not only did he love her, he loved their child. They named him Pharaoh because Ellie wanted something regal. *Something that announces him before he does*, she had said. He didn't mind, a name was a name. Sam ruffled his son's white-blond hair as he walked past.

They have lived in a little bubble for the first few years, and now the bubble extended to Pharaoh, it was even sweeter. He didn't even mind being an almost thirty-year-old part-time bartender. It gave him something to do, to feel like he was making some sort of contribution. His parents still sent him money every month, the payments had never stopped so he didn't question it. Ellie never asked him where the money was coming from. She wasn't stupid, she must know it was more than a part-time bartender's wage. It wasn't like they needed the money, Ellie's job as a paralegal in Lisbon paid her well because she spoke English as well as Portuguese.

Sitting on their tiny balcony with his right foot on his left knee, his shirt open, his skin trying to catch the slight breeze in the humid air, he took a glug of his now warm, beer. He looked out at the terracotta rooftops that spanned his eye line, sloping gradually down until it hit a haze of blue sea. He wondered idly how different things would be if he hadn't continued to travel after coming home from Thailand. If he had settled in Paris instead of Porto or even if he had gotten the right coffee order the day he met Ellie. So many things could be different if he had made just one wrong decision.

Being a dad was easier than he thought it would be, but that was probably because Ellie was so good at being a mum. She did most of the meals and bedtimes as well as reading to him and playing games with him and arranging playdates. All while working thirty hours a week. That didn't leave much for Sam to do. But he did make sure that if Pharaoh woke in the night, which he still did four or five nights a week, he would be the one to get up with him. Usually taking him into the living room and talking to him quietly. He had figured out early on that his son was comforted by the sound of his voice, so he calmed his tears by telling him stories he made up and some that he didn't. About before he met Ellie and the places he had been the people he had met. It was freeing to talk so openly to another human being without worrying anyone else could hear it, even if he didn't understand most of the words he said. He thought about his parents and the first words he remembered his mum saying to him *"I don't know where you came from Sam, but you're not mine."* He hoped that Pharaoh knew that he was wanted. That he was his. His and Ellie's. The best of them both.

Sounds of Ellie rushing around behind him drew his attention, so he finished the bottle and walked back through the thin net curtains that divided the living room from the open balcony doors.

"OK, so no sweets or biscuits or anything before bed. I know he looks cute and I know he gets fussy, but I want a lie in tomorrow," Ellie said. She was packing a small bag on the sofa, while Pharaoh sat on a padded blanket on the floor drinking a bottle with one hand. The other tucked behind his head, drawing small circles in his hair. His huge, bright eyes, inherited from his mother, looked up to his daddy as he walked over and picked him up. Holding him on his hip, Sam took hold of the bottle for him as he walked back to Ellie.

"He looks knacked, so I don't know how much of a lie in it will be, but don't worry, I will be a responsible parent this evening Sergeant Mummy," Sam replied, giving a small mock salute.

Ellie walked to the mirror and looked at his reflection as she put a pair of

CHAPTER 27

large silver hoops in her ears and smiled. "I know, I'm annoying but I get weird feelings about going out without him."

Sam looked at Pharaoh with feigned shock. "It's you she would rather go out with huh? I mean, I think I'd be better conversation but obviously, you still win."

"I'll miss you too," she kissed them both on the cheek. "Love you both," she said as she walked out the door.

"Come on Roey, it's boys night, what are we doing?" he asked his son, blowing a small blond lock out of his eye.

Pharaoh squeezed his eyes shut and smiled, dribbling milk down his chin.

"Fancy a bit of poker?" he asked jokingly.

Pharaoh rested his head on Sam's shoulder and pointed to the TV.

"OK, Baby Shark it is."

* * *

Ivy pressed the speaker button on her phone. "Hey, we're on our way. There was some accident on the ring road," she said.

"It's cool. Is Al with you?" Jessie asked over the sound of cupboard doors slamming.

Ivy and Thea exchanged a look. "Should he be?" Ivy asked.

"No, it's just that he said he would come over early and help me set up, but he never turned up," she answered.

"Have you called him?" Thea asked.

"Yeah, no answer,"

"He's probably tied up at one of the restaurants or something. We can swing by The Maple on the way and check if he's there?" Ivy offered.

"Um... no, no it's fine. He'll be here," Jessie responded only sounding half convinced.

"He wouldn't miss his own goddaughter's birthday, Jess," Thea said.

"Yeah, yeah you're right he would. How far away are you?"

"About ten minutes from yours," Thea replied.

"Okay, I'll see you when you get here then. Any chance you can help me with the food? The little monsters will be here in half an hour and I'm not even close to done,"

"What are godmothers for?" Ivy replied.

* * *

The party was a success. Four hours of party games, presents and cake made for a pack of excited, screaming, sugar-crazed children. Ivy was wiped but she and Thea helped to clear the house for Jessie, who had been greeting parents and ushering kids out the door for the last half hour. She collected paper plates and pulled half-eaten chicken nuggets out of the matted rug while Thea did the dishes and wiped sticky handprints from the surfaces over.

Ivy battled with a bin bag, overflowing with torn wrapping paper when Thea caught her off guard "So I was thinking about that friend of yours,"

"Huh?"

"Your friend? The guy who sent you the postcard?" she asked, she dunked a dish into the soapy water and glanced over her shoulder at Ivy.

Oh God, why is she mentioning him? It had been more than a year since Ivy had received the postcard, that was probably still on the fridge, buried under Freya's drawings and preschool photos. "What about him?" Ivy replied, trying to hide the furrow she felt forming in her forehead.

"Well, we have space, so why don't you invite him to the wedding?" she asked. "Like a sort of olive branch, you know? You said you guys used to be close." Thea continued.

It was weird, Ivy had always thought Sam would be at her wedding if she ever had one. "No, it's weird. I haven't spoken to him for almost ten years. I'm not just gonna message him and be like "come to my wedding, which is in a different country to where you are right now, and spend some more money on bringing your family with you," Ivy dismissed it.

"That's fair enough, I just wanted to make sure you were happy, that you have everyone you wanted there."

"I will. As long as you turn up, I'll be golden." Ivy finished tying the bin bag off and flashed her fiancee a smile.

CHAPTER 27

Thea smiled and shrugged and continued with the dishes. Grateful for the excuse to leave the room, Ivy took the bin bag outside. *It would be weird, wouldn't it?* When she was with Thea she was completely wrapped up in her but every now and again thoughts of Sam still crept into her and cloaked her with guilt. She wasn't sure why she felt guilty. She wasn't exactly *cheating* on Thea by thinking about him. But maybe she should feel guilty, at least guilty that she hadn't told Thea the whole truth, but she didn't love Thea any less for wanting Sam. *And aren't we all entitled to certain omissions?* Perhaps she had been clinging on to the idea of being in love with some version of Sam, but the fact is that version if it ever did exist, wouldn't now. Just like her, he would have changed since the last time they spoke.

Ivy closed her eyes and remembered the moment Thea proposed, one night a few months ago in front of the TV.

"I'm going to get a glass of wine, do you want one?" Ivy asked, with a mouthful of crisps. She put the bag onto Thea's lap as she got up.

"Marry me," she said as if it were a statement and not a question.

Ivy almost missed it over the crunch of the crisps she was still chewing. She swallowed. "OK," Ivy replied. They both grinned at each other for a second. Ivy bent down, and they kissed, still both smiling widely.

They didn't talk about it again until the following weekend, to the point Ivy wasn't even sure it had happened when Thea took her to a jewellery shop and they picked out engagement rings.

Thea said she didn't need one; she was the proposer, but Ivy wanted her to feel just as special as she did. Ivy chose a large, oval sapphire with small diamonds on either side, while Thea chose a princess cut solitaire diamond.

"Co-ordinated, but not the same," she said and Ivy smiled. That was what they were, two complementing colours on a murky canvas.

She shook herself from the memory and walked back into the house. She stood in the door frame of the living room for a moment. She thought about how much she loved Thea. Then a little voice in the back of her mind spoke. *Maybe. Maybe if Sam was there, at your wedding, it would finally close that door. Maybe you would finally get some closure.*

"I am exhausted," Jessie said, coming downstairs and interrupting Ivy's thoughts.

"I bet. Where's Freya?"

"Upstairs with Alden. Did he mention why he was late? I heard the door go but I was distracted with the cake," Jessie asked.

"Not really. I asked him where he was and he just got caught up with work, but he didn't seem to remember that he was supposed to be early,"

Jessie pulled a face. "He told me that his family had pulled their investment from the new one, The Beech?"

"The Birch. Did he say why?"

"He made out it was no big deal, just a business decision, no hard feelings and that. Maybe that's how families with money are. I don't know."

"Something's going on with him. Like he's forgetting things, he's being flaky. I ask him about work and he gets kind of defensive. Is it just me?"

"It's not just you."

"Should we be worried?" Ivy asked.

"No, it's probably fine," Jessie said.

"If there was something wrong, he would tell us. At least one of us. Right?" Ivy asked.

Chapter 28

It was to be a fairly understated affair. Ivy chose to wear a plain white jumpsuit that was open at the back and tied at her neck, just below her recently cut hairline. On a whim, she had decided to cut her hair into a pixie cut just before the wedding and looking in the mirror that morning, she felt beautiful. Her hair was slicked down and tucked behind her ears to add an edge to the softness that comes with being bridal.

"Damn, Miss Ivy you look hot!" Jessie said as she walked up behind her with both of their bouquets. She smiled back at her reflection in the mirror.

"What, you mean this old thing?" she flashed her eyes up and twirled on the spot in mock humility and they both laughed.

Alden poked his head around the door at the sound of them laughing. "Does this mean you're read- Oh, Ivy, you look—"

"Beautiful, I know, but do go on." They all laughed and Ivy began to tear up slightly. She walked to the edge of the bed and sat down while holding her hands out to them both, which they quickly took.

"You guys..." she began. The emotion closing her throat.

"We know," Alden said, squeezing her hand.

"Yeah, you love us, we know," Jessie said jokingly, wiping the few tears springing to her own eyes.

"Yeah. That was it really," Ivy said, pulling her hand back whilst still holding Jessie's to wipe her tears. Her throat was a little hoarse as she tried to push the words out. "Just thank you. For being with me for the last eight years. Who knows where I would be if you hadn't found me," They had not grown up together. They had not seen her, fatherless and with longing. But the truth was that they had also watched her bloom.

"Girl, please stop or we'll all be a wreck and we haven't even watched you get married yet," Jessie said, fanning her face with her free hand. She sat next to Ivy on the bed and hugged her tightly. Alden followed suit and they sat there for a minute.

"Thea is a lucky woman," Alden said just as Rachel knocked on the door.

"Car's here. Oh God, look at you lot." The trio laughed through their tears and Ivy gave them both a quick squeeze before getting up and going to the mirror to fix the makeup that had smudged around her eyes. Alden and Jessie began collecting their things and were soon waving goodbye as they made their way to the venue.

Just as Ivy and Rachel were about to leave, Ivy hesitated. "Mum…"

"I wish she was here too," she said, stroking the side of her face. Rachel went into her purse and pulled out a crumpled ten-pound note which she tucked into the side of Ivy's jumpsuit. "Something old. You're wearing something new and here is something both borrowed and blue," she said as she reached back into her bag for a silver bracelet Ivy recognised as Agatha's. It was studded with alternating small blue and clear crystals. "I'm sure she wouldn't mind you keeping hold of it for a while."

Ivy's eyes began to well up again as did her mum's. Thinking of her sister's absence reminded her of the self-loathing she held that made her feel so empty. She had resigned herself to the knowledge that it would always be there, but she was grateful for the loves she now had. They stopped her from feeling as empty as she would have without them and that was enough for now.

She held her wrist out, shaking a little as her mum fixed the clasp around it. Ivy took her mum's hand and they both walked to the car. She wondered if her mum was thinking about her dad, about her own wedding day. But she didn't want to break the intimacy of the moment.

The rest of the day went by in a blur of toasts and confetti. Ivy looked in Thea's eyes and thought of how truly themselves they were. Thea had worn a simple white gown, with long sleeves just off her shoulders, nude stained lips and shimmering eyes. She was every bit the blushing bride Ivy knew she would be, complementing Ivy's jumpsuit, dark eye makeup and red lips perfectly.

CHAPTER 28

Surveying the scene through the large patio doors that opened up onto the grounds where she was perched on a bench with Thea. Ivy rubbed her thumb back and forth on her new wife's hand. It warmed her to see all their friends and family meld together. Thea's mum Valerie, leaning on Rachel's shoulder, removing her heels. Ivy's Uncle Donald chatting up Thea's friend Jo nearby and Freya running around the dancefloor with Thea's younger cousins while the DJ set up for the evening. It was a perfect day. Alden stepped out and put a glass of champagne in both hers and Thea's hand.

"Thanks, Al, I'm gasping," Ivy said, throwing two-thirds of the drink back.

"Well, the speeches are over so it's not dutch courage?" Jessie said as she came up behind her.

"Just thirsty!" Ivy said finishing the glass off and swapping her empty for Jessie's full glass. "Cheers, Thea King," she said clinking her fresh glass to Thea's. She smiled back and kissed her, to some cheers around them. They were interrupted by a small hand tugging on Thea's arm. Thea broke away from Ivy and looked down to Freya, whose loose curls fell around her tiny shoulders beneath a beautiful flower crown, which by now was sliding down and hung by just a few grips.

"Can I take this off now Auntie Thea? It's itchy," she said and scratched her hip through her dress as if to demonstrate.

"If you like, I think mummy has some PJs for you to change into?" Thea looked to Jessie.

"Just a bit longer sweetheart," She said, pulling the dress down at the skirt to straighten it. "We're going to go soon, so we can put your PJs on in the car huh?"

Freya sighed a big sigh. "Okay mummy," she said, walking over to look at the cake that was Alden's wedding gift to them. The grown-ups laughed to each other quietly.

"Okay, I better follow her before she has that cake all over her face."

"It's fine — I got it," Alden said and followed her over but Jessie went over with him. He had been spending more and more time at the restaurants lately so Ivy was glad to see him enjoying himself today. The chef at The Birch, Alden's newest restaurant, specialised in sweets and pastries and the cake he had made them was beautiful, filled with fresh raspberries and pistachios with giant folds of white chocolate standing on top.

"You know, we could do that," Thea said, bumping her shoulder affectionately. Ivy looked at Thea and smiled. "A conversation for another day though, I just want to bask today."

They watched Alden holding Freya up to snap off a sheet of chocolate. Her cheeky smile as she bit into it made Ivy's heart melt. The music started up and Ivy pulled Thea up to dance. They danced outside for a moment, Thea's head resting on Ivy's shoulder and almost as if on cue, large droplets of water came hard and fast. They both jumped up and ran to the sheltered doorway where they lingered a moment watching the rain.

"Almost lasted the whole day without seeing the rain," Ivy said.

"Well there is a whole song around April showers so it was always a risk, but I think we did pretty well to make it this far," Thea replied.

"Are you talking about the Bambi song?" Ivy asked.

"Of course."

They danced all evening, barely making it a few steps from the dancefloor before someone else took their hands and led them back. Later, when the DJ had packed away and the only sound was the waiters collecting glasses. Ivy walked over to Thea, who was hugging her aunties goodbye.

"Come on. I think it's time to go home, wife," she said.

"No problem wife, I'm gonna go grab us some cake for the road," she said walking towards the rest of the room.

Ivy found her mum collecting the organza sashes from the backs of the chairs. "You don't need to do that, Mum,"

Rachel placed her collection of sashes on the table in front of her and hugged her daughter. "I'm so proud of you, girly. You found a perfect match in Thea. I once worried you would be too soft for her, but she brings out a strength in you I never knew you had."

"Thank you," Ivy replied. Her mother was always an affectionate drunk. Looking around for Jessie and Alden she could see the pair were talking heatedly so she decided against interrupting. Freya was asleep in Alden's arms, her head resting in the crook of his neck.

CHAPTER 28

"Make sure Alden still has the marriage certificate, please? And don't forget the cake."

"Don't worry. I've got it, go home. Enjoy your wedding night," Rachel replied, kissing her hair.

She stepped away still holding Rachel's hand, only letting go when she was too far away to hold on any longer. Her head was buzzing when she got in the back of the taxi with Thea but she fell asleep before they got home. Thea gently nudged her when they arrived and Ivy was so grateful for her wife.

She later found an envelope from Sam's parents with the rest of the cards from the day, congratulating her and including a cheque.

"Old family friends," she said to Thea.

Chapter 29

"That's the last of them," he said over his shoulder to George as he unloaded the last box from the car. He closed the boot of George's car with his elbow as he turned to walk through his parent's door.

It felt strange to be back in England, but especially strange to be staying in his old bedroom, in his parents' house. He felt like he had regressed somewhat. He was no longer the thirty-four-year-old living and working in Portugal with a beautiful girlfriend and a toddler that could be his double. He was almost his twenty-two-year-old self, just slightly more sober and a little more weathered.

Slightly more sober. He should have known it couldn't last. Sobriety or happiness. Both had left him when Ellie did. *But that isn't strictly true,* he thought. He had begun drinking again after his last visit home to his parents. They had stayed in Sam's room because it was bigger and it meant Pharaoh could have the guest room next door. When they arrived, Vicky scooped her grandson up and whisked him off to his bedroom. *"This is your room Pharaoh. So you can always come and stay with Nanny and Granfer."* They made cupcakes in the kitchen, with ingredients from a fridge that usually held only wine and cheese. He had even walked into the garden to find his dad planting vegetables with Pharaoh and teaching him the names of the plants.

He should have been happy but it hurt. It hurt because he always thought that his parents neglected him because that was who they were as people. Having children isn't for everyone. But seeing them doting on Pharaoh showed him that they were capable of loving him. *They just didn't want to.*

He dumped the box just inside the front door and checked his phone, sure he felt it buzz in his back pocket, but there were no notifications. No Ellie checking in on him, no updates on Pharaoh. He stared at his phone screen for a moment, looking at the photo he had saved to his background. It was a close-up shot of Pharaoh. The light was behind him highlighting the tips of his face. Only his blue eyes, fringe across his forehead and the edge of his smile could be made out.

Sam thought about all the things he was going to miss now he was now a two-hour flight away. He had just started school the week before he left and looked adorable in his school uniform.

"He's a cute kid," George said as he walked down the stairs.

"Yeah, he is," Sam replied, putting his phone in his back pocket.

"Have you guys figured out the whole splitting between two countries thing?"

"Not really, no. Well, yeah. He stays with his mum and I just work around that. He's going to come over for Christmas, Ellie is going to be staying with friends and he's going to stay here for Christmas night and boxing day for Christmas round two with the Johnsons."

"Sounds good mate." George patted him on the shoulder ."I should get going," George said, fishing his keys out of his pocket, his words tinged with pity.

"Yeah, thanks for helping me out. Appreciate it."

"It's cool mate. I'll ask on Monday about that job at my place for you as well."

"Yeah, cheers. I know it's been a few years but at least I still know how to fix a car."

George held his hand up and walked out the door. Sam closed it behind him and sunk to the floor, his back to the door, still looking at the photo on his phone.

His mum came out of the living room, her attention on her phone typing. "You all in then?" she asked without looking up.

Sam locked his phone and put it in his pocket. "Yep, I won't bother unpacking or anything though 'cause I'll hopefully find a place pretty quickly."

She waved a hand in his direction as if to say 'he could stay as long as he wanted' but still didn't take her attention from her screen and walked into the kitchen. Only putting her phone down to pour herself a glass of wine. His mum was the only person he knew who drank almost as much as he did. It didn't take a degree in human behaviour to know that watching Vicki self medicate herself into a numb stupor was the reason he did the same. What we see we perpetuate.

She left the bottle of red on the corner of the counter, in Sam's eye line. *Seems as good an idea as any,* he thought, as he pulled himself up and took the bottle from the side and up to his room.

Their split had been almost amicable, but it didn't take long for Ellie to move on and find another guy. Someone she worked with, Juan or something. *Not that it was important.* She was happy.

* * *

Getting the job at George's garage ended up being a blessing. It gave him something to focus on during the day. He always enjoyed working with his hands and forgot how good he felt concentrating on a problem and solving it. Then in the evenings, he could just drink in front of the TV. His parents just left him to it. If he walked into the living room, they would make some excuse or other to leave the room and just wouldn't come back.

The dynamic, although familiar, was pretty excruciating. Especially since he had spent most of the last twelve years away from it and worse still for spending the last six in a somewhat normal functioning family. He didn't want to think about that too much though. He didn't want to dwell too much on what he had lost. Especially when he didn't think it was him who had fucked it up for a change. *Or did I? Maybe you didn't do it directly but you do always find a way to ruin something good.* The alcohol blurred these thoughts a little, and he hoped it would continue to do so until it wouldn't anymore and then he would have to find something else to block it out.

He walked out of the Tesco Express that was a few minutes from his new flat. Luckily it was only around the corner because he thought he probably overestimated how much red wine he could carry. He wondered if it was too

CHAPTER 29

late to go back and ask for a box to carry it home in instead. But that would mean more time pissing about when all he wanted to do was open one of the bottles.

Reaching the door to the building, he dropped one bag on the ground and pushed the handles of the other bag up his wrist to reach into his pocket for his keys. The door opened just as he went to put his key into the lock.

"Hi Sam," his seventeen-year-old neighbour said as he held the door for her to scoot past.

"Hey Briony," He said, looking more towards his feet than at her. He noticed she had a way of looking at him like he was something. Like he was cool and older and she had a crush on him.

"Special occasion is it?" she asked as he leant down to pick the bag up from the floor.

He was probably imagining it though. She probably just wanted someone to buy her alcohol and he seemed like the type of irresponsible acquaintance who wouldn't tell her parents.

"It's my birthday," Sam said.

"Oh, well Happy Birthday," she said as he pushed his shoulder against the door, holding it open with his frame as he pushed through.

He looked back to say thank you but she had already flounced off. Maybe she was going to meet some friends or go drinking in the park. *Of, course, the child has a better social life than I do. When did I become so sad?*

Ambling into the flat, he dumped the bags on the kitchen counter and kicked his shoes off. He picked one of the bottles from the bag and twisted the cap off, before drinking directly from the bottle. It seemed pathetic to pour it into one solitary glass. His phone buzzed in his pocket, he pulled it out hoping it was Ellie. She promised to video call with Pharaoh that evening. But it wasn't Ellie, it was Clara.

```
Wanna see you tonight x
```

He had been sleeping with George's sister Clara on and off for a few months now. Pretty much since he had come back to England. She kind of hung around in the same circles as George so it was pretty inevitable one drink-fuelled night at the pub would lead to them going home together.

George knew something was going on between them but he didn't acknowledge it. There was no "stay away from my sister" talk, but Sam still knew it wasn't the best set up. George was the only proper friend he had left. He had workmates and there were a few lads from school he still met up with at the pub occasionally but he was always on the periphery of the friendship groups. Like he wouldn't be missed if he didn't turn up one night and he noticed that he was sometimes left off the invite list. Not intentionally, but just like he was forgotten about, which was somehow worse.

So, all in all, it wasn't a great plan to start shagging Clara but it was easy and she didn't expect anything from him which suited him. He thought about texting her back to invite her round but decided against it. The only thing sadder than spending your thirty-fifth birthday alone was spending your thirty-fifth birthday with your twenty-nine-year-old side piece. He closed the message and left it unanswered.

Ellie hadn't called yet and it was about 6 p.m. Lisbon time, which was almost Pharaoh's bedtime. He took a big swig from the bottle and put it on the counter before video calling Ellie's phone. It took a minute to connect and when it did, the picture was blurry, made from big square pixels.

"Hang on, lemme go out to the balcony Sam," she said. The picture began to clear as she moved from the darker interior to the light of the balcony.

"Look Pharaoh, it's Daddy," she said as she sat him on her lap and held the phone out.

"Hey buddy," Sam said over the ball of air in his chest. He didn't realise how much he missed him. He had only spoken to him a handful of times since he left.

"Daddy!" he cried and tried to grab the phone from his mum's hands.

"Let mummy hold it darling, what are we supposed to say to Daddy?"

"I got a truck Daddy, it's a bin lorry. Mummy, can I show Daddy my new truck?"

"Not now darling, what do we say to Daddy?"

Pharaoh looked at his mum perplexed before Ellie whispered into his ear.

CHAPTER 29

"Happy Birthday, Daddy," he said pushing his face close to the camera and grinning.

"Thanks, Roe, what have you been up to today?"

"I got a new truck, Juan bought it for me and it's binman day tomorrow so I am going to show the binman my new truck."

"That sounds great, mate,"

"Why don't you go get it Pharaoh?" she said. The camera shook a bit as he climbed down. "Sorry I didn't call earlier, it's just been manic"

"Yeah it's cool, I get it," he replied.

"Listen, I wanted to talk to you about Christmas. There's been a change of plan,"

"What do you mean a change of plan?" He asked, not liking where this was going.

"Juan has booked us a cabin to spend Christmas in. I didn't know he had booked it but he wanted to surprise us. Anyway, he's put the deposit down and Pharaoh is really excited, so I don't think we're gonna be able to come to England this year."

"But El, we agreed. My parents have already started buying him gifts and mum was going to take him to see Santa. Plus it's been three months since I've seen him."

"I know, I'm sorry, but it's just…it's all sorted and I'm happy Sam. Juan does make me happy and he's there you know? Like body and spirit."

"What and I wasn't, is that what you're saying?"

"Sam, come on, things weren't working for a long time, you know that."

"And Juan has been on the scene all of five minutes, but he's your number one priority," he replied.

"That's not fair. Don't put that on me," She sighed. "I will book flights for us to come in the new year. He has two weeks off for Easter so we will come over then. Or you could come to us? I don't mind making up the spare bed for you?"

"No, it's ok just…just come over here. It will be good for him to see his grandparents."

"Yeah, OK." Something crashed somewhere in the background. "Juan?

What was that?" she said, taking her attention away from the phone. Pharaoh began crying in the background.

"Look, Sam, I'm sorry, I have to go. Happy Birthday. Hope you like the gift." she said before the phone beeped three times, signalling she had hung up.

Sam looked over at the large frame that he had partially opened earlier. It had a photo of him and Pharaoh together at the top and below that, two handprints with *Pharaoh, aged 6* underneath and in large handwritten letters "I love you, Daddy". You could see where Ellie had put the dots to spell it out and he had traced over the top.

Chapter 30

Ivy ran the cloth around the inside of the wine glass before dunking it into the warm soapy water. It was the first of January but the sounds of Christmas songs were still playing from the TV in the other room.

They had spent Christmas Day at Thea's parents opening gifts and eating too much food. Rachel had joined them as she had the previous three Christmases. Val had kindly invited her to Ivy & Thea's first Christmas as a married couple so they didn't have to choose and Rachel was never left having Christmas alone. Sat around the table of food-stained plates and cracker jokes splattered with gravy was the kind of Christmas Ivy always wished for. The closest she had before was when her family was whole. Her mum teaching Agatha how to roast potatoes in the kitchen and her dad lifting her to pick chocolate from the tree. But unlike those memories, she wasn't waiting for the inevitability of her parents getting into a screaming match and her dad to walk out.

Boxing Day her mum cooked a curry with the leftover turkey Val had wrapped up for her. Alden, Jessie and Freya joined them and they all opened presents again and watched Kung Fu Panda. Alden napped in the armchair and Rachel did a jigsaw with Freya on the dining table. And just like every year, it was all over too quickly and all the adults returned to work tomorrow, except Alden who had worked in between Christmas and the New Year.

"Don't worry about that love, I'll sort it out in the morning," her mum said as she walked into the kitchen.

"It's alright mum, you did all the cooking, again," she replied.

"Here," — Rachel said handing Ivy a tray of After Eights — "Take these into your beautiful wife, will you,"

Ivy wiped her hands in the tea towel hanging from the edge of the cupboard door beneath her before taking the box. Her mum knew exactly how to play her. She loved After Eights but they had always been a treat her mum bought at Christmas so it was the only time of year she would ever have any, making them all the more delicious when she did.

She tried to think of the first time she had had them, or at least the first time they had appeared on the coffee table on Christmas Eve as she carried the box into her mum's living room, unwrapping it as she went.

"Isn't it funny how you attach so many memories to certain things?"

"Like what?" Thea asked. "Oh, no thanks, I'm still stuffed from dinner," she said, waving a hand at the open box of mint chocolates Ivy held out to her.

Ivy shrugged and took three before putting the box in the middle of the coffee table. "Like After Eights, they always make me think of Christmas. I can't even imagine having them at any other time of year, it would be like sacrilege", she said, pulling one of the chocolates from the wrapper and putting it into her mouth.

"Yeah, I know what you mean. I don't think I even remember they exist at any other time of year," she replied before leaning over and taking one from the box despite her earlier protests. "Can you believe we have to go to work tomorrow?" she asked, rolling her eyes, with chocolate in her mouth.

Ivy raised her eyebrow and smiled. "Can you believe I start my new role tomorrow? I thought it would sink in over the break but it still feels weird that I'm gonna have a team of publishing assistants looking to me for what to do,"

"I don't think it's weird, you've worked your ass off and you have been doing the job anyway since your manager left,"

"I know, but as of tomorrow, it's official. Like they can't change their minds...or maybe they can, can they change their minds?"

Thea got up and walked over to Ivy, she ran her hands through her wife's hair before clasping her face. "Honey, you've got this. You are a badass bitch and you can do anything," she said before kissing her gently.

"Hmm, you taste good, do that again," Ivy mumbled and Thea leant down and kissed her again more deeply. "I love you, Thea Green-King"

Rachel walked in at that moment. "Right, is there anything I can get you,

CHAPTER 30

ladies?"

"No Mum, we're good, we should be heading off really. Back to work tomorrow."

"Ah of course. Do you want to take anything with you?" Rachel yawned.

"It's fine Mum, head up to bed and we will lock up," Ivy said, kissing her mum's cheek.

Ivy bent down to pull her shoes on as Thea grabbed their coats from the hall cupboard and noticed the corner of a book tucked under the shoe bench. She picked it up, intending to prop it on the shoe bench without a thought, but caught the title "Tender Is The Night" by F. Scott Fitzgerald. It was a book she read for school. Distant memories danced at the edge of her mind and she smiled a little before placing it back on the bench.

She put her hand to her throat and pulled gently at the necklace that hung there. She had unfollowed Sam on Instagram a year or so ago, but she couldn't stop herself from wearing the necklace he bought her.

"Ready?" Thea said, holding her coat out at her.

"Yeah, yeah I'm ready." she smiled.

* * *

"Ow," Thea said as Ivy injected her thigh with hormones.

"It's over, no more for today," she said as she kissed her thigh, just below where she stuck the needle.

"Thanks, hopefully, these ones work," she replied with a small smile that didn't look hopeful.

They had been trying for a baby for just over a year. At first, the doctor said not to worry, she was healthy, they were using the best sperm and it would happen when she relaxed about it. Then after eight months, he tried her on some tablets. Thea had said she felt humiliated when the doctor pointed out she was an "old" mother at thirty-eight but she took the tablets because she knew the end result would be worth it.

That was a few months ago now and the doctor had since moved her onto daily hormone injections. Ivy couldn't bear to let Thea do them herself, she was going through so much for this pregnancy so she wanted to help any way that she could. And at the moment, that meant administering the daily injections.

But every month she was given sperm from a stranger and every month her period came anyway. The doctor suggested Ivy try conceiving but it was Thea's dream to get pregnant and Ivy wouldn't take that away from her.

"Don't forget, the doctor is going to phone at two with your last lot of test results. Hopefully, they will tell us what's going on," Ivy offered.

"Yeah, I set a reminder so I can nip out of the office if I need to," she replied. She sounded distracted and Ivy knew the results were playing on her mind, just like they had done for the past two weeks.

When Thea came home from work that evening she walked in and pulled a bottle of white wine from the fridge before walking to the cupboard and pulling out a glass. She poured a large measure and swallowed around half of it before she even acknowledged Ivy, so she knew the news wasn't going to be good.

"I can't get pregnant," she said flatly and Ivy saw the tears glistening on the edges of her lashes. "The egg won't implant. He said it was like an "entrance exam", that the embryo needed to pass the exam to implant and it keeps failing."

Ivy didn't say anything but she moved closer and took her hand, rubbing her thumb back and forth on her skin as she did.

"So all those times we went to the clinic, the sperm was making it to the egg, and there was an embryo but I've effectively miscarried eleven times. What is the point of a uterus that turfs a baby out huh?" Her voice cracked on the last word.

Ivy pulled her close and smoothed her hair as she cried into her chest. "Come on, why don't I run you a bath? We can talk about options,"

Thea didn't answer but pulled herself back to let Ivy know that was OK. Once the bath was full, Ivy threw as many different liquids and salts in as she could find, she found a tub of lavender Epsom that she emptied. She didn't know what else to do in this situation, but she could be there for her wife at least.

Thea climbed into the warm water tentatively, wrapping her arms around

CHAPTER 30

her bent legs, resting the side of her face on her knees. Ivy climbed in behind her, perching on the edge of the tub in just her underwear and a vest top. She picked up the empty pot that used to contain the lavender Epsom salts and filled it with the bathwater. She guided her broken wife's head back and carefully poured the water over her hair, using her other hand to stop the water falling into her eyes. She washed her hair gently while they sat there quietly, just being together for a few minutes.

"Did they say IVF was an option?"

"Um, he said it was, but only a slim chance so probably not worth going through. So I suppose we are going to have to go with plan B," Thea said, turning to look at Ivy questioningly.

"I've obviously thought about it, but how would you feel about that?" she asked.

"I mean, a bit sad, but at the end of the day, we would be having a baby so that kind of trumps everything really. Don't you think?"

"Yeah, I do think," she replied.

After a beat, she continued, "It doesn't make you any less, you know. It's just one of those things as they say," Ivy said quietly.

She knew Thea had registered what she said but she took a minute to answer. "I know," she said in a small voice and nodded slightly. "But I just want to be sad for a while. Is that OK?"

Ivy leant over her shoulder and kissed her neck, burying her face and wrapping her arms around Thea's wet body. "OK, let's be sad for a while, together,"

Ivy's mind briefly flicked to a blurry memory of Sam washing her vomit out of her hair one drunken night at his parent's house. She didn't remember much of that night until she tiptoed out in the early hours of the morning, leaving him sleeping in the empty tub, fully clothed and walked home with wet hair.

* * *

Ivy got pregnant almost immediately, she thought as if to twist the knife slightly, but Thea was over the moon. She had been on a high for weeks now as she tracked Ivy and little pip's progress. Named for the fact they were the size of an apple pip. Ivy couldn't tell who was more excited; Thea, Jessie or Freya.

"You know she's already calling them her sister right?" Jessie said one evening on the phone.

"That's adorable, but it might be a boy," Ivy replied.

"We will have to see," Thea chipped in.

"Anyway, tell me about the new man," Ivy said.

"There's a new man? No one told me there was a new man?" Thea said.

"Shut up and let her speak then," Ivy laughed.

"The new man has a name — which is Henry by the way," Jessie replied. "He is smart and kind, a—"

"Send me a picture," Ivy said and Jessie immediately sent a photo to her phone. He had dark black skin, a strong brow and plump, ardent lips surrounded by a short beard and moustache. Ivy showed Thea who pulled a face like she might find him attractive if she liked men.

"Wait, Henry as in Dr Henry? Your lecturer?"

"Potentially," Jessie said, trailing off.

"Is that even allowed?"

"I don't know, we're both grown adults so why the hell not?"

"I don't know, wouldn't he give you special treatment or something? How old is he?"

"There's only an eleven-year difference, but I've always preferred an older man. And as for special treatment, I hope so — PhDs are hard!"

"Age ain't nothing but a thing baby," Thea said. "Besides, none of that matters when you get to our age anyway," she added.

"Will you stop saying that like we are old," Ivy said, swatting at the air near her wife.

"Well, I'm just saying we are all forty next year, we are much too mature to still sweat the small stuff,"

Ivy rolled her eyes at this. "So when do we get to meet him then?" she asked.

"Soon. I think this is the real deal guys, I mean I'm solid on my own and

Freya and I are a unit. So only someone special will be able to break into that but I think that's him. It's only been a few months though so I don't want to get ahead of myself,"

"I'm happy for you Jess, you sound made up about him. You really do," Ivy said smiling genuinely as she spoke.

"Well he's gotta pass the Freya test yet, he's coming over for lunch next Sunday so I will let you know if he's still around after that."

"He will be putty in her hands, I'm telling you now,"

Jessie laughed, "As long as she doesn't chase him out I'm happy, but she has been a bit moody recently. I think she's already full of teenage angst and hormones. It is a minefield. I can't ever remember being that bitchy."

They laughed, "Oh trust me, with you it never went away!" Ivy joked.

"In all seriousness, if I could get a tiny bit of what you guys have, I will be living free and easy. Anyway, I have to go. Freya has food tech tomorrow and only told me twenty minutes ago she needs to take in all the ingredients for a moussaka!"

"OK, I was definitely guilty of that at thirteen," Thea said.

"We will catch you later, love you lots," Ivy said.

"Love you both!" Jessie replied before hanging up.

"Maybe we are getting old, Thee,"

"Why do you say that?"

"Well, I think ten years ago I would be out drinking and partying and now I'm sitting at home, pregnant with my wife watching Celebrity Gogglebox while my friend dates her PhD professor,"

"Wanna trade it?"

"Not really no. In fact, not at all. I love my life. Don't you?"

"More than anything," Thea replied, rubbing Ivy's belly.

* * *

The sun hit her shoulder one morning and she dreamed of him. She dreamed of a morning in Thailand, where the sun streamed through the translucent curtains. The crisp, white sheet parachutes over them as he wraps around her, kissing her from head to toe. The sheets billow and he's gone. She opens her eyes knowing the bed was full of sand, feeling it rub between her fingers and smelling him on her skin.

Chapter 31

Ivy had never imagined herself pregnant. She had a vague idea of future kids but not the practicalities of it. When she and Thea had talked about it, Thea had always been the pregnant one but even before Thea, she didn't ever really think of what it would be like to have a baby inside her.

Isn't there supposed to be a glow or something? Nice little stomach flutters that make you feel like you're not alone? Jessie was a glimpse into normalcy and she complained about some of it, but she never said how lonely she felt. How she no longer knew her own body. After nearly forty years with this body, Ivy thought she knew every contour, every freckle, every blemish but she seemed to find something new every day recently. A darker patch of skin here and there, a voice that sounded foreign to her own ears, not to mention the boob sweat.

She stood in front of the mirror wearing just her bra and underwear and held her tiny bump. *Who would have thought such a tiny thing would make such a big difference?* But she would never share these thoughts with Thea. It was bad enough she was the one that was pregnant, but she knew it would gut her to know that Ivy hated it. *Hate is such a strong word* she thought, but she had no inclination to change it.

Thea would be glowing, she would love all of it. She forced a smile on her mouth and stared at it in the mirror. *Good enough* she decided before walking to the dresser to get dressed. As she bent to get to her bottom drawer she tripped over her foot slightly and bumped into the unit, knocking her jewellery box off and the contents all over the floor. *Is clumsiness a weird pregnancy symptom? Or is Thea just rubbing off on me?* She thought as she lowered herself onto the floor and began collecting all the jewellery back into the box. She picked up handfuls of earrings and dumped them into the box. Then reached under the dresser to pick up the pieces she could see shining in the shadow.

She was surprised when she pulled her hand back and it contained the silver V-shaped necklace that was a gift so many years ago. She couldn't remember the last time she wore it or when she stopped thinking of him as a solid person and not just a memory. Not even a memory of her own, more like a memory of a dream.

Thea called asking if she wanted a coffee, decaf of course, so she got dressed and put the jewellery box back where it belonged and went to join her wife.

As she came down the stairs, she heard a knock on the door. She could just make out the shape of her mum behind the clouded glass.

"Mum, what a nice surprise," she said as she opened the door.

"I'm not interrupting anything, am I? I did text, but you haven't seen it."

"No, course not. Come on in," she said. Rachel removed her jacket and hung it on one of the hooks behind the door, which she closed behind her.

"Coffee Rache?" Thea shouted from the kitchen, hearing her mother-in-law's voice over the sound of the water boiling.

"Tea if you have it?" Rachel replied and followed Ivy into the kitchen.

Ivy kissed Thea on the cheek as she took both hers and her mother's cups and walked to the back door that was ajar letting in a slight breeze. She pushed the door open further with her elbow and walked to the small patio table to bask in the warmth of the August sun.

Thea had spent a lot of time in the garden, making it home to beds of wildflowers for the bees and butterflies which always flitted around at this time of year. She sat down placing the mugs in front of her and Rachel sat opposite her. Rachel pulled her mug closer and saw a slight sparkle near Ivy's chest.

"That's a nice necklace love, is it new?"

"This?" Ivy's hand went to her throat instinctively. "No it's not new, it was a graduation gift," she smiled, but the smile didn't touch her eyes.

* * *

CHAPTER 31

Thea chose this moment to join them. Walking out into the sunshine, she squinted slightly at Ivy and looked at the necklace the two were talking about. It was the silver one she had seen many times before but admittedly, not for a while. She was puzzled, as she thought back to when Ivy opened the gift and she could have sworn she said it was from Rachel. Maybe she was getting it mixed up or maybe Rachel had just forgotten she had given it to her. Ivy didn't seem to notice this train of thought though as the two had already begun talking about other things.

"How are you getting on at work Thea?" Rachel asked, knocking Thea gently from her thoughts.

"Hmm. Work? Um. Not great actually. I thought once I got a big project to sink my teeth into I would start enjoying it again but honestly? It's a shit show at my place and I am so done with it." While Ivy had stayed at Braitons their entire relationship, Thea had been working in advertising since she left uni. First working for a start-up then moving onto bigger and bigger agencies. She had been given an account for a weight loss app at the tail end of last year and although she had initially refused to work with them, her director had convinced her it would be her stepping stone to bigger accounts. But almost a year on she was still managing them and it was starting to eat at her ethics. She hadn't even mentioned it to her parents because she knew they would be disappointed. They knew as well as she did how diet culture affected and even caused eating disorders, so it felt like a betrayal to her younger self.

"Oh, you're going to start looking elsewhere then? Good for you. I always thought your talents were wasted at that place," Rachel encouraged.

"Yeah, I am. I'm not one-hundred per cent sure what I wanna do yet, but something different. Something to excite me, you know?"

"She's a bit fed up with the whole soulless corporation thing. Otherwise, I told her she could walk straight into a job at my place, easy," Ivy added.

"Would you consider a startup then? Or maybe a charity?" Rachel asked.

"I'd love to work at a charity but the pay isn't usually the best and with Pip on the way, I haven't got the luxury of taking a step back pay wise."

"Well that's not true, you just haven't been looking in the right places. And worst-case scenario if we had less money but you were happy it would be worth it." Ivy said.

She and Ivy had discussed this most evenings and she was so encouraging but Thea felt like she had already let Ivy down by not being able to carry this baby and no matter what Ivy said, she didn't want to let her down by not being able to support them once the baby was born. It had been the only point of contention in their twelve-year relationship and even that was because they both wanted the best for each other. "Yeah, I think I just want to feel valued, you know? But also feel like what I am doing has value to others,"

"I know exactly what you mean and good for you for knowing what you want," Rachel said, reaching her hand to Thea's and tapping it lightly twice before taking it back. "I'll keep my eyes open for you. See if any creative roles are going you might enjoy," she added.

"Thanks, Rache," Thea replied.

The talk rolled around to the baby and Ivy's morning sickness that was still present even though she was over four months pregnant by now and it still lasted most of the day, not just the morning. Rachel just smiled and nodded, like she was remembering her own pregnancies before remembering only one of the babies she carried was still here. Ivy used to worry about her mother being alone, and to an extent so did Thea. She couldn't imagine what it must have felt like to lose her daughter so young and it had just been her and her girls for so many years so she was more than happy to have Rachel so involved in their lives. She had become a second mum to her over the years and it was warming to see how the dynamic has altered since Ivy had been pregnant. Even though Pip wasn't here yet, Thea already loved them so much but she understood now that no matter what, you are always a mother. Whether you could see and hold your child or not.

"Agatha would have been a great Aunty," Ivy said aloud.

"She would have," Rachel smiled. "Fussing all over you and the little one, when they arrive. She'd have done all the fun things because that's the best bit about being an aunty, doing those things and then giving them back at the end of the day — full of sugar and excitement,"

"Oh God, I can only imagine," Ivy smiled into her hand as a tear fell from her eye. She wiped it quickly and the three of them sat there silent for a moment

CHAPTER 31

and looked towards the small vacant space at the table as if allowing space for Agatha to join them.

Chapter 32

Returning to work helped Ivy massively. She spent the first few months of motherhood feeling like a sausage in a skin that was too tight. She was no longer at home in her own body, her hair was falling out and her stomach didn't look like it belonged to her anymore. She spent time thinking how none of this mattered though, Josh was perfect and he was a piece of her and a piece of Thea. But returning to some semblance of her life before Josh, somewhere she wasn't just a milk machine or *mummy* as Thea affectionately called her, was the breathing space she needed to be one-hundred per cent mummy when she returned home.

Thea didn't seem to have the same problem. She adapted to motherhood perfectly and thrived on the new identity she had taken on. Not once did Ivy see any sign she wanted to hang the mum coat up for a while, even just for a few hours. Although this was hard for Ivy to understand, she was grateful. She was grateful that Thea was on when she was off and that she could have time away and fall back into her family every evening seamlessly, mainly down to the role that Thea took.

Finally, after years of hating her job, Thea did something for herself and got a new job as Youth Worker at a local eating disorder clinic while she trained to be a Councillor. She spent her days helping people with something that almost destroyed her and although it was a dramatic pay cut from her old job, she had flexible hours so she could spend more time with her son. Which meant that childcare wasn't an issue. Josh was cared for by Thea's parents while both mums worked and Thea finished at 3 p.m. to collect Josh from her parent's house and return home to feed him before Ivy got home and was able to give

CHAPTER 32

him another small feed and a bath before bed.

By the time Josh's first birthday rolled around, the trio seemed to have settled into an easy routine of family life and Thea loved it. It felt like Josh was her missing piece and now she could start the rest of her life, just the three of them. She voiced this to Ivy one night and Ivy agreed, she felt at peace with their lives right now. But, what Ivy didn't say, was that she still couldn't help but think there was something more. Something she wasn't quite grasping.

She knew that life wasn't going to be sex, drugs and rock and roll anymore and she wasn't lying when she told Thea she was content, because she was most of the time. But now and again a tiny little voice reared from the dark crevices of her mind to say *it's not enough* and sometimes it even said *you are not enough* to which she replied *I know*.

The doorbell rang, breaking Ivy from her thoughts.

"I'll get it," Thea said, balancing Josh on her hip. Ivy heard the door opening and the muffled voices of both Thea and what sounded like Alden.

"Hey, I didn't realise you were coming over," Ivy said as she rose to hug him. As she stood, she noticed the sombre look on his face. "What's wrong?" she said.

"I fucked up, Ivy. I really fucked up," he said as tears welled in his eyes.

"Whatever it is, we can fix it, just tell me what's wrong."

He sat on the edge of the sofa cushion and closed his eyes and breathed deeply in an effort to calm himself. Ivy exchanged a silent look with Thea who nodded before taking Josh upstairs. By the time Jessie had arrived, Alden had told Ivy everything. Ivy let her in and after closing the living room door on him, she filled Jessie in on Alden's story.

"He's completely broke, but not just that, the restaurants are bankrupt too," she told her. Jessie pushed her hands into her hair, the blood had drained from her face. "He hasn't paid his mortgage in six months so the bank evicted him last week,"

"Fuck," Jessie responded, half shouting half whispering.

"I knew something was...he asked to borrow some money, about April time. Said he was having issues with a supplier, but...where has he been sleeping?"

"In the back office at The Maple."

Jessie exhaled. "Come on then, let's get in there and see if we can fix this," she said pushing open the door. Alden looked up his face puffy from tears that were threatening to start anew at the sight of Jessie. "Hey, boo,"

"Hey,"

"Do you wanna tell me what's going on?" she asked, sitting in the armchair facing him. He looked to Ivy. "Ivy's told me the basics, but I want to hear the whole thing from you," she answered for him.

"It started at uni, a bet on the football here, a trip to the casino there. I didn't think it was anything to worry about, I figured all students were in debt you know?" Ivy thought back and wondered if this was part of the reason he started skipping classes and cut his degree short, but she didn't want to interrupt him so she let him continue. "My dad helped me with the cash to buy The Maple and I used the profits to buy The Oak and The Birch, but it started getting really bad about three years ago. I started using one of those online casinos late one night and spending a lot more than I meant to so I had to keep going, you know to win it all back and it just kind of snowballed from there really." He wiped a tear from his cheek. "So about six months ago, I stopped paying our suppliers,"

"Which is why you asked to borrow the money," Jessie said.

"Yeah, and I hate to say it, but I didn't exactly use it to pay them back," he looked at the floor. Jessie swallowed and nodded. Ivy folded her arms and leant on the door frame.

"Okay, but what do we do about it now?" Ivy asked.

"Well, I can't afford to keep the restaurants going, I've lost the house…I've hit rock bottom,"

"Good," Jessie said. Ivy looked at her sceptically.

"Good, because there's only one place to go from here right?" Alden said.

"Right. First things first, you need to get some help," Ivy said, looking up the nearest Gambler's Anonymous group. "There's a GA meeting on Church Street on Thursdays at eight. We can drop you off and pick you up—"

"We *will* drop you off and pick you up," Jessie interjected. "And give me your phone," she added. Alden handed it over and Jessie fiddled with it for a moment. "Okay so I am setting parental locks on your phone so you can't get onto any gambling sites and I am disabling your mobile banking apps." She looked up from the phone. "Benefits of having a teenager: I know how to lock down a phone when I need to."

"You should give us your debit cards as well. We can sort out some sort of allowance system or something. Plus you need to cut up your credit cards so you don't keep digging this hole," Ivy added. Alden hung his head in his hands, over his knees and took a deep breath, exhaling loudly through his mouth. "We're not trying to punish you, Al, we just want to help," Ivy said. He nodded without lifting his head for a moment, then jumped up and pulled his wallet out of his back pocket before throwing it over to Ivy.

"You can move in with us. Immediately, in fact. Freya will love having you around," Jessie said, reaching out to clasp Alden's hand.

"What about Henry? Isn't he supposed to be moving in next week?" Ivy asked, almost under her breath so as not to make Alden feel unwanted.

Jessie just waved her hand as if to say *we can deal with that later* and continued. "And we will sort out the mess with the restaurants, I'll call in sick tomorrow and we can sit down and look at the books together and if necessary we can go to the bank."

"Alden smiled tightly. "Thank you, both of you, thank you. I thought you would be ashamed of me or...thank you."

"We just wish you had trusted us with this sooner. You are our best friend and we never want you to struggle alone," Ivy said, crossing the room to rub Alden's back.

A few days later Jessie called Ivy to fill her in.

"It's worse than we thought," she said. "He's going to have to sell The Birch, straight off the bat. We asked the bank for a loan so he could keep The Maple and The Oak, but they would only give a partial loan, which means he will most likely lose them both,"

"Well that's OK, I'm sure his parents can lend him all of it can't they?" Ivy asked.

"Not exactly," she said. "He told me that he hasn't spoken to either of them in years. They knew about his gambling so cut him off,"

"Wait — what? How did we not know this?"

"He was too ashamed I think, but more than that, I think keeping it under wraps was part of his compulsion," Jessie said.

"OK, so what do we do?" Ivy said. "How much does he need?" She looked to Thea who nodded supportively, giving her a look that said *do what you need to do.*

"About one hundred and fifty k for both of them," Jessie replied. "So the bank is willing to give him one hundred and I'm going to give him thirty."

"Are you sure?" Ivy asked.

"Well, I have the cash. I've been saving for a while and I have been looking to invest it."

"Okay, well count me in for the other twenty. But we need some sort of contract in place so he can't just run them into the ground and we end up owing money to a lot of people,"

"Way ahead of you, I hired a solicitor to draw something up this morning but I'll get him to sort your side out too."

"How did Henry take it?"

"Good, I mean not great but he understands."

"Is he still moving in?"

"He will, just not yet. I don't want Alden to feel like he is intruding, you know? Like we're a happy family and he's stepping in on that,"

"That makes sense," Ivy said. "You're a good friend, Jess," Ivy said.

"There's something else too...I quit my job," Jessie said.

"You did? Why?"

"So I can keep a better eye on him and our new investments. I'm going to be handling the books from now on. See if I can dig us out of this mess with the suppliers,"

"What if you can't?"

"The lawyer thinks we might be able to buy him out and then bring him back on board so it basically wipes the debt but we can still deal with them but it seems quite underhand to me,"

"I agree, let's avoid that if we can, even if it means we buy him out but pay them as much as we can."

"Agreed. I'll be at The Maple this week going over it all but I'll keep you updated."

"Okay, speak to you soon," Ivy hung up. She couldn't believe it. She thought they had all become boring adults and nothing would upset that but she was wrong. If Jessie was going for the best friend award, she had certainly won. Although she wasn't surprised she would quit her job for Alden she was sad that she had spent twenty years studying and working in her field, because she loved engineering so much. She was also relieved because although they could have more than comfortably afforded to invest twenty thousand pounds before Thea started working at the clinic, it would be a push now. That would be most of their savings, but what use was money when you couldn't help those you loved?

Chapter 33

It turned out to be much harder to pack with a child than when it was just the two of them. It required more planning, and manoeuvring and a much bigger car. Ivy thought that was probably why they hadn't had a holiday in three years, but it was needed at this point.

Work for both of them had become increasingly more consuming with Ivy's company acquiring and merging with other publishing houses and Thea's work being so altruistic that she could always find more to do. When they did sign off from work for the day, their evenings were capitalised by the routine of a two-year-old. It wasn't something they resented but it was usually around 9 p.m. before the two sat down together to spend time on themselves and that usually meant dinner in front of the TV or alongside a new manuscript Ivy had been approached with while Thea worked on advertising campaigns for the restaurants.

"Is that all of it?" Ivy asked as Thea closed the boot.

"Man, I hope so," she replied, looking at the car apprehensively.

"If we've forgotten something, it isn't the end of the world. We are only going for the week, and worst-case scenario, we can buy whatever we need there," she replied.

"Well if we do end up buying anything we will also have to buy a new car to bring it home in," she smiled and thrust her arms in the air, looping them around Ivy's neck and planted a kiss on her lips. Ivy gripped her wife by the waist and kissed her back.

Despite the changes adult life has brought, Thea and Josh were by far the best part. Ivy couldn't imagine loving anyone more than she did them. Even if after

CHAPTER 33

all these years, she still wasn't sure she deserved them. But a week away from work in a cottage by the seaside was her chance to focus completely on them, which they did deserve. They had been forewarned the phone signal and wifi would be practically non-existent so they wouldn't have much contact with the outside world which made Ivy anxious as Henry and Jessie were moving into their new home over the weekend and Alden had arranged to visit his parents. He had been speaking to them over the last year, keeping them updated on his recovery and businesses but this would be the first time he had seen them since they cut him off. She worried she was being a terrible friend but they both assured her they needed to do these things themselves which she understood.

"You'd better get going then, it's getting dark already and it's not a short drive," Rachel said, emerging from the house with Josh on her hip.

"We're going on our holidays Joshy!" Thea said in a silly voice that made Josh giggle, his bright golden eyes shining. Thea held her arms out to him and he reciprocated.

"Where's Nanny's kiss?" Rachel said, turning her cheek to him, and he dutifully pulled her face closer to his with splayed palms and kissed it. Ivy smiled. She loved seeing how close her mum and son were. Ivy thought she would find it hard having a child around when she was missing one of her own, but they have had such a special bond from the moment they met, she needn't have worried. She still wondered if now and then, her mum saw her sister in Josh's face like she did.

Rachel waved them off from their drive as they pulled away before heading back to her own car. They made good time and were near Cardiff within an hour, but the skies took that moment to empty themselves and rain thrashed down around them. All the drivers on the motorway ahead of them had slowed dramatically and Thea was struggling to see anything in front of their car.

"Look their all pulling onto the hard shoulder, Thee,"

"Yeah, but what if someone skids into us?" she replied warily. "There's a service stop there, I'll pull off and we can wait it out there,"

Ivy looked back to Josh who was sleeping soundly in his car seat and when she looked back up Thea had pulled into a car park of a small service station. She shakily turned the car off before clicking the radio back on for some accompanying noise to the rain chucking down on the roof above them.

"I can't believe he is sleeping through this," Ivy said, leaning close to Thea to be heard above the rain.

"I know but thank God for small mercies." Thea took a deep breath and leant her head back against the rest and closed her eyes. Ivy looked at her silhouetted against the water covered window. These were the moments that Ivy appreciated most when they weren't in any rush to be anywhere and they could just sit there appreciating each other's company. They didn't even have to talk, they were content in the silence and their presence was enough.

When the rain didn't let up they began talking, first about home and work and Josh, then distant memories of who they used to be before they found each other before circling back to home and work and Josh.

They talked for hours and didn't even notice the rain had gradually eased off and stopped completely while they were wrapped up in conversation.

They both looked back at Josh together, almost bumping heads in the centre. He was still sleeping and looked like a perfect cherub in the glare of the service station lights hitting the still wet windows.

"Come on, let's make a move before he wakes up and ruins this perfectly calm moment with tired toddler tears," Ivy said.

Thea smiled and turned the key in the ignition before slowly following the one-way arrows through the car park and back onto the motorway.

By the time they reached the cottage, it was just past 9 p.m. but they were both exhausted. They feasted on a dinner of Babybel cheese and crackers they had packed for Josh before turning in for the night.

Ivy tried to read a book that she hadn't been tasked with for work but fell asleep before her eyes had read three words.

* * *

The next day the trio went to the beach. It was warm for April but the sky was overcast. Josh loved the feel of the sand between his toes and running into the sea, feeling the cold water rush against his ankles. Ivy didn't know they could enjoy themselves so much on a Welsh beach in spring. They spent hours building sandcastles and Thea dug a moat around Ivy and Josh as they built grainy towers together. They collected buckets of water and filled the moat before leaving it for someone else to find. They tried looking for shells and other washed-up treasures but settled for collecting litter and filled a bag to throw away.

"Are you guys hungry?" Ivy asked.

"Famished," Thea replied.

"Yeah Mummy, famish," Josh chipped in, squinting against the bright sky to look up at Ivy.

"Shall we go to the pub then? It's a bit late for lunch but we might be able to catch the kitchen or we can hang around for the dinner service if not,"

"Sounds good to me," Thea replied.

"And me," Josh shouted, jumping in the air.

Both women took each of his hands and they began walking up the beach in the direction of the seaside pub they had spotted on their way to the cottage the previous night. Ivy wasn't looking ahead. She knew the direction she was headed, muscle memory from long ago holidays with her mum and sister after her dad had left, but she spent most of her attention looking at Josh as she and Thea counted to three and swung him into the air, much to his delight.

"Ivy?" It wasn't quite a shout but the sound, as soft as it was, cut through the family reverie and crashing waves beside them.

And that was when she saw him.

Part Four

"I don't have an explanation as to how you pull me in, you just do. You've always had a gravity that I've never been able to overcome." — JmStorm

Chapter 34

Ivy couldn't sleep. No matter how she lay on the bed, she just couldn't find a way to be comfortable. Thea was sleeping soundly next to her. Every time she exhaled, she made a small sighing noise that broke Ivy's heart a little bit more each time she heard it. She stopped tossing and turning for a moment and turned to study her sleeping wife. Her cotton camisole vest hugged her breasts, which perched above the duvet. Ivy watched the steady rise and fall of her chest and traced the outline of her collarbone with her eyes. She dare not touch her and wake her, but she wanted to feel her, to commit her every curve to memory.

She reached up and held her hand an inch or so from her face and slowly moved it down the side of her cheekbone drawing the edge of her jaw. Her hand moved further down, and outlined her shoulder and down her arm. She could feel the warmth radiating from Thea's skin in her fingertips. Stroking the air along her arm and stomach before reaching the edge of the duvet, she pulled her hand back. She loved this woman. More than anything. So why could she not stop thinking about Sam? Her mind flew back to their meeting that afternoon.

"Sam. Hi," It was awkward and she knew Thea could feel it too.

"It's nice to see you. You look good," he said in a voice that carried across the waves to sound far away from where they were standing.

Did she have mum hair? He had always liked it when it was long. She smoothed a hand over her hair to try and catch some of the flyaways. "Um, yeah thanks. You do too. I didn't know you were back - are you visiting or...?" He still looked the same. His hair was peppered with a few coarse greys and his face was a little more drawn but he had lost nothing of his looks.

"Well visiting Tenby, yeah, but I'm back in England for good now. Things... didn't work out."

The sentence hung for a few seconds before Ivy blurted out: "Sorry, I'm being rude. This is my Thea. I mean my wife, Thea."

"Nice to meet you, Thea," Sam said before shaking her hand. Did he actually shake her wife's hand? Is this how adults behaved?

"Nice to meet you too, uh, Sam is it?"

"Yes, Sam, Sam is me,"

She could tell he felt just as weird as she did but he still seemed to pass it off better than she ever could, with an air of coolness around him even now.

"And who's this little one?" he asked, bending slightly to give Josh a high-five. Josh high-fived him but then hid behind Thea's legs, shyly.

"This is our son Josh, he's two. Aren't you, baby?" Thea said. Josh poked his head out but didn't respond.

She snapped back to the present moment, climbed carefully out of the bed and crossed the room to the door. Tiptoeing to the bathroom she went to sit on the edge of the bath, but made a decision before allowing herself to put her weight down, and stood up. She walked out of the bathroom, grabbing her cardigan off of the bannister on her way down the stairs.

Stopping at the foot of the stairs, she waited a moment, expecting to hear Thea or maybe Josh stirring from the deafening noise of her pounding heart, but she heard nothing. She walked over to the door and pulled on her wellies that she left there that afternoon after coming back from their family walk, and she very carefully turned the key in the handle.

Stepping out onto the decking, she turned and just as quietly, closed the door behind her, before taking a deep breath. It wasn't too late to change her mind. She could just go back inside, take off the boots, climb back into bed with Thee and carry on with her life. Because she knew that every step she took toward Sam was a step away from that, from the comfortable slot that she fit into. She wasn't sure what was waiting for her in Sam, or why he was back in her life again, but she knew she just wanted him closer, even if it was just for a moment. Before she could argue with herself more, she stepped off

CHAPTER 34

the porch and onto the beach.

"So who was that?"

"An old friend, an old school friend actually,"

"Is he the one who moved to Portugal? He sent you a postcard once?"

"What? Oh yeah, yeah he did. I'd forgotten,"

She knew he would be there before she saw him and that was why her feet had taken her there. Sam was a dark figure sitting on the sand in front of her. As she got closer, she could see he was hugging his knees to his chest and smoking a cigarette, staring out at the black sea that looked like it was covered with a huge piece of white lace in the barely lit night. She sat down beside him, wrapping the cardigan tightly around her waist and pulling her hands up into the sleeves to try and protect herself from the cold wind coming off the water.

She said the word like it had two syllables like the second syllable regretted the first but had to follow anyway. "He-ey,"

"Hey," he replied.

Ivy looked over and saw there were fresh tears on his cheek, glistening in the sliver of moonlight they were allowed tonight, before turning back to the sea. They sat there without speaking or looking at one another for a while, with just the noise of the waves crashing to shore to keep them company.

"I feel like I've lived a whole life since I saw you last." she began. "But I wish that this could be the first time we had met. I would still have Agatha and me and you...we would be okay." She didn't turn to look at him as she said this but felt his eyes slide to her.

He didn't say anything for a while. He sat there digesting her words fully before replying. "You came so much further without me though. The life you had without me is much better than anything I could have been a part of."

His response surprised her. That was all so separate from Sam, that he almost didn't have the right to judge how well it had turned out. She tried not to acknowledge that she had thought this to drown out the voice inside her that told her he was right.

"What about you? How was your life without me?" She asked, hoping he would say it was empty without her and hating herself for it.

"Dull." He said flatly then turned to her and smirked. "I'd have preferred your company to my own most of the time." They lapsed back into silence for a moment. "Look about that night. That night, fuck, twenty years ago. I shouldn't have done that to you. I just, I knew I was never good enough for you. I wasn't a good enough friend...or anything else, but you have to know that I did love you." he said quietly and turned back to the sea. His words were cutting but she was numb. The only thing she felt was tired. She was tired of it all.

"I knew. I just...I needed to be alone for a while," she replied in a small voice.

They both fell silent again. Ivy started to think back to the last time she was honest with Sam and how she had ended up on another beach. But at least this time, Sam was here. She wanted his comfort so badly, to just fall back into that rhythm of Sam and Ivy and Ivy and Sam, to quiet those voices in her head, even if it was just for a second.

She was a mess, she knew it. She didn't want to admit to herself that she chose it; the mess, but she did. She was still choosing it and the only person she knew that could understand that was the person next to her. She turned to face him.

He looked at her and leant across, closing the void between them and hovered his face in front of hers for a second, looking her in the eyes, waiting, asking permission.

"Are you done being alone now?" He asked.

And in a way she was, alone in being the broken one inside her perfect life. Her face must have betrayed her because he kissed her and it was as if her mind had rewritten her whole life in that kiss. She was twenty-two again, her sister had never killed herself and she had never gone to that beach alone and high. This other life she had lived belonged to someone else and she was with Sam again. She followed him back to his hotel and there they cut through the layers of noise until she was just a line meeting his, and making a corner.

* * *

After, she led there naked on top of the sheets and watched him sleep. He looked so young and innocent when he slept. Young as he was before, he was never innocent, not even then. She stroked his chest and noticed a smooth patch, the size of her thumbprint, where the hair didn't grow. She tried to remember if he always had it or if she remembered where he got it, but she couldn't.

He smelled so good. Of nostalgia and sex and it was a comforting smell, like finding an old perfume from your childhood. But it wasn't the smell of home. That was Thea. She felt sad for Thea, but she wasn't sure she felt guilty. For her to feel guilty she had to feel bad and she wasn't sure that she did. Was it bad if what she was doing didn't even feel good? Last night was a confirmation of what she had believed since her dad had left. That she was undeserving of happiness, but with Sam, she could be both miserable and happy somehow. There was nothing more intimate than being hurt the way you want to be hurt.

The noise was creeping in again and it was time to go home. Her reprieve was over. She had to leave. The sheet caught around her as she climbed out of the bed, pulling it from around his waist, she noticed a small square tattoo on his hip. It stopped her for a second and she bent down to pull the sheet up over him again. Just like the scar across his chest, she didn't remember that tattoo but she hadn't known him for so long. He was entitled to have lived a life without her but it hurt that he had for some reason. Like she expected him to have frozen like the image of him in her mind had. She had always held him to a different standard than she did herself.

She got dressed quickly and left the hotel. The night manager smiled at her when he saw her face leaving reception, then his gaze dropped to the rest of her and the smile slid from his face. Taking on a knowing look that Ivy tried not to recognise.

Chapter 35

Thea was already awake when she arrived back at the cottage. She was sitting in the kitchen drinking coffee when Ivy slipped in. Ivy had prepared for this on her walk back to the house and walked in as breezily as she could and walked into the kitchen.

"Nothing like an early morning walk to wake you up huh? Bloody cold out there," she said pouring the freshly boiled water into a coffee mug for herself, all the while keeping her back to Thea. It felt easier lying than she ever would have thought. She turned and bent to kiss Thea's cheek, cautious not to linger too long, in case she smelled of Sam. But Thea moved her face to duck the kiss.

"Sit down," she said and Ivy knew that she knew. "Don't insult me by lying, I know where you were. I woke up in the night and found you gone," she said.

Ivy wasn't sure if she expected her to sound more upset but she wasn't sure how Thea felt or how this was going to go.

"Do you love him?" Thea said as sternly as before.

"No," Ivy replied quietly and Thea began to cry, but they looked like tears of relief rather than sadness. Seeing her cry was like a punch to the chest but knowing she had caused her tears felt much worse. She wanted to reassure her and reach out to her but she couldn't. Couldn't bring herself to comfort her, and potentially make it worse. Thea's feelings were so abstract to Ivy just hours ago when she was in Sam's bed. Guilt wasn't real until you had to witness it.

Thea partially held her tears and cleared her throat. When she trusted her voice to work again she said: "So where does that leave us?"

"I'm sorry. I love you and I don't want to lose you. I don't know why I did it, I just... I don't ... I can't really understand it myself so I don't know how to explain it."

"Did you arrange to meet him? Actually no, I don't want to know that. What I want to know is if you will do it again. If you *want* to do it again." she asked, her voice cracking on the last word.

Ivy thought for a moment and realised she hadn't even asked herself this question. Did she want to sleep with Sam again? Whether she wanted to or not, she felt like she *could* fall back into what they were before so easily. But what kind of future could they have exactly? The Sam and Ivy in her head hadn't changed even though the Sam and Ivy of the real world had. She didn't know how to answer, but she saw the fear creep over Thea's face with every second that passed without answer and eventually opened her mouth to speak.

"I don't love him, but he does represent something, a very difficult time for me, but it is one I want to go back to because it was a time when my sister was alive." Ivy looked up and felt the shame in her throat and knew what Thea must be thinking. "That is not an excuse! I'm not trying to play the dead sister card, I swear. I'm just... trying to be honest with you."

She paused for a minute and thought about how Sam is all around her. Last night proved he was in her, but he wasn't a part of her, not like Thea is. Sam was like the grains of sand in their bed that morning in Thailand and Thea was the comforting wrap of the sea. She felt contaminated with him, but with no urge to wash him off. Ivy thought she had left her self destructive impulses in her twenties, but it looked like he had brought that old side of herself with him. It was true, she didn't love him, how could she when she didn't even know him anymore. But regardless of the logic, she was still drawn to him.

"If it was a one-time thing and you've gotten it out of your system, I can... I can accept that." Ivy felt relieved like she had released a breath she didn't know she was holding. "I can understand a moment of weakness. But I am not willing to put myself or Josh through the pain of an affair. Especially if you will eventually leave us for him. So if that's what you... want... then you need to tell me now." Thea looked at Ivy hopefully.

"It was a one-time thing. I love you and I love Josh. I don't want to break up our family." Ivy said. *But I still can't help but want him.*

"OK, I can cope with that," Thea replied. Ivy leant forward to kiss her, but Thea pulled away. "I'm not ready for that yet. I need some time to forgive you," she said. Ivy nodded but felt tears stinging her eyes. She wondered why they hadn't come before. Did she not care that she had put her marriage at risk? Or almost lost her family in one selfish night? Or was she just broken? *Broken people will always break good people.* Josh chose that moment to run into the kitchen and Ivy quickly swiped at the tears on her face and smiled.

"Mummy!" he shouted and ran to Ivy. She scooped him up onto her lap and squeezed him tight. How could she even think about giving this up? How could she give up this small creature that loves her so much, he is *this* excited to see her when he wakes up? She looked to Thea who was wiping her cheeks. Ivy didn't deserve her, she knew. She pulled Josh back so she could see his face.

"Does Mama get a cuddle too?" she asked him. Josh nodded, still beaming at her and climbed down from her lap to go cuddle Thea.

"Thank you, baby," she said as she pulled him up.

"Are you sad Mama?" he asked curiously.

"A little bit, but I'm much better for seeing you," she said cupping his cheek.

"Can we have toast and watch Paw Patrol?" he asked, oblivious to adult life and although Ivy was grateful for his ignorance she was also heartbroken at his innocence.

"Of course we can. You go put it on and I'll bring you some toast," Thea replied.

Josh smiled and climbed down from Thea's lap, running into the living room. Ivy was always shocked at how much energy he had in the mornings, he definitely got that from his Mama, not her. She looked at Thea smiling and the smile slipped when she saw her. Thea got up and began making toast. Clattering dishes and pouring the end of her coffee down the sink.

"I'm gonna go take a shower then," Ivy said. Thea didn't respond. Ivy went to the bathroom and shut the door. She took a deep breath and imagined Thea was doing the same on the other side of the door. She turned the shower on and undressed before stepping under the running water, hoping it would cleanse her soul and make her new again.

CHAPTER 35

* * *

Thea still hadn't forgiven her a few weeks later. They had planned to go for cocktails with Jessie and Alden together, but instead, Thea chose to stay home with Josh. They planned these nights a month in advance mainly so the women could sort out appropriate childcare but also because if they didn't, they probably wouldn't get around to seeing each other.

"So we're back on track with the restaurant now, mostly down to Jessie," Alden said.

"I mean, it's been great for me, I'm really enjoying it. I can be flexible for Freya, it fits around my PhD and I get to hang out with my best bud all day," Jessie said.

"I can't believe you're doing a PhD in engineering when you aren't even an engineer anymore," Ivy said just as a round of drinks arrived at the table.

"Who ordered these?" Alden asked as Jessie's phone pinged.

"It's Henry," she read the text aloud: "Hope you guys have a good night, have a round on me. P.S. I won't wait up."

"You are obviously doing something right, that man is still completely hooked on you," Alden said and Jessie smiled into her drink and blushed a little, finishing it before taking the new glass.

"Well cheers then," Ivy said, bruised by her friend's happiness and they clinked glasses. Ivy swallowed a mouthful of her mojito and asked "How are the meetings going Al?"

"Yeah OK, I mean it's all a bit self-indulgent really isn't it? "Hi I'm Alden and I have a gambling problem, oh woe is me,"" he laughed a little awkwardly, "But my dad came with me last week."

"Does that mean you guys are OK now?" Ivy asked.

"We're getting there, I think. Neither of them wanted to lose me but they couldn't cope with why I was doing it. They thought they had done something wrong and messed me up, but it had nothing to do with that. Don't get me wrong, some addicts had some sort of tragedy but for me, I realised that the machines were just calming. The symbols going around, the short-lived joy when I would win, the whole system is geared up to trap people like me. That's the real reason people gamble and do drugs and cheat on their spouses and whatever else. They think they want to be happy but really they want to be excited. But just 'cause I know that doesn't mean I'm cured, you know?"

Ivy winced a little at the mention of cheating. Her heart ached. She should be proud of Alden for making such breakthroughs but she was jealous. Jealous that he could see his toxic behaviour for what it was and recover from it. Something she didn't think she was ever likely to do.

"With that in mind, there's something I wanted to ask you both," he said and cleared his throat. "I'm thinking about opening a third restaurant again. I've found a new location, over on Queen's Road that would be ideal and I'm still on good terms with Andy — you know, the chef from…that we had to let go? Anyway, the point is I appreciate all of the help you guys have given me and for getting me out of the mess I made and was wondering if you both want to increase your investment?" He took a sip of his drink before continuing. "Obviously, if you want to be bought out or don't want to expand, I totally get it, but I think with both of you guys owning the shares you do, and with Jessie running the money side of things, this would be a great opportunity you know?"

He looked at both of them hopefully and Ivy answered first. "Yeah, I mean, you will have to give me an idea of costs of course but I am definitely in and I'm happy to continue being a silent partner who gets free food every now and then," she smiled.

Alden reached across the table and squeezed Ivy's hand. "Thanks boo," he winked and looked over to Jessie.

"I'm surprised you even have to ask, I'm in. It sounds like fun." She held her glass up to the centre of the table. "Besides, I'm not leaving you alone with the money again," she smirked tightly. Alden and Ivy clinked their glasses around hers.

"Harsh, but fair," Alden replied.

"Harsh, but fair. I feel like that should be the title of her autobiography," Ivy said and they both smiled at Jessie who seemed to agree before changing the subject.

"So how was the seaside?" Jessie asked and sipped her pink margarita. Ivy had forgotten for a brief moment but here was reality to greet her again.

"Pretty horrible actually. I've got something to tell you both." Alden and Jessie looked at each other and frowned before looking back at Ivy. "I can't say it paints me in the best light," she said.

"Just spit it out will you woman, you're starting to worry us," Jessie said.

"I-I slept with someone. I cheated on Thea."

"What?!" Jessie stared at her wide-eyed.

"Are you serious? With who?" Alden said.

"Sam."

"Who the fuck is Sam?" Jessie asked loudly.

"Sam. My Sam. *The* Sam," she said quietly.

"Is she making sense to you or are you as confused as I am?" Jessie said, turning to Alden.

"No, I get it," he said just as quietly.

Jessie frowned harder. "Somebody needs to start explaining to me because I am fucking lost."

Ivy stared into her drink, swishing the mint around with her straw. "Look it's a long fucking story but he is *that* person you know? The one that fucks you over but you still go back for more, the one that for some reason you never have closure with," she said without lifting her eyes.

"He was her best friend in school. I remember seeing you both together. I knew you guys must have had a falling out because you used to be inseparable but you never mentioned him to us. I guess I didn't think too hard on it. I didn't exactly know you back then," Alden added.

"So you're leaving Thea?" Jessie asked, lowering her voice slightly.

"No, oh god, no. I love Thea. It was...it was a mistake. I don't know we just bumped into each other and—"

"You tripped and fell on his dick?" Jessie added with a snort.

"Jess," Alden looked at her, silently communicating a warning.

"We have this history you know and I saw him and I was twenty-two again and life was easy and—"

"You don't have to explain, we get it," Alden said, reaching his hand over to hers. Jessie gave him a look as if to say *"we do?"* but he seemed to ignore her.

"Are you going to keep sleeping with him?" Jessie asked.

"No," Ivy said out loud but the voice in her head said *maybe*.

"Well that's fine then, I mean, it's not great but you have your closure now," Alden said supportively.

"Yeah, and you're going to have to live with that closure now, for your family's sake," Jessie added.

Ivy looked up to meet her eye. "I need to go to the bathroom, I'll be back in a bit," she said, getting down from her stall. Ivy knew Jessie would react badly, but realised it was because she was hurt. She had been carrying around this big secret for their whole friendship and then just dropped it on her like she was supposed to know and be ok with it.

Alden was a little more understanding, probably because he had his own demons, but she could see the disappointment on his face which felt awful. She had made such a mess of things and managed to hurt the closest people to her, she had put her marriage on the line and her son. Her beautiful, baby boy. Her phone vibrated in her small bag and she pulled it out, thinking it was probably Jessie threatening to come in after her. But it wasn't.

```
I need to see you
```

She stared at the screen for a moment before putting it back in her bag and walking back out. She caught a waitress on her way back to the table. "Can you please send six shots of tequila and a long island iced tea to that table there please?" Sam 101: what to do when you hate yourself? Get rip-roaring drunk.

They tried to continue the night as if nothing had been said, but it was like a small cloud was hovering over their table. Ivy had passed the point of tipsy and was on her way to drunk when she messaged Sam.

```
Come pick me up? I'm at Jack's bar in town
```

CHAPTER 35

```
Be there in 15
```

When her phone buzzed in her pocket she excused herself for a moment. The atmosphere had changed between them as they all got progressively more drunk. They were laughing and joking almost as usual when Ivy snuck away. She walked towards the toilet before changing direction and heading outside.

He was standing away from the door smoking a cigarette, which he dropped and stepped on once he saw her. She walked quickly towards him, barely feeling the cold around her. She threw her arms around his neck and pushed him into the dimly lit doorway to the building next door. He stooped down to kiss her hard and pressed her back into the wall. *This is nice. This is…this is terrible. What am I doing?* But after a minute her thoughts went silent again and it was just her and Sam and peace. He eventually pulled back but kept his face close to hers, cupping her cheek.

"Do you want to get out of here?" he asked.

"Yes. I mean — can you just take me home?" *Did she just ask her lover to take her home to her wife? Her judgement was getting worse by the minute.*

"Of course. My car's around the corner." he went to walk away grabbing her hand. She tugged his hand slightly so he turned to look at her.

"I need my jacket and stuff. And I need to say goodbye."

"K, well I'll go grab the car — meet you back here in five?"

"Yeah, see you in a minute." She turned to walk back in and saw Jessie waiting by the door. *Fuck.*

"What the hell do you think you're doing?"

"Back off Jessie, this is none of your business." she tried to pass her and open the door.

"Oh, so you're none of my business now? Here's me thinking you were my best friend."

Ivy closed her eyes and took a breath. "Look, he's just giving me a lift home."

"Do you think I'm stupid? I saw you together! If you want to throw your family away for some high school hook up, that is up to you, but don't think you just get a free pass and I'm not going to say anything."

"God forbid you keep your mouth shut," she muttered under her breath, but loud enough for Jessie to hear. Jessie stared at her wide-eyed and mouth open. "Look, Jessie, I'm sorry I didn't mean—"

"Oh I know you didn't, but you kind of did. I may be a loudmouth but you know what your problem is? You are still stuck on shit that happened twenty years ago. I get it, your sister died, you weren't there for her, but at some point, you have to stop punishing yourself. You have to stop throwing any ounce of happiness away and you most definitely have to stop being so selfish." Ivy glared at her but didn't say anything. "What about Josh? Have you thought of him in all this? Or how about, I don't know, your wife? When are you gonna realise it's not just you that you're punishing anymore? Why can't you be happy unless you have some sort of internal conflict? This isn't some teen drama Ivy, it's your life and you need to grow the fuck up."

"You know what the stupid thing is?" Ivy turned, tears began falling freely down her cheeks. ". I was making decisions at twenty-two I should be making now. I cut him out of my life then, so I should be able to do it now, but I can't. I don't know if I am too long in the tooth or I'm past caring about what's best for me and as you so kindly pointed out, everyone else around me. Aren't you supposed to get wiser as you get older? 'Cause I feel like I'm just growing more tired and stupid."

"Then stop," Jessie said, quietly looking Ivy in the eye, trying to appeal to the woman she knew calmly.

Ivy didn't say anything but opened the door and walked over to the table. She pulled some cash out of her purse and put it in front of Alden. "If I owe more, then text me and I will pay you back."

"What's going on? You're leaving?" he said.

"Yeah, I'm leaving. I'll talk to you soon OK," she kissed him on the cheek, picked up her stuff and walked out. Sam was waiting in his car outside and Jessie hadn't moved from where she left her. Ivy strode over to the car and got in.

"You wanna be careful with that one mate, she has a habit of fucking over the people that care about her," Jessie shouted towards the car before going back inside.

Fresh tears fell from Ivy's eyes and as Sam pulled away he put his hand on her knee and rubbed it comfortingly, but the contact made her wince.

***

It was selfish, he knew. But he also knew what life was like without Ivy. He wasn't going to kid himself and think that she loved him. Of course, she didn't, but since Ellie had left him he was lonely. He wasn't a daddy anymore. How could he be when he was never there? Juan was the one who took him to school and watched him play football on the weekends and cooked his dinner. Sam was just the guy he saw a few times a year who would buy him gifts to make up for not being around. So despite his best efforts, he had turned into his parents after all; substituting affection for things.

There was Clara. She was good for nights he couldn't bear to sleep alone and he knew she wanted more than that, but it wasn't something he could give her. And he did feel guilty for that but he had been upfront about what he could offer and if she chose to keep coming around that wasn't his fault.

He looked over to Ivy, her face lit periodically by the streetlamps they drove past. He had only been back in her life for a few weeks and so far she'd had an affair and fallen out with her best friends. He thought things would be different now. Like they had both grown up and they could make this work now. But he had been on that beach in Tenby intending on walking into the sea until his lungs were full of water or he was dragged away by the tides when he saw her. And he couldn't shake the thought that she was an angel there to save him. *I have no right to you, but I love you all the same.*

It all led back to Ivy. And he saw her, happy with her family, happy without him but he recognised something in her eyes he knew too well. That seed of self-hatred that burrowed itself into your brain and threatened to pull you down. And like a scab, you keep picking at it and picking at it until it bleeds. And eventually, it scars. He knew because he had the same scars. So even if what they were doing wasn't right, even if it ruined everything, that was OK, because he had her.

Chapter 36

It had been eight months and Ivy had gotten no better at covering up her affair. Thea had taken to sleeping on the sofa, but climbing back into bed around 5.30 a.m., so she was there when Josh woke them up.

Ivy cried herself to sleep most nights. One moment she was leading a perfect life full of love and friendship and now she had a wife who could barely touch her, two best friends who hardly spoke to her and a toddler who could sense something was off, but couldn't quite understand what. And what did she have in exchange? Moments of respite with Sam, but that was all they were. She was living on the leyline of her own life, not quite in one or the other, just awkwardly straddling the two, and the ones she loved were suffering the consequences. But she couldn't bring herself to close one or the other off.

She told herself she would stop seeing him, cut him out of her life just like she did the first time, but as soon as she saw a message from him, pushed her fingers into his hair and inhaled him she was hooked all over again. Being with Sam was like taking morphine for a headache. It dulled the senses, numbed the pains of life, but you knew it would be back in two to four hours and next time, you would need a stronger dose.

Life with Thea wasn't like that. The past eight months have been painful. The pair were surrounded by broken glass, doomed to tread carefully around the other and brace themselves for pain whenever they crossed it. It wasn't lost on Ivy that it was all her fault, but that only reinforced her self hatred and drove her further towards Sam. She was a completely different Ivy when she was with Sam, more herself and less herself at the same time.

Thea bent forward and picked her wine glass up from near her feet. Her

CHAPTER 36

clothes were baggier and hung from her in a way they didn't before. *Had she stopped eating?* Ivy tried to think about when the last time she had seen her eat was. She was so wrapped up in her head and the pain she was causing Thea that she hadn't noticed if her wife was inflicting pain on herself. *If she was skipping meals that is your fault though, not hers.*

Part of her wished that one of them would leave her. She would create bitter scenarios in her head and watched Thea take Josh and walk out on her and then she saw Sam getting on a plane, and flying out of her life forever. Neither was what she wanted but she also knew it would force a decision on her one way or the other. But she knew which version was best, the one that would make her happy. That version just happened to be the opposite of what she wanted.

"I've invited everyone round for dinner on Thursday," Thea said, breaking the silence that had been held since Josh went to bed an hour and a half ago. *Dinner. What a normal prospect,* Ivy thought and looked at her wife on the other sofa despite the fact there was plenty of room for both of them on the main sofa and it had a better view of the TV. She wore her pain like an invisible crown.

"Oh yeah? Who's everyone?" Ivy asked and cleared her throat. Her voice was raspy as if she hadn't used it for weeks. And she realised she hadn't. They barely spoke anymore and when they did it was about Josh. Thea was punishing her. Not punishing her exactly, but it was as if talking to each other meant she was condoning her behaviour. She wanted to touch her, to feel her soft skin against her own, but it would be insulting to try. *After you've touched him?*

"Jessie, Freya and Henry — I asked Alden too but he's holding some charity function at the restaurant or something,"

"Yeah, that um, sounds great," Ivy said, another thought popped into her head. "That reminds me, the new restaurant opens next month."

"Did he mention what he was going to call it?" Thea asked.

"The Ivithica,"

"No more tree names then, huh?"

"I guess he wanted to thank us."

"He did?"

"The Ivy-Thea-Jessica: Ivi-th-ica. I put it on the calendar but are you...I mean, will you be able to come? With me that is?" she asked.

"I'm not sure, it depends on childcare," Thea responded although it didn't sound like childcare was the issue.

"Yeah, course. It would be great if we could go together though," she said.

"Are you sure it's me you want to go with?" Thea asked her pointedly. Ivy winced a little. *I deserve that* she thought.

* * *

When Thursday rolled around, she made sure to set the table without being asked. She bathed and dressed Josh. He was too big for the high chair now but still needed a cushion to sit on to be able to reach the table.

When the bell rang, Freya ran to Ivy to hug her and then ran off in search of Thea to do the same. Jessie and Henry were not far behind but neither of them looked as happy to see her. She hadn't had more than a handful of conversations with Jessie since the argument they had almost a year ago and poor Henry was so new to the group, he rightly chose the path of least resistance and kept his girlfriend happy.

Alden had been the glue holding the group together through sheer determination more than anything. Ivy's heart palpitated at the thought of an evening without him to ease the tension. It was even worse to think of how anxious she felt around her own best friend. If it hadn't been for the restaurants, and especially The Ivithica's imminent opening, she wondered whether she would have spent any time with Jessie at all.

Sometimes she wondered who gets to keep the friends when relationships end. It looks like Jessie had made her decision. Although she had been her friend first, she didn't resent Jessie choosing Thea over her. If the situation was the other way around, Ivy didn't think she would choose herself either.

"Hey,"

"Hey,"

"How's work?" Ivy asked her.

CHAPTER 36

"Fine — how about you?"

"Yeah, it's fine thanks. Actually, we have this big book we are about to launch. I'm trying to do the marketing for it, it's a debut you see, the author she—"

"Is there anyone else joining us tonight?" Jessie asked.

"No, no, it's just us,"

"I will open the wine then," Henry smiled and carried the bottle he had brought through to the kitchen.

Ivy could hear Thea talking to Henry and Freya above the noise of the bubbling stove. "We're having chilli," she said as she sat down, not sure what else to say.

Jessie stood for a moment and then decided to take a seat diagonally opposite her. "So you were saying? About this book?" Jessie asked.

"Uh, well, it's not important, just...I'm busy at work, that was the point," Ivy said quietly.

"Good, busy is...good," Jessie replied.

Ivy felt the tears sting her eyes. She used to be able to talk to Jessie about anything, but Jessie just didn't get it, she didn't get *her* anymore. But she couldn't blame her for that. She blinked a few times to push the tears back down.

When they sat down to dinner, Ivy concentrated on Thea physically putting the food into her mouth, so she at least knew she was eating and breathed a bit easier when she saw that she was. The group tried their best but it was tenuous at first. The most predominant noise was the sound of cutlery hitting plates and Freya helping Josh with his food. Ivy watched her take on a maternal role that she must have learnt from watching others and smiled. She has turned into such a strong, capable child and Ivy knew that she would take the world by storm once she got the chance.

By the time the third bottle of wine had been opened the conversation began to flow again, almost as it used to. They began to reminisce about old times before Henry and describe the parts he missed that they had found hilarious but Henry didn't understand.

By the fifth bottle of wine, Ivy and Jessie were facing each other, centimetres apart holding hands on the sofa. They had taken themselves away from the rest of the group and the privacy of the moment fuelled by wine, gave Ivy the confidence to blurt out what was really on her mind.

"I'm so sorry, Jessie,"

"I know," she said straight-faced. And then she laughed. "OK, I'm sorry too. I just feel like you have turned into someone I don't know anymore,"

Ivy looked across to Thea who was dancing with Freya and Henry in the kitchen, while Josh slept on his hands on the dining table. "I'm not even sure I know. I think I've changed myself so many times, I'm afraid of all the people that knew who I used to be. I worry they will expose me for the sad broken girl I really am. Fucked, is what it is. I fucked it," she said, turning back to Jessie.

Jessie drunkenly grabbed Ivy's face with one hand and pulled her even closer. "So unfuck it," she said, then kissed her lightly before getting up from the sofa and joining everyone dancing in the kitchen.

Ivy watched them from the sofa and made her decision. She tried to take in every detail and be truly grateful for this little family she had made herself. She might not have filled the space her sister left but she found something great along the way and she knew she needed to make the most of the time she had with them. Making her way into the kitchen, she gave Thea a questioning look. Thea held out her hand to Ivy and smiled with fresh tears in her eyes. Ivy took her hand and kissed it before beginning to dance with them. She looked at Thea and she knew she truly didn't deserve such a wholly beautiful person.

Chapter 37

She reached up to the white PVC door, pressed the buzzer for Flat two and waited. It swung open almost immediately. "Hey," Ivy said.

"Hey," replied Sam. He stood back and let her inside and she followed him through the short corridor to the flat with a wedged open door. She took a step inside and was hit with the usual smell of stale smoke that had got inside every fibre of that flat. She thought about Sam like that. It wasn't very fair of her, but it was easier than thinking of herself as the poison on her life.

Ivy dropped her overnight bag by the door. She didn't have to tell him she had left Thea. He already knew. Her bag contained a few bits of clothes and sentimentals, but she left pretty much everything. She didn't need any of it. Plus she didn't want to hurt Thea more by letting her come home to an empty house. She would know. But at least this way, she can make the decisions as to what to keep or throw away and it can be on her terms. On hers and Josh's terms.

If she thought about how she might not see Josh's bright little face again, she would... but, she wasn't sure what she would do. She clearly wouldn't leave Sam and go back to them or she wouldn't be here at all. *It's like a part of me wants it, wants to hurt, if only to avoid the boredom of happiness.* She would never take him away from Thea either. She was an amazing mum and Josh deserved stability. The thing was, the real soul of the thing was that she loved them. She loved them both, but it just wasn't enough. In choosing Thea, she would be choosing her peace and nothing scared her more.

Sam was broken, but in the end, so was she and her family deserved better than that. She didn't know what would happen from here on out. *What happens if we're both broken? Do we get more broken or do we fix each other?* She knew that being with Sam wouldn't be plain sailing. Or maybe it would be, but there would be no place for Josh, or anything of her old life in the waters.

Sitting down on the sofa, she pulled her feet into her lap. Sam sat back down at the small dining table that was barely big enough for two. Newspaper and pieces of wood were spread across the whole table so Ivy felt like it was only really big enough for him. After a few minutes of staring she realised he was fixing a wooden photo frame.

"I'm going to take a shower," she said. It wouldn't help. She could never wash away the dirt spilling from every pore of her body. She had to make peace with the fact that she was and always had been the villain in her own story. That she couldn't climb out of her skin, no matter how tight it gets.

Getting up from the sofa, she walked over to Sam and bent to kiss him on the cheek. She hung her arm around his neck to steady herself as she did so. She looked down at the photo he was putting inside the now fixed frame and it was of the two of them. They were both smiling up at the camera with the view of the beach and the light of a low sun behind them in Thailand. It wasn't a photo she could remember posing for or one she remembered seeing before.

"I'll join you. Give me five minutes," Sam said. She smiled into his face. Still hanging there for a beat, before standing up and going towards the bathroom.

She pulled two big towels out of the airing cupboard en route and dumped them in a heap on the floor before reaching in to turn the shower on full. She took her jeans and underwear off in one, unhooking them from her heels and dropping them into a pile by the sink. She pulled her vest top over her head, dropping it on top of her jeans and unhooked her bra letting that also fall onto the pile.

Thinking of the picture in Sam's hands, she stared at herself in the mirror for a moment. She was older now, dark rings lived under her eyes, her boobs were closer to her waist than her chest and her hair was shorter, but she was surprised to see she wasn't suddenly the same girl she was at twenty-two. You shrink as you get older. Not just physically but you take up less space than you did before. As if you are no longer worthy of taking up space and the space you used to occupy now belonged to those younger and bolder and brighter than you.

Even in her older face, she saw Agatha in every line and crease. Even though Agatha never got to make one for herself, she was encoded into the lines and contours of Ivy's entire life. A tear rolled down her cheek, which she quickly wiped away and stepped into the shower.

The warmth of the steam was so inviting, and it almost cleansed the doubt from her mind for a second. She stood still under the showerhead, looking up, letting the water pelt her face until she couldn't hold her breath anymore. Bending down, steadying herself against the wall she began inspecting the few bottles of colourful gels Sam had. She picked one up and opened the cap, sniffing it before squirting some across her chest and rubbing it in. It smelt like plastic apples, familiar, but synthetic at the same time and it was oddly comforting. *Somewhere in another world, there was another Ivy who was getting it right. She was loving Thea as she deserved, she was there for her son, she was happy being happy.*

Sam stepped into the shower behind her. Ivy didn't hear him coming until he had already put his arms around her, but she didn't have the energy to be startled. She was growing more tired with every day that passed but she turned smiling. Showing the face she needed to, but not the one that reflected her heart, she pulled Sam under the flow of water. He knew she would never be happy as well as she did but they both lied to themselves about it because the truth was too shameful. The truth was that Ivy couldn't be happy with anyone, not even herself and she now knew that was how Agatha had felt too. *I don't want to be me anymore. I don't like the person I have become.* If she couldn't fully be herself with Thea, and still can't fully be herself with Sam, who even was she? *Aren't I supposed to know the answer to that question by now?* She rested her head on Sam's chest and stood there together for a minute, she let him stroke her hair and hold her close when really she felt miles away from herself.

She thought back to their prom. *Posing for pictures together in the hallway, him giving her a corsage to match her dress. Dancing all night. Sneaking sips of vodka from his flask.* Sam kissed her head. She pulled herself back and moved to look at him. They kissed, tentatively and tenderly. *Do our shared secrets make us taste the same?* Sam lifted her off of her feet and pushed himself inside her. Ivy reciprocated but didn't look at him.

She thought about when he carried her on his back from the bars in Thailand. *Her heels in one hand, her legs threaded through his arms, arms wrapped around his neck. Her whole body bounced hard, up and down with each step he took.* Feeling herself bounce against Sam now, her thoughts slipped back into the present. She still didn't want to look at him. She was relieved to feel his head buried in her shoulder. The water dripped from his nose down her back and she could hear him breathing raggedly into her.

Her mind wandered again. She thought about the night they built a fort out of the sofa cushions in his parent's flat. *He read Tender is the Night, their English assignment, aloud, while she, head in his lap, drew Ivy on the blank skin that lived on the inside of his thigh in sharpie until she drifted off.*

She felt it building in her, she was going to come and as she did, tears streamed down her cheeks, masked by the shower. Her fingers kneading into the skin on his shoulders. Sam came not long after. He lifted her off of him and put her down, back onto her feet. He kissed her cheek and exited the shower.

Ivy watched the blur of him fade away into the hall. His semen travelled silkily down her right thigh, around the contours of her shin and pooled at her feet. She watched it slide down the drain.

Broken People
by Agatha King

Broken people, break people.
That is what they say,
But if we are all broken,
Who is it we are breaking?

Broken people make the prettiest of poetry,
The words shine through the cracks and inclusion,
You turn them in the light and see new faults at every angle,
So many fractures that rattle when they walk.

They run so deep, my fingers catch along the veins,
The skin is stained with breaks of rust and gold,
And the lines of bright and worth blur hard,
Against the poison streaks so that they don't know,
What's good, what's light, what's canker.

Yes, you can make pretty poetry out of broken people,
But broken people will always break
Good people and that is never pretty.

About the Author

Laura is a Marketing Exec who has a degree in Business with Marketing. She spends most of her spare time writing essays and poetry. She is a proud feminist and is passionate about highlighting bi-erasure, everyday racism and encouraging self-love. She lives with her husband Nic and three-legged Frenchie, Luna. Alongside work, she is currently writing an anthology and eating copious amounts of vegan doughnuts.

You can connect with me on:
- www.instagram.com/lozbarber93

Printed in Great Britain
by Amazon